# TROY STORY

## ROMANCING THE RUINS #2

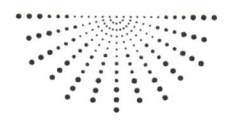

CARLA LUNA

MOON MANOR PRESS

This is a work of fiction. Names, characters, organizations, places, events, and incidents are either products of the author's imagination or are used fictitiously. Any resemblance to actual persons, living or dead, or actual events is entirely coincidental.

Copyright © 2023 by Carla Luna

All rights reserved. No part of this book may be reproduced or used in any manner without written permission of the copyright owner except for the use of quotations in a book review.
For more information, contact: carlalunacullen@gmail.com

First paperback edition: May 2023

Cover Design: *Bailey McGinn*
Editing: *Free Bird Editing*
Proofreading: *One Love Editing*

ISBN: 978-1-7368661-9-1 (paperback)
ISBN: 978-1-7368661-8-4 (ebook)

Published by Moon Manor Press
www.carlalunabooks.com

❦ Created with Vellum

*Dedicated to the memory of my mother, Dulcie Luna, a truly gifted artist who marched to the beat of her own drum.*

AUTHOR'S NOTE

In some international publications, the country of Turkey is referred to as Türkiye. To avoid any confusion, I opted to use the familiar spelling of the country's name in this story. The archaeological site of Troy, located in northwestern Turkey, has been under excavation since the 1870s, when amateur archaeologist Heinrich Schliemann began digging there. In the years that followed, numerous teams of international scholars have excavated at Troy. The most recent investigations into the site began in the 2010s, led by a Turkish team of archaeologists.

To the best of my knowledge, at no point in the last twenty years have there been any scandals at Troy involving smuggling, artifact tampering, or other archaeological misdeeds. However, in creating a compelling story, I've taken a few liberties, including the creation of a fictitious American university that had its excavation permit revoked. For all you archaeological purists, I apologize but hope you still enjoy the story!

# CHAPTER ONE

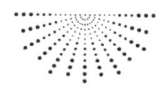

Dusty Danforth had faced down venomous snakes, deadly scorpions, and surly camels. None of them had proved quite as intimidating as her mother when she was in a disapproving mood. Her anger hardly seemed rational. If anyone should understand the need to spend the summer working on an excavation, it should be Dr. Louisa Danforth, world-renowned archaeologist and scholar of Egyptology.

But while Dr. Danforth had a PhD, Dusty did not. Hence the argument.

Dusty sat across from her mother on the balcony of their family's apartment in Cairo. Despite the sweltering June temperature, Dr. Danforth was drinking Earl Grey tea from a china cup. Even during her years in the field, she'd allowed few things to disrupt her afternoon tea break.

She frowned at her daughter. "You can't keep flitting from one project to the next. No matter how alluring they've seemed, none of them have resulted in a worthy dissertation topic. That's where you should focus your attention this summer. Not at some dig site in Turkey."

Dusty cast a wistful glance at the Nile, shimmering in the distance. "It's just for two months. I don't see how—"

"Dulcinea Danforth. You have spent five years in graduate school, and you have nothing to show for it except a handful of drawings. You need to get serious about your future."

Not for the first time, Dusty fought back a surge of resentment. It wasn't like she'd been doodling in a notebook. She was a trained archaeological illustrator whose artwork had appeared in dozens of scholarly publications. She had a master's degree in Classics. And she *hated* the name Dulcinea. She'd been going by Dusty since she was three.

But if she didn't offer a concession, her mother wouldn't stop nagging. "Once the summer ends, I promise I'll go home to Boston."

"You won't go jetting off to Cyprus again? Or Tunisia? I realize you're old enough to make your own choices, even if you dress like you're sixteen instead of twenty-six."

Another hit. Her mother had brought out the big guns today. But not everyone could pull off a cream linen pantsuit and a perfectly coiffed bob the way Dr. Danforth could. Dusty preferred comfort over style, which was why she usually opted for baggy cargo pants and graphic tees. Today's shirt was a vintage Muppets tee that she'd scored at the Dolapdere flea market in Istanbul.

"If you can acknowledge that I'm a fully grown adult, then it's time you treated me like one," she said. "My clothes are my own business. Same with my summer plans."

Her mother gave a world-weary sigh—the kind that made Dusty feel like a naughty little kid. "I realize that, dear, but sometimes you need a nudge. You get so caught up in these short-term adventures you lose sight of your goals. If you want a doctorate, you need to put in the work."

Dusty was well aware her efforts to finish grad school had stalled out. Though she'd completed the coursework for a PhD in

Classical Archaeology and passed all her exams, she had yet to start writing her dissertation. Mainly because she vastly preferred drawing to writing. Only when she was immersed in her artwork did her creative spirit truly run free. She could spend hours sketching without noticing the time passing. Writing, however, was like a slog through a murky lake where she struggled to dredge up the words.

But no matter how much art she created—whether it was her detailed technical commissions or her fanciful, Egyptian-themed drawings—none of it would aid her in writing her thesis. The only way to complete the Herculean task was to settle on a topic, stick to it, and set everything else aside.

"Sorry. I don't mean to keep letting you down," she said. "Starting in September, I won't take on any new projects until I've written my dissertation."

"Why wait until then? What's so important about this dig in Turkey?"

Dusty bit back a grin. "It's pretty special. Located near the Dardanelles in a place called Hisarlik. Ever heard of it?"

The briefest of smiles crossed her mother's lips. "Naturally. The site believed to be the legendary city of Troy. I was eight when I read *The Iliad* for the first time. What an epic—the agony of the Trojan War, with its tragic heroes and meddling Greek gods. I wanted so badly for all of it to be true."

"Some of the stories could be. No one knows for sure. But I didn't accept the job just because of the location. Stuart's serving as the assistant director of the American excavations there. It's the first time he's ever had this much responsibility, and I want to support him."

Unlike her, Stuart Carlson—her best friend and fellow dig buddy—had finished his dissertation last winter. Upon receiving his doctorate from UC San Diego, he'd landed a plum teaching job at the University of Boston. Though he wasn't scheduled to start teaching until September, he'd been asked to help run the university's dig at Troy. When he'd invited Dusty to join the team as the site illustrator, she'd accepted without question.

Fortunately, her mother had a soft spot for Stuart because his father was an archaeologist who'd spent years working with the Danforths in Egypt. As a result, Stuart and Dusty had grown up together, weathering countless seasons on their parents' expeditions.

Dr. Danforth set her teacup on the wrought-iron table. "I would never dissuade you from helping Stuart. He's like a part of the family." She arched a perfectly sculpted brow. "But is that the *only* reason you agreed to join him?"

A flush of heat crossed Dusty's cheeks. In a moment of weakness, she'd told her mother how she really felt about Stuart. Big mistake. "Of course. We've always been there for each other. But we're just friends. That's not about to change."

"No? Because I heard from Stuart's father that the poor boy is finally free of that vapid Shelby."

Dusty gave an involuntary shudder. Tall, blond, and athletic, Shelby was the quintessential California girl, almost too perfect to be true. While Dusty couldn't fault her for achieving perfection, she *did* blame her for putting Stuart through a lengthy and toxic relationship that had left him emotionally gutted.

"If you ask me, he wasted far too many years on Shelby," Dr. Danforth said. "She was never right for him. Whereas you—"

"Nope." Dusty held up her hand. "We're not going to talk about this."

"Fair enough. But Dusty..." Dr. Danforth narrowed her eyes. "After this summer, if you don't get serious, I'll have to cut you off."

Dusty's mouth fell open in shock. "What are you talking about? I earn my own living." In addition to her academic commissions and her on-site gigs as an archaeological illustrator, she made a fair amount through her popular Etsy shop, where she sold her Egyptian-themed pieces.

"Your drawings may pull in enough to keep you clothed and fed, but you've spent years pillaging my frequent-flier miles and making use of our family's apartments without paying a dime. I let it happen because I wanted to encourage your passion for travel, but you need to be grounded for a spell."

*Grounded.* A hypocritical demand, coming from a woman who'd never managed to settle in one place. When not excavating in Egypt, Dusty's mother split her time between an apartment in Cairo, a condo in Boston, and a town house in London. Even then, she never passed up an opportunity to give a guest lecture, lead a tour, or speak at a conference, no matter where it took her.

Dusty's father—also a fellow Egyptologist—had once accompanied her everywhere. Now that he was retired, he spent most of his time in Boston, which was why Dusty had chosen to attend graduate school there. But like her mother, she found it hard to resist the lure of travel. An incessant need to keep going, in the hope she might one day figure out where she truly belonged.

Before Dusty could protest, her mother gave her the no-nonsense frown that effectively ended any argument. "After this project ends, I want you on a flight back to Boston. You need to stop running and focus on your future. Got it?"

"Got it." Dusty offered a conciliatory smile. "Who knows? Maybe this dig will inspire me. I could write about the site of Troy for my dissertation."

When her mother didn't smile in return, Dusty knew better than to promise something she couldn't deliver. She'd gotten just as fired up on her last three digs, only to have her ideas fizzle out before she started writing.

She stood, eager to put some distance between them. "Can I go now? I'm supposed to Zoom with Stuart."

"Tell him hello from me, will you? And offer my congratulations. Not just for the Troy project but for landing a teaching job in Boston. I'm so proud of all he's accomplished." Dr.

Danforth gathered up her teacup and saucer. "I won't be home tonight since I'm having dinner with the people from Ancient Excursions. They want me to lead another VIP tour through Egypt this fall. Quite honestly, I don't know if I have it in me. Tourists can be so tiresome."

"Like that tech bro who insisted aliens built the pyramids? Dad said you blew up at him."

"I would never do anything so uncouth." Her mother gave a wicked smile. "I just made certain he got an obscenely grumpy camel during our jaunt around Giza."

Dusty had to hand it to her—as prim as she appeared when she was off duty, her mom was tough as nails in the field. Even while leading pampered millionaires around Egypt, she didn't put up with any shit. Thanks to her, Dusty had never let anyone belittle her because she was a woman.

She retreated into the apartment, taking momentary pleasure in the feel of the cool tiled floor against her bare feet. After grabbing a bottle of water from the fridge, she went into her bedroom and shut the door.

The tiny room contained two twin beds, left over from the days when Stuart's family would stay at the apartment after the dig season ended. She and Stuart would room together while their parents spent weeks in Cairo, networking with archaeology professors, museum curators, and dignitaries. Since both of them were only children, they'd grown up like siblings. As adults, they'd stayed close friends, no matter how many miles separated them.

But they'd never been anything more. Until that soul-crushing night, two years ago.

At the time, Stuart had been single, still reeling from a recent breakup with Shelby. When he'd come to Boston for an archaeology conference, Dusty had invited him to crash at her family's condo. Since her parents had been in London, she'd had the place to herself. To distract Stuart from his misery, she'd taken him on an epic bar crawl. But their drunken foolishness had led to a passionate session on the couch where he'd fulfilled almost all her secret fantasies, including the tender words he'd whispered to her in the heat of the moment.

Thankfully, she'd been sober enough to hit the brakes before they had sex. In the short time it took her to fetch them some water, Stuart passed out on the couch. He woke the next morning, bleary and hungover, with no memory of anything they'd done. Dusty, on the other hand, remembered every detail. All weekend, she agonized over whether to tell him, but before she could summon up the courage, Shelby reached out to him, and they reconciled.

Since then, Dusty's feelings for Stuart had progressed from an embarrassing crush to full-blown longing. Now that he was finally single, she needed to seize the moment this summer.

She plopped down on one of the beds, pulled up her laptop, and logged into her Zoom account. It was only 7:15 a.m. on the West Coast, but Stuart was the type who woke at six without an alarm clock.

When his face appeared on the screen, his thick, sandy-blond hair still looked sleep-mussed. He was cradling an insulated tumbler, no doubt filled with piping-hot coffee. His ocean-blue eyes danced in amusement at the sight of her. "Hey, Dusty. I like the new hair color."

She patted her short, dark hair, which now bore a vivid purple streak. "Thanks. I dyed it yesterday. Naturally, Mom hated it. When we went out to the market, she insisted I wear a hat." She returned his grin. "I see you've grown a beard, Dr. Carlson."

"You like it?"

"Definitely. You're totally rocking a distinguished professor vibe." *And making me swoon more than ever.* She'd always been a sucker for hot guys with beards. To stop herself from drooling on camera, she directed her attention to the mountain of boxes behind him. "Why does your place resemble a storage unit?"

"Because I'm in packing hell, trying to box up my entire life in San Diego. I sold most of my furniture, but I still have too much crap for someone who's only twenty-seven."

"You're such a pack rat. I'll bet you could ditch half that stuff and not miss it. When are you driving out to Boston?"

"Next Monday. Please thank your parents—*again*—for letting me store everything in their condo. I've got a place lined up near the university, but the lease doesn't start until August. I thought I'd have the entire summer to deal with this shit, but the Troy dig sped everything up."

"So, basically, you're driving to Boston, off-loading your boxes, and then hopping on a plane to Istanbul. All in the space of about ten days?"

He raked a hand through his hair, messing it even further. "That about covers it. Other than catching up on decades of excavation reports. Do you have any idea how many archaeologists have worked at Troy? It's overwhelming. I'm hoping to make some headway on the plane ride over."

She snorted. "You're so disciplined. The only thing I ever do on those long-ass flights is watch movies."

"Speaking of flights, are you coming? Did you get the green light from your mom?"

"I don't need her approval. I'm my own person."

"Says the woman who's sitting in her parents' apartment on a child-size bed."

"First of all, child-size fits me perfectly since I'm not a six-foot-tall giant like you. Second, why wouldn't I stay here? This little room isn't much, but it's the one place I can call home in this corner of the world." The wall facing her bed held a trio of bulletin boards, where she'd pinned dozens of drawings, photos, and postcards. The sight of them always improved her mood. "Anyway. I *am* coming. I can't wait to spend the summer digging at Troy with you. I'm flying to Istanbul, then taking the bus to

Çanakkale. I figured I'd come a day early so we'd have time to catch up. Any chance you could get me at the bus station?"

"I'll give it my best shot." He flashed her an affectionate smile. "I can't tell you how glad I am that you're going to be there."

"Really?" Her heart did a skip-jump. Was he thinking the same thing she was? That this might be their chance to take their friendship to the next level?

"Yeah. This dig's going to be stressful, but having you around will make a big difference. You're such a great friend."

*A friend.*

That was all she'd ever been.

But maybe this summer, that could change.

## CHAPTER TWO

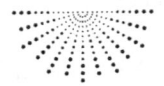

Talking with Dusty was the boost Stuart Carlson needed, and not just because of her unabashed enthusiasm. Even though they were seven thousand miles apart, her presence on his laptop screen was so vivid he felt like she was in the same room with him. As always, he found her completely irresistible, with her impish smile, expressive hazel eyes, and hair that had seen every color of the rainbow. She might have been a foot shorter than him, but she was more fearless than he would ever be. If he could choose anyone in the world to have his back, it would be her.

And right now, he needed all the support he could get.

He'd always been prone to anxiety, but the past month had raised his stress levels to new heights. On the one hand, he was immensely grateful he'd landed a teaching job at the University of Boston. Most students with a newly minted PhD in Classical Archaeology weren't so lucky. But he'd expected to have the entire summer to get ready—to pack up his apartment in San Diego, prepare for his classes, and move across the country. Instead, he'd had to rearrange his entire schedule when the chair of the Classics Department, Dr. Valeria Fiorelli, had asked him to start the job three months early so he could assist with the university's excavations at Troy.

Not that he was complaining. Working at a legendary site like Troy was one of the reasons he'd gotten into archaeology. The more he read about recent discoveries at the hilltop site, the more his excitement grew. But the job also came with a staggering amount of baggage.

When Dusty disappeared from his screen, he startled, wondering if she'd wandered off, but her face reappeared a minute later.

Grinning, she saluted him with a bottle of beer. "Sorry, I needed something stronger than water. Before I forget, Mom sends her congratulations. She's impressed you landed a tenure-track position, right out of the gate. I know you were hoping to score the assistant professor spot at UC Santa Barbara, but I think Boston's a better fit."

"I only wanted the Santa Barbara job because of Shelby. She was adamant that I find a post in California. But when I didn't get it...well, that was the beginning of the end for us." He winced inwardly, remembering her furor when he'd told her the news. "I'm glad Olivia was offered the position instead."

If anyone else had beat him out, he might have been resentful, but he had nothing but respect for his colleague Olivia Sanchez, who was not just a brilliant scholar but one of his closest friends.

"Olivia was thrilled when she told me," Dusty said. "The location's perfect for her since she and Rick both have family in California. But trust me, you're going to love Boston. It's filled with amazing universities, great museums, and tons of incredible restaurants."

"And you'll be there, right?"

"Indeed, I will, by order of my mother. Once you're settled, I'm taking you to Gourmet Dumpling House. Best dumplings in the city. And we have to go to the North End for Italian food and pastries." She gave an audible shiver. "It's going to be so much fun."

"I can't wait." Despite the frantic nature of his move, he was looking forward to starting fresh in Boston. Not only would he put some much-needed distance between himself and Shelby, but he'd also get to spend more time with Dusty.

"Back to this Troy gig." She leaned closer to the screen, her eyes gleaming with excitement. "Again, mega impressive. But I'm guessing there's more to the story. How'd you score the assistant director spot? Technically, you're not even working for the university yet."

"I am now. This is just between us, but the whole situation is kind of messed up. How much do you know about the American excavations at Troy?"

"Not that much. I'm familiar with the history of the site, and I watched a show about it on the Discovery Channel last week, but I don't know all the dirt. Get it—dirt?"

A terrible joke, but it made him smile. "Nice. Well, starting in the '90s, the University of Boston led a series of digs there. The guy running the project was Professor Rutherford Hughes. I'm sure you've heard of him."

Dusty's eyes widened. "Yeah. He was a big deal back in the day. Wrote a couple of books about Troy, did the lecture circuit. But then he dropped off the map. Is he still teaching at Boston?"

"He is, but..." Stuart swallowed as he recalled what he'd learned from Dr. Fiorelli. "His reputation isn't what it used to be. Ten years ago, during a summer season at Troy, he got into a dispute with the German archaeologists working there. I don't know what happened, but the Turkish Ministry of Culture got involved and revoked the University of Boston's excavation permit. They haven't been back there since."

"Not for ten years? That's harsh."

The severity of the sentence had shocked Stuart. *Ten years.* Whatever Dr. Hughes had done, it must have been bad.

"It was a huge blow, but they worked out a new agreement this spring," he said. "I'm not sure if money changed hands, but we got permission to go back. But then, the woman who was supposed to serve as Hughes' assistant turned down the job. They had a big falling-out, to the point where she called him a 'sexist asshole' and swore she'd never work with him again."

After learning about what she'd dealt with, Stuart had been leery of taking on her role. But as the Classics Department's newest hire, he wasn't in a position to turn it down.

"Damn. I had no idea he was that bad," Dusty said.

"Me neither. When I watched some of his earlier lectures online, I caught a few sexist remarks, but nothing too extreme. He came across as more of an old-school ladies' man. But his former assistant said his behavior was completely inappropriate."

"If he's such a liability, then why's the university letting him go back to Troy? Aren't they afraid he'll screw up again?"

"Honestly? I think it's a huge mistake, but you know how it goes in academia. He's a tenured professor and an expert on the site. Like you said, he literally wrote the book on it. I'm just hoping he doesn't mess with the Germans again."

Dusty put up her fists, as though preparing to do battle. "He'd better not. But no matter what shit he pulls, I've got you. Remember our motto, bud? Ride or die."

He remembered, even if he hadn't been living up to his end of it. For the past six months, he'd been a terrible friend. Instead of responding to Dusty's texts right away, he'd let them linger, too ashamed to admit what a shit show his life had become. Ending his relationship with Shelby had been painful enough, but applying for jobs in academia added a whole new level of misery. Each time he learned he'd been passed over for a position, his morale sunk lower.

But all that was behind him. Now that he was on the other side, free of Shelby and gainfully employed, he was determined never to shut out Dusty again.

"Stuart?" Dusty's voice shocked him out of his reverie. "What about the rest of the team? Do they look solid?"

He glanced at the paperwork Dr. Fiorelli had sent him. Besides a lengthy document outlining the budget and parameters of the dig, he'd received a bibliography of background material, a set of rules, and the university's code of conduct. He'd been so busy he'd barely scanned through any of it. "God, there's, like, fifty pages of stuff here."

"Don't stress. It's the same old crap on every dig. The only thing you need to worry about now is the list of students and when they're arriving."

He found the list buried at the bottom. "We got a lot of applications but only accepted a few. Since it's our first year back, we want to see how it goes. A smaller team means less chance for problem children."

"Speaking of 'problem children,' I got another lecture from my mom about my dissertation." Dusty gave an exaggerated eye roll. "She was haranguing me for taking the summer off to work in Turkey."

A twinge of guilt tugged at Stuart's conscience. "You don't have to come if it's going to cause trouble. I'd love to have you there, but—"

"No, I want to come. Working at Troy could be just the inspiration I need. Maybe you could help me. In exchange for my fabulous drawing skills, you could motivate me to settle on a thesis topic, then kick my butt into gear."

"I'm totally down for some butt kicking. Metaphorically speaking, of course."

If he was being honest, he often wondered whether Dusty really wanted to get her doctorate. Unlike him, she had no interest in teaching. She was happiest when focused on her artwork. Maybe this summer, he could do more than just motivate her. He could have a heart-to-heart with her and help her figure out her future. It made no sense for her to struggle with academia if it wasn't something she wanted.

She flashed him an adorable smile. "Thanks, Stuart. You're the best. I can't wait to see you again."

Whenever she bestowed one of those smiles on him, he felt a pang of longing. A secret wish he could reveal how he really felt about her. As children, they'd been raised like siblings. But when he turned thirteen, he developed a ridiculous crush on her. Even when they'd dated other people, his feelings for her had always simmered on the back burner.

For years, he'd held out the hope that they'd end up together, despite their different temperaments. While Dusty was constantly in motion, finding it hard to settle anywhere for longer than a few months, he craved stability and commitment. So when he found those qualities in Shelby, he stopped dreaming of a future with Dusty. In hindsight, it had been a terrible lapse in judgment.

But now, after years of Shelby drama, he was single. He could finally tell Dusty he wanted more than friendship. Or could he? If she didn't feel the same way he did, he'd be putting her in an awkward position. His confession could drive a giant wedge between them. But he didn't know how much longer he could hold in his feelings.

After chatting with her a little longer, he signed off and resumed packing, pausing at nine for his call with Dr. Fiorelli.

At first, the call went well, as his boss reviewed the logistics of the dig. But as the conversation continued, her cheeriness gave way to a more somber tone.

"It's vital we get through this season without a hitch," she said. "It took a lot of finessing to get our excavation permit renewed. If Dr. Hughes makes any trouble, this might be the last time we're ever allowed at Troy."

*No pressure or anything.* "With all due respect, is there a reason he's being allowed back?"

When she didn't answer right away, Stuart cursed himself for sounding impertinent. What right did he have to question a professor who'd spent forty years in the field?

Then again, that same professor had been kicked out of Turkey for ten years.

"Have you heard of Mortimer Jones?" Dr. Fiorelli asked. "He's an alum from way back. Got his degree in business and made a fortune. Thanks to his passion for ancient history, he's donated generously to our department."

Slightly baffled over the way she'd changed topics, Stuart tried to recall what he'd learned about one of the university's most affluent donors. "Doesn't the school offer an archaeology scholarship named after him?"

"That's the one. He's also contributed to quite a few of our other endeavors. Without his funding, we wouldn't be able to afford a full season at Troy. But he made his donation on the assumption that Dr. Hughes would be leading this year's dig."

Stuart bit back a groan. "Let me guess. He's a big fan of the professor's work?"

"Indeed. Apparently, he was thrilled to support a dig that would 'get Professor Hughes back in action.' His words, not mine. But you understand what's at stake here."

*Shit.* No wonder the university was letting Dr. Hughes' reputation slide. When a wealthy donor asked for a favor, you didn't say no.

"I get it," Stuart said, "but I'm surprised Dr. Hughes wants to go back. Being exiled must have been so humiliating."

"I'm sure it was. But he thinks if he can find something newsworthy this summer, he could restore his former glory and erase the stigma of his past mistakes."

Just what had the guy done? "Any chance you could tell me what happened?"

"I can't. To absolve the university from further embarrassment, we had him—and everyone associated with that dig—sign a confidentiality agreement. For now, let's keep our focus on the upcoming season. Dr. Hughes has an ambitious goal. He wants to find a cemetery dating to the Late Bronze Age as proof that the Trojan War took place. He's hoping to present his findings at an international symposium in Amsterdam this fall. Your job is to support him as best you can while making sure he doesn't do anything illegal."

*Illegal?* Did that imply he'd broken the law before?

Taking a deep breath, Stuart bottled up his frustration. If he couldn't get the truth about Dr. Hughes from Dr. Fiorelli, he'd ask Dusty to do a little digging. Thanks to her mom's keen ear for academic gossip, she'd kept up with most of the scandals that had rocked the archaeological world over the past two decades.

He kept his voice even, not wanting to reveal the uncertainty coursing through him. "I promise I'll keep things on track. Is there anything else I need to know?"

"Well, actually...there's another complication. As I said, Mortimer Jones has been one of our biggest donors. Now that he's retired, he's decided to cross a few things off his bucket list. Like joining an archaeological dig."

*Dear God, no.* He sounded like one of those entitled millionaires Dusty's mom dealt with on her VIP tours. "He's joining us? Does he realize how rustic the conditions are?"

From what Stuart had heard, the field house where they'd be living contained dorm-style rooms and communal bathrooms. Hardly the lap of luxury for a wealthy business executive.

"He won't be staying with the crew. He's arranged a long-term rental at a local hotel."

*Perfect.* Maybe he wouldn't be too much of a burden.

"But his daughter wants to stay in the field house," Dr. Fiorelli added.

Stuart's stomach churned, making him wish he'd had more for breakfast than two cups of coffee. "Wait. His daughter?"

"Clarissa. She's a high school art teacher. Graduated from the

University of Boston five years ago. She's passionate about ancient history, so she wants the full experience."

*Of course she does.* Despite his unsettled stomach, Stuart forced himself to sound enthusiastic. "Great. Anything else?"

"That's about it. I wish you the best of luck. I know I'm asking a lot of you, but I trust you'll keep things under control and have a great season."

"Thanks." After ending the call, Stuart slumped down in his chair and cast a weary glance at the boxes around him. This summer wasn't going to be easy.

At least Dusty would be there. With her by his side, he could get through anything.

# CHAPTER THREE

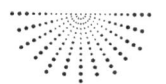

After riding the bus from Istanbul for four hours, Dusty was growing restless. She'd downloaded an audiobook of *The Iliad* as a quick refresher on the Trojan War but was losing patience with all the aggressive male posturing. So much of the conflict could have been avoided if the Greeks and the Trojans had gotten their massive egos in check.

She glanced out the window, taking in the flat farm fields, the rolling hills, and the groves of olive and oak trees. Occasionally, she glimpsed the blue-gray waters of the Dardanelles, the strait separating the European and Asian sides of Turkey. When their bus crossed over a long suspension bridge spanning the strait, she perked up. Less than an hour to go.

At five, the bus pulled into the Çanakkale Otogar, a small station that paled in comparison to the chaotic transport hub in Istanbul where she'd started her journey. She grabbed her messenger bag and waited patiently as the other passengers cleared out. Emerging from the bus, she blinked at the bright sunlight. Even at this hour, the day's heat hadn't ebbed, though it was less intense than Cairo in July.

As the bus driver opened the side hatch and unloaded the

luggage, she reached for her giant backpack, only to have it snatched away. Stuart towered over her, looking more tanned and muscular than she remembered. His sandy-blond hair was covered with a blue baseball cap bearing a stylized version of the Trojan horse.

She grinned at him. "Nice hat. Any chance you could score one for me?"

"Already done. It's at the field house." Setting down her pack, he pulled her into a hug.

For a moment, she wished he would greet her as a lover. That he would kiss her passionately, then promise to whisk her off to bed at the first available opportunity. But being enfolded in his arms and pressed against his solid chest was a decent consolation prize. She inhaled the familiar scent of cedar and cypress, the same body wash he'd used for years.

When he released her, she stepped back and gave him a once-over. "You look good, bud. Thanks for trekking out here to get me. I wasn't sure if you'd have time to pick me up."

"I wouldn't leave you in the lurch, not after you came here a day early." He gestured to her oversized backpack. "Is this all you have?"

"Yep. You know I travel light." Other than her drawing supplies, her tablet, and her laptop, she usually made do with a small selection of well-used dig clothes and a couple of nice outfits for the occasional party or night out.

He hoisted her pack on his shoulders. "Come on. Our ride's this way."

She followed him across the paved parking lot to an ancient Land Rover that had clearly seen better days. Once he stowed her pack and got behind the wheel, she hopped in next to him.

He placed his hand over hers. "I know I said this before, but I'm *so* glad you're here."

Despite the warmth of his touch, he sounded so vulnerable

that her bare arms prickled with goosebumps. "You okay? Did something happen with Shelby that I don't know about?"

"Nope. It's totally over."

She wanted to believe him, but Shelby had left him before, and he'd always taken her back. Still, this time, he'd been the one to initiate their breakup, which might mean he'd moved on for good. "No backsliding?"

"None whatsoever. It's been five months now. I even tried dating." Releasing her hand, he started the engine and pulled the Land Rover out of the lot.

*Shit.* She'd wanted to get to him before he got in deep with someone else. "You did?"

"Don't sound so surprised. One of my running buddies set me up with a friend of his, but it didn't go well. When we went out to dinner, she was so rude to our server that I left a huge tip as an apology. And all night, she kept asking me about dinosaurs."

Since the Land Rover didn't have air-conditioning, Dusty cranked down her window and let the warm breeze ruffle her hair. "Let me guess. She thought you were a paleontologist?"

"Exactly. We spent an hour discussing the *Jurassic Park* franchise."

Dusty snickered. Maybe she didn't have much to be worried about.

"After that, I almost hooked up with a grad student from Irvine," he said. "We met at a conference in Portland and really clicked. But..."

"You didn't go through with it?" She cringed at the hint of desperation in her voice.

"I didn't even get her number. You know me—I can't handle casual hookups." He maneuvered through a tricky roundabout and headed south on the highway. "Not like you."

"What do you mean?"

"Most of your relationships have been short-term flings, but you somehow manage to have fun without getting your heart involved. I'm not like that."

Rather than reveal how much his comment stung, she looked away, focusing on a tall hill dotted with a row of wind turbines. "You make me sound so ruthless."

"I didn't mean it that way. But seriously, have you fallen in love with anyone since you started grad school?"

*If only you knew.* She swallowed past the painful knot in her throat. "No, but that doesn't mean I wouldn't be open to it." She needed to redirect this conversation, stat. Ten minutes with Stuart and she was already too close to revealing her feelings. "If you're not hung up on Shelby, then why do you need moral support?"

"Like I said before, this job is a ton of responsibility. I still haven't read through all the paperwork they sent me, and I'm not sure why Dr. Hughes was banished from the site ten years ago. Did you dig up any good dirt?"

With Stuart in full anxiety mode, she needed to tread carefully. But she didn't want to lie to him, either. "I asked my mom what she knew about it. Back when he was exiled from Troy, she heard a few rumors, but no one seemed to know what really happened. She suspected the university went to great lengths to cover it up."

Stuart drove out a harsh breath. "That's what I thought. Dr. Fiorelli told me everyone on the dig had to sign an NDA."

"That's messed up. Mom *did* say that he's an asshole. She led an Ancient Excursions tour with him through Egypt and Turkey about fifteen years ago. I couldn't get her to tell me what went down, except that she can't stand him. Apparently, the feeling is mutual and…" She gnawed on her lip, hesitant to say more, but Stuart saw right through her.

"Out with it."

"She tried to talk me out of coming here. Claimed Hughes

was so toxic that I'd have a miserable time. But you know me. I'm stubborn as hell."

As his hands tightened around the steering wheel, she regretted her honesty. She placed her hand on his thigh. Just a quick touch for reassurance. "I'm sure it'll be fine. You know how abrasive my mom can be. If Hughes pissed her off when they were on that tour, she probably went into Queen Bitch mode around him. But you're a lot more easygoing. And no matter what happens, I'm here for you."

The thought of being needed filled Dusty with a warm glow. It wasn't often that anyone needed her. Though she had no doubt her parents loved her, they were so busy with their academic careers that she often felt like unnecessary baggage.

"Thanks," Stuart said. "Even if I'm stressed, I'm excited to be working at Troy. Do you remember when we watched the movie together?"

One of the things she loved most about Stuart was his nerdy passion for films set in the ancient world. Whether they involved gladiators, mummies, or Greek myths—he'd seen them all. Over the years, she'd done countless watch-alongs with him.

"How could I forget *Troy?*" she said. "We watched it together when we were in Cairo over Christmas break. It was a total cheese-fest."

"Maybe so, but you couldn't stop drooling over Brad Pitt."

When he gave a warm chuckle, her breath snagged in her throat. How was it possible he'd gotten even hotter over the past year? It had to be the beard. She yearned to feel those coarse bristles under her fingers.

She defused her momentary bout of weakness by nudging him playfully. "Can you blame me for ogling Brad? He was the perfect Achilles, and there were two scenes featuring his naked butt."

They drove past a long stretch of farm fields until the sea came into view. The sight of the dark blue water shimmering along the coast made Dusty eager to jump in and cool off. "I'm hoping you weren't stringing me along when you said we'd be staying near the beach."

"Believe it. The field house is a mile south of Güzelyali, which is right on the Aegean. Should make for some great swimming on the weekends."

"How'd you swing that?"

"The American Research Institute in Turkey owns the land and the building, so we're renting it from them. Since it's only fifteen minutes from Troy, the location's ideal, but it's an old building. The plumbing's janky, it doesn't have AC, and the decor is from the '70s. But it's a lot better than spending the next two months living in army tents."

"You got that right." Dusty had been on enough digs to appreciate any lodgings that included indoor plumbing and actual beds.

Güzelyali contained the usual amenities of a seaside village—boutique hotels, luxury villas, outdoor restaurants, tiny cafés, and touristy shops. After they drove past the edge of town, Stuart headed down a side road until they reached a small compound bordered by a row of olive trees. At the center was a sprawling, one-story house; beside it was a storage shed and an open garage containing another Land Rover and a battered Ford truck. One side of the yard held a tented area with two rows of picnic tables underneath. Not a bad setup, especially compared to some of the rustic projects she'd worked on.

Stuart parked on a gravel stretch beside a shiny Volkswagen Passat. "Here we are. Home sweet home for the next two months."

Dusty frowned at the other car. "That doesn't look like a dig vehicle. You said no one else was coming today."

"It probably belongs to the housekeeper. She cleaned the whole place yesterday but needed to drop off more towels and bedding. We also have two local women coming during the week to cook our midday and evening meals. But tonight, I figured we could hit a place on the beach and have a nice dinner."

*Yes.* An intimate dinner would be the perfect opportunity to gauge Stuart's feelings for her. "That would be great. It's been ages since we've really talked."

In the months following his breakup, Stuart had been oddly uncommunicative. Dusty had found his behavior frustrating but hadn't pushed him on it.

He released a drawn-out breath. "That's on me. Sorry I was so evasive."

She looked down, not wanting to reveal how hurt she'd been. "I get it. Shelby did a number on you. But you could have talked to me about it."

"I could have, but it was embarrassing to admit that you—and everyone else—were right about Shelby. She was totally wrong for me. I can't believe I spent so much time with a woman who never respected my profession. It took me a while to come to terms with it, but now that I'm on the other side, I'm ready to make amends." He placed his hand over hers. "Okay?"

A shiver danced along her spine. Her evening with Stuart was looking more and more promising. "Okay, but you're buying me dinner. I might even splurge and order dessert."

He laughed. "You can order whatever you want. Let's get you settled first."

"Perfect. Thanks." As Dusty unlatched her door and hopped out, a booming male voice made her freeze up. "Stuart, my boy. About time you showed up. And who's the little lady?"

*Little lady?* She stood there in shock as a portly older man walked over to greet them. He was clad in a safari hat, a matching vest, and a pair of khaki shorts, like a colonial explorer. Next to him was a woman in her twenties, tall and slender, with wavy blond hair, who was a dead ringer for Shelby.

Like a ghost from the past come back to haunt them.

∼

STUART HATED BEING BLINDSIDED. Whenever he took on a project, he made sure he was completely prepared so that he'd come across as a professional. Right now, he felt anything but as he faced down Mortimer Jones and his daughter, Clarissa. When he'd spoken to them earlier in the week, he'd written down their itinerary. They were supposed to be spending the night in Izmir. Or had he gotten the dates wrong? If so, it was a huge gaffe on his part.

He strode over to Mortimer and shook his hand. "Mr. Jones. It's a pleasure to meet you in person. I'm sorry I wasn't here to greet you earlier. I thought you'd be arriving tomorrow."

The older man gave his hand a vigorous shake. "Call me Mort, please. Mr. Jones sounds like a stuffy businessman. As you can see, Clarissa and I are ready for adventure."

While Mort looked as though he were outfitted for a Victorian-era safari, Clarissa was dressed more like a typical tourist in a wide-brimmed hat, a loose cotton blouse, and shorts that displayed her long legs to their full advantage.

"Sorry about the change in plans," she said. "Father decided to pass on Izmir. The housekeeper was here when we arrived, so she let us in and showed us around."

"Glad to hear it," Stuart said. "She cleaned the field house yesterday, so it's ready for occupation. Although you mentioned staying at a local hotel?"

Mort nodded. "I'm at the Iris a mile down the road. A little shabby compared to what I'm used to, but it has a pool and a spa." He placed his hand on Clarissa's shoulder. "I can't convince this one to join me. She wants to rough it with the rest of you."

Clarissa offered Stuart a dazzling smile. "I want the full experience. The dirt, the heat, the bonding over dig stories. I can't wait."

"Um, Stuart?" Dusty said. "Okay if I drop off my stuff inside?"

*Damn.* In his haste to placate the Joneses, he hadn't thought to introduce Dusty. "Right. First, I'd like you to meet Mortimer Jones—I mean Mort—and his daughter, Clarissa. They'll be working with us this season."

Rather than offer her hand, Dusty gave the two visitors a quick nod. "Nice to meet you. I'm Dusty Danforth, the site illustrator."

Though her tone was genial, Stuart wasn't fooled. She was pissed. If he wanted to defuse her irritation, he'd need a few minutes alone with her. "If you'll excuse me," he said to Mort and Clarissa. "I'm going to get Dusty settled."

After grabbing her backpack from the trunk, he hustled her inside, leading her past the communal living area, then down a hall where the bedrooms were located. He'd put her in a large, dorm-style room outfitted with four twin beds. Along one wall were two large wardrobes and a shared sink.

Once inside the room, Dusty shut the door behind them and whirled around to face him. "Who the hell are they?"

He stared at her, stunned by her burst of anger. Though Mort had arrived a day earlier than expected, it was a minor glitch. Nothing like the disasters they'd experienced on their parents' digs in Egypt, when they'd dealt with cave-ins, dust storms, and bouts of dysentery.

Even so, he felt the need to apologize. He set her pack next to one of the beds. "Sorry. I was going to warn you tonight at dinner. Mort is a big donor who wants to dabble in archaeology, and Clarissa is his daughter. They'll be working with us on-site, and she'll be living here with the rest of the crew."

Dusty dumped her messenger bag onto the bed. Hoping to soften her up, Stuart was about to point out the Trojan horse cap he'd bought for her. He'd left it on the pillow as a surprise.

But she was staring at the bed opposite hers. She gestured to the luggage propped against it—a black suitcase, a matching carry-on bag, and a travel pillow. "Looks like she's already made herself at home. Are you supposed to look after her? Is that a part of your job?"

"I just need to make her feel comfortable. It shouldn't be too hard. She'll be like any other member of the team."

"A member who needs extra TLC," Dusty muttered.

Stuart's jaw tightened. What was up with her? For all her snark, she rarely criticized anyone for their lack of experience. She'd worked with lots of newbies before, and she'd always treated them decently. If anything, she was good at taking anxious students under her wing.

Maybe she was just disappointed they wouldn't get to talk alone tonight. He was disappointed, too, since he hadn't seen her in person for almost a year. He'd wanted to reconnect with her before everyone else arrived, but he had a job to do.

"Come on," he said. "We can tell Mort we already have plans."

She gave a brittle laugh. "Right. I don't think he'll be that easy to offload."

Sure enough, once they went back outside, Mort greeted them with a jovial grin. "Since it's just the four of us, how about I treat you both to dinner at my hotel?"

Stuart held up his hand. "That's very generous of you. I appreciate the offer, but—"

"No buts. I insist you join us. This way, you can fill us in on the excavation."

Clarissa clasped her hands together. "Please come with us. It's the least we can do for showing up early."

Stuart managed a weak smile. He couldn't say no, not when Dr. Fiorelli had asked him to keep Mort happy. "Sounds good."

Somehow, he'd make it up to Dusty. He owed her that much.

# CHAPTER FOUR

Dusty sat beside Stuart at the outdoor restaurant of the Iris Hotel. If they'd been alone, the setting would have been perfect. Shaded by a wide canopy, their table was protected from the sun and cooled by the breeze blowing off the ocean. In the distance, the Aegean Sea provided a soothing soundtrack, the waves breaking against the shore in a steady rhythm. A banquet of mezes had been laid out before them—olives, cheeses, stuffed vine leaves, stewed eggplant in tomato sauce, and plenty of pita bread to accompany the delicious bowls of hummus, baba ghanoush, and fava bean dip.

But instead of bonding over a romantic dinner, they were sharing a table with Mort and Clarissa.

When Mort wasn't bragging about his recent cruise through the Mediterranean, Clarissa was gushing with excitement over the dig. "I'm so thrilled to be working at Troy. When I was at the University of Boston, I minored in Classics and read *The Iliad* twice. It's amazing to think I could uncover artifacts from the time of the Trojan War. But when I read about the site, it seemed so confusing, what with all those layers of history."

Stuart nodded. "Ten layers, covering thousands of years of

occupation. But we'll be concentrating on the layer dating to the Late Bronze Age. That's when the Trojan War supposedly took place."

"It's all so exciting. I've always dreamed of joining a dig, but I never imagined I'd work on one of such significance."

"Go big or go home, right?" Mort said. "Who knows what treasures we'll find?"

*Probably broken pottery. And then, more pottery.* Based on her experiences in the field, Dusty suspected they'd devote most of their time to hauling up buckets of potsherds, animal bones, and the occasional bronze tool. Or they'd spend hours scraping their trowels along rows of stones that might be architectural features. But she wasn't about to burst Mort's bubble.

If anything, she was trying to behave, to make up for the way she'd snapped at Stuart earlier. She knew her snark had been unwarranted, but she hadn't been able to stop herself. Even now, she was overcome with a peevishness she couldn't explain. It didn't help that Mort and Clarissa were doting on Stuart as if he were an archaeological wunderkind.

*Let it go. If you let them upset you, you'll have a miserable summer.*

"Dusty?" Stuart asked.

She startled, suddenly aware the others were looking at her. "Sorry. What was it? I'm a little tired from today's bus ride."

"I was telling Mort that you've been on more excavations than I have," Stuart said. "You're in such high demand as an illustrator that we were lucky you agreed to join us."

A warmth spread through her, easing a little of her heartache. But before she could speak up, Clarissa beat her to it. "That's wonderful. I'm something of an artist myself."

"She's being modest," Mort said. "Not only is Clarissa a fabulous art teacher, but she's truly gifted. A friend of mine runs a children's publishing firm in Boston, and he's used her work for two of their picture books. One of them won a library medal, if you can imagine."

Dusty knocked back the rest of her wine in one quick swallow. Illustrating children's books was a dream of hers, along with creating her own graphic novels. And this woman, this beautiful Shelby-clone who'd appeared out of nowhere, had already achieved it. "Congrats."

Clarissa reached for the wine bottle and refilled their glasses. "It's just something I do on the side. When I'm not reading up on Greek mythology or volunteering at the animal shelter."

*Or saving the world.*

Aware Mort was staring at her, Dusty stiffened. Had she allowed her resting bitch face to peek out? Even if she was wallowing in jealousy, she couldn't let it show. "Mort? Were you about to ask me something?"

"When you introduced yourself earlier, your last name sounded familiar," he said. "I just put the pieces together. You wouldn't be related to Dr. Louisa Danforth, would you?"

*And there it is.* "Yep. She's my mom."

"Well, then. Color me impressed. I've been a fan of hers for years. In fact, I'm hoping to go on one of her Ancient Excursions jaunts this fall. She's giving an exclusive tour of Egypt, with access to places tourists aren't allowed to visit. Any chance she'd be interested in joining us for part of the dig? What a thrill that would be."

Dusty sucked in a tight breath. She couldn't think of anything worse than having her mother show up and spend all summer in full nag mode. "She doesn't work in the field as much anymore. Besides, she's an Egyptologist, so she's all about Ancient Egypt. Mummies, pharaohs, hieroglyphics, you know what I mean?"

Mort harrumphed. "I'm well aware of what an Egyptologist studies, and—"

"We'd still love to meet her," Clarissa said quickly. "When she hosted the show *Ancient Histories—Ancient Mysteries*, we watched every episode. She's brilliant."

If it were possible, Dusty felt even smaller now.

*Why am I here? Why not invite my brilliant mother to take my place? And hire Clarissa to do all the archaeological illustrations?*

Thankfully, Mort began peppering Stuart with more questions about Troy.

For the rest of the evening, Dusty didn't say another word. She didn't need to. Her presence was entirely inconsequential.

∼

AFTER DINNER, MORT DROPPED THEM OFF AT THE FIELD HOUSE AND returned to his hotel. Dusty dashed inside, desperate to put some distance between herself and Clarissa. She needed to get her emotions under control before she said something she'd regret. But no sooner did she enter her room than Clarissa followed. Even if the field house was nearly empty, it was just Dusty's luck she was sharing a bedroom with the person she least wanted to see.

Half watching as Clarissa began unpacking her carry-on bag, Dusty plopped down on her bed. Only then did she notice a baseball cap bearing a logo of the Trojan horse, propped up on one of the pillows. It was identical to the one Stuart had been wearing earlier, except in a navy blue that almost matched the purple streak in her hair. As she picked it up, a lump formed in her throat. More than ever, she felt terrible that she'd lashed out at him.

Clarissa glanced over at her. "That's a cute hat. Do we all get one?"

"No. I mean, you could buy one if you wanted. I'm sure the Troy Museum has a gift shop. But Stuart got it for me yesterday. He knows I love cheesy shit like this."

Clarissa raised her eyebrows. "Are you and he...?"

Here was Dusty's chance. If she were smart, she'd stake her claim before Clarissa got any ideas about pursuing him. But she couldn't bring herself to lie. "We're just friends. His dad worked with my parents on a huge excavation project in Egypt for ten years off and on. Because of that, Stuart and I spent a lot of time together when we were kids. But there's nothing else between us."

"Okay. Good to know."

Clarissa's smile darkened Dusty's mood even further.

*Great, I practically told her to go for it.*

"I know it's not that late, but would you mind if I got ready for bed?" Clarissa asked. "I thought I was doing okay, but today's travels just caught up with me."

"Sure, no problem." Dusty was tired, too, but if she went to sleep now, she'd wake at four in the morning. Better to push herself until ten, in the hopes of getting a decent night's sleep.

After leaving the room, she checked out the rest of the field house. The wing they were in reminded her of a college dorm, with four shared bedrooms, two single rooms, and a set of men's and women's communal bathrooms. The bathrooms looked recently cleaned, though they wouldn't stay that way with a bunch of grubby archaeologists using them every day.

The back side of the house was research-oriented, containing a lab for processing their finds and a field library. One wall of the library displayed photographs of Troy over the years, spanning from nineteenth-century photos in black and white all the way to the present.

Dusty made her way to the front of the building, which housed the communal living space—a comfy seating area with worn plaid couches and mismatched armchairs, a set of long wooden tables for dining indoors, and a spacious kitchen with wood-paneled cupboards, avocado-green appliances, and laminate countertops. Like Stuart said, the decor was firmly stuck in the 1970s.

Tacked next to the fridge was a tally sheet for keeping track of beverages. She grabbed a beer from the fridge and added her name to the sheet. Wanting to take advantage of the cool night air, she ambled outside but stopped short at the sight of Stuart. He sat by himself on the patio located on the far side of the building. Like her, he had a beer in hand, but he was staring into space, as though lost in thought.

Had he come out here in search of solitude? Too bad. Now that she'd caught him alone, she needed to talk to him.

She planted her butt in one of the hard plastic patio chairs and held up her bottle in a salute. "Greetings."

He frowned at her. "What's going on? You were sulking all through dinner."

Sulking? Really? Maybe she hadn't been on her best behavior, but she doubted Mort and Clarissa had noticed. They'd pretty much dismissed her once she told them her mom wasn't about to jet over to Turkey and join the dig. Still, she didn't want to make Stuart feel bad.

"Sorry," she mumbled.

"Not good enough. You were glad to see me when I picked you up, but you barely said a word tonight. Then, when Mort asked you about your mom, you were totally condescending. I know you were hoping for a quiet dinner, but we'll have other chances."

*No, we won't. Literally everyone else is showing up tomorrow.*

"It's not that. I was just tired."

"Seriously? Your flight from Cairo to Istanbul was only a few hours. It's something else, isn't it?"

"I also rode a bus for five and a half hours, which isn't my idea of fun." When Stuart's expression didn't soften, her shoulders sagged in resignation. "I was caught off guard by Mort and Clarissa. But it's more than that. Clarissa looks just like *her*."

Stuart chuffed out an angry breath. "You think I didn't notice? Before they flew out here, I had to check in with Mort on Zoom. When Clarissa's face showed up on the screen, I could barely speak. I couldn't believe how much she resembled Shelby. After we were done, I checked to make sure she wasn't related."

"Is she?"

"Nope. Just another gorgeous blond with long legs and a killer tan."

*Gorgeous.* That meant he was halfway in already. Dusty swallowed painfully, washing down the ache with a swig of beer. "You remember what happened the last time we had a gorgeous blond on one of our digs?"

It was a low blow. But she'd never forgotten how Shelby had treated him. He'd only been dating her for six months when he left for a summer dig in Greece. Though he'd warned her that an archaeological dig wasn't a true vacation, she'd insisted on coming for two weeks. And she'd been pissed as hell when she realized their remote hilltop location was nothing like the *Mamma Mia*-inspired fantasy she'd conjured up in her head. After she left, Stuart had been a mopey son of a bitch for weeks.

Shelby had done a lot of shitty things to Stuart, but this was the one thing Dusty couldn't forgive because she'd made him feel miserable in a place he loved.

"You don't have to remind me," he said. "That summer was a disaster, but this isn't the same. Unlike Shelby, Clarissa loves archaeology. You heard her at dinner—she's a huge ancient history nerd. She'll fit in fine."

The thing was, she probably *would* fit in fine. She'd love it and bond with Stuart, and he'd have a new Shelby all over again. Except this time, she'd be perfect for him because she'd respect him for going into archaeology. She also lived in Boston, so if things developed between them, they'd be able to stay together after the dig ended.

Dusty looked away, trying to hide her heartache. She was so screwed.

"Dusty?"

"What?" she snapped.

"Don't be mean to Clarissa, okay? She's not Shelby."

She glared at him. "For the record, I wasn't mean to Shelby, either. I treated her decently, even though it wasn't easy. Do you remember what she said when I told her about my childhood?"

Now it was Stuart's turn to look ashamed. "She just didn't get it."

"She felt sorry for me because I didn't have a 'normal' childhood, whatever that means. Because I had the misfortune to spend a chunk of my life in Egypt instead of good old America." Her voice rose. "I had an amazing childhood. Not everyone can be Malibu Barbie."

He placed his hand over hers. "I'm sorry. I think she was jealous of us and all the fun we'd had together. But she told me she liked you."

*She pitied me. There's a difference.* Shelby had never acted jealous of Dusty because she didn't consider her a threat, not in terms of looks or personality. Shelby had once said to her, albeit jokingly, "You're lucky you don't care about your appearance. Must make life so much easier."

Dusty shook off the memories. She didn't want to rehash any of it. And she didn't want to fight with Stuart, either. "I'm sorry, too. I know this dig won't be easy. Just let me know how I can help."

"Be nice to Clarissa. Even if she seems confident, she's taking a leap outside her comfort zone. The first season in the field can be really challenging. Think of all the times we've worked with nervous undergrads. You've always helped them fit in."

Dusty nodded. As beautiful and talented as Clarissa was, she'd never worked on a dig before. Rather than seeing her as a threat, Dusty should be helping her adapt. Making her feel comfortable. And maybe, if they became friends, Dusty might not resent her as much.

But it would be a hell of a lot easier if she didn't look like Shelby.

# CHAPTER FIVE

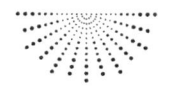

Stuart stood in the kitchen, waiting as the coffeepot filled at a glacial pace. Making American drip coffee in a land known for its thick, rich kahve seemed like sacrilege, but he was preparing breakfast for a dozen people. He'd already poured a full pot into the urn on the counter and had started another in case everyone needed an extra hit of caffeine. Since most of the group had arrived in Turkey yesterday, they were still recovering from jet lag.

With that in mind, he'd planned an easy first day—a visit to the Troy Museum, followed by a tour of the site. In addition to letting the students sleep until eight, he'd also laid out a traditional Turkish breakfast—sliced tomatoes and cucumbers, cheeses, olives, dried apricots, and thick peasant bread accompanied by pots of sour cherry jam, Nutella, and honey.

When Dusty ambled into the kitchen, wearing her Trojan horse baseball cap, her bright smile filled him with a warm glow. Two nights ago, after they'd argued about Clarissa, he'd worried that her sullen mood might linger. But yesterday, she'd given him her full support, even picking up the incoming students from the bus depot in Çanakkale. When it came to driving in foreign countries, she was fearless.

She leaned on the breakfast bar and snatched a slice of beyaz peynir, a tangy white cheese similar to feta. "Look at you, setting out a whole feast. You're going to spoil them."

"This is just to ease them into the first day. After that, we'll shift to a normal dig schedule. Wake-up call at six with coffee, tea, and biscuits. Arrive at the site before seven, break at ten for a full breakfast, and work on-site until two. Clarissa and I did a grocery run yesterday afternoon and stocked up the fridge and the pantry."

Dusty's expression clouded over briefly, but she kept her voice upbeat. "Nice to know we won't go hungry."

Her forced cheeriness didn't fool him. For whatever reason, Clarissa's presence was still bothering her. It shouldn't. Even if Clarissa bore a striking resemblance to Shelby, she was nothing like his ex. But he didn't want to bring up the subject again. "Thanks for doing pickup yesterday."

"No problem. That Land Rover's a cranky pain in the ass, but it did the job. I also had a few students help me sort through all the crap in the shed. Some of the smaller picks need new handles, and we're low on buckets, so we might need to do a supply run." She pointed to the clipboard on the counter. "Everyone here and accounted for?"

"Yep. Fourteen of us: you, me, Mort, Clarissa, and ten students, including the two from Turkey. We'll be meeting the Turkish archaeologist at the site today. Since he lives in Çanakkale, he's planning to stay here during the week and head home on the weekends."

"What about your boss, the esteemed Dr. Hughes? Any sign of him?"

"Nope. I've emailed and texted and...nothing." The professor's lack of communication was not only unprofessional, but it was also frustrating as hell. "Last I heard, he was giving a lecture in

Istanbul, but that was three days ago. He should have arrived yesterday."

"Do you think he bailed?" Dusty's eyes widened in excitement. "Wouldn't that be fabulous? Then you'd be in charge."

The thought had crossed Stuart's mind when he'd woken at 5:00 a.m., too anxious to fall back asleep. Given everything he'd heard about Dr. Hughes, he'd grown exceedingly leery of working as the man's second-in-command. But leading a team of grad students on a site of such significance was a daunting level of responsibility. Besides, Mort was expecting Dr. Hughes to run the show. Wasn't that why he'd given such a generous donation?

Stuart poured the contents of the coffeepot into the urn and tightened the lid. " "I don't think I'm ready to take on the role of dig director yet."

"You could totally handle it. Plus, isn't Dr. Özgen actually the lead archaeologist? He's worked at Troy for years."

"Right. He's the real expert." He was grateful they'd be digging under the guidance of Dr. Kerim Özgen, a university professor from Çanakkale who was intimately familiar with the Troy excavations. "He's expecting us on-site at noon, so I'm going ahead with today's tour regardless of whether Hughes shows up."

"Good plan." Dusty flashed him a saucy grin. "I like this take-charge side of you, Dr. Carlson."

Whether his decision would come back to bite him in the ass, he couldn't say. But he didn't want to waste anyone's time by hanging around the field house all morning. He grabbed a set of mugs and placed them next to the urn, along with a box of sugar cubes. Dusty filled a cup for each of them. He took a sip, then winced, realizing he'd made it too strong.

"Do I smell coffee?" a strident female voice exclaimed. "Thank the goddess because I'd be a right bitch without it."

"Oh, is that why you were so grouchy yesterday?" a male voice grumbled.

Stuart grinned at the sight of two familiar faces—TJ Mayer

and Emilia Flores. He'd met TJ last year while teaching at a field school in Cyprus and Emilia three years ago while digging in Greece. Though TJ and Emilia were both graduate students working toward their doctorates in archaeology, they'd never dug at the same site before.

TJ looked the same as Stuart remembered—shaggy brown hair, glasses, and a lanky frame, though he'd put on more muscle since last summer. Maybe he'd been lifting. Stuart could relate. After he and Shelby ended things, he'd channeled his depression into a grueling workout regimen.

Dusty smiled at them sweetly. "Everything okay, you two?"

"I'm fine, but Em is still pissed about Istanbul." TJ glared at her. "Let it go, girl."

"Did you call me 'girl'? Don't dismiss me like that." Emilia turned to face TJ, her eyes blazing with fury. Tall, slender, and toned, with light brown skin and long black hair, she was truly striking. Like Dusty, she didn't let anyone steamroll over her just because she was a woman.

"What happened in Istanbul?" Stuart asked.

Emilia scowled. "When we found out we'd be arriving there on the same flight, TJ offered to find us a place to stay for the night, using his 'connections.' Some connections. It was the dumpiest, one-star fleabag in the entire city."

"We were there for one night," TJ said. "What does it matter if it was a little run-down?"

"Run-down? It stunk to high heaven, probably because the bathroom hadn't been cleaned since the days of the Ottoman Empire." As TJ started to speak, she held up her hand. "Don't call me a diva again. I worked in the jungles of Mexico for two months with nothing but pit toilets, and they smelled better than our hotel room."

Stuart couldn't help but laugh. When it came to hard-core experiences, he had nothing on TJ or Emilia, both of whom loved to flaunt their ruggedness. Emilia's point of pride was the two seasons she'd spent digging in the Yucatán Peninsula as an undergrad, while TJ never missed a chance to boast about his experiences in the Jordanian desert.

Dusty smirked. "How about some coffee, Em?"

"Yes, please." Emilia pushed past TJ to grab a mug. "I'm still groggy. How are you so damn perky, Danforth?"

"Dusty's been around the world so many times she's probably immune to jet lag by now." TJ glanced around the kitchen. "Nice place, other than the disco-era decor. But this Troy dig is low on the hard-core scale. We've got running water, beds, flush toilets, and a decent kitchen. It might be a little *too* luxurious."

Emilia snorted. "If you're really hurting, you can drag your blankets outside and sleep under the stars. Would that make you feel better, *bro*?"

Ignoring her, TJ grabbed a mug and filled his cup. After taking a sip, he shuddered. "A little bold for my taste. Got any cream or evaporated milk?"

Stuart found a can of evaporated milk in the pantry, opened it, and passed it to TJ. When he'd first learned that TJ and Emilia were joining the dig, drawn in by the lure of working at Troy, he'd been excited to see them again. Hopefully, they could set aside their animosity for the summer. It didn't help that they were academic rivals; TJ was doing his graduate work at Harvard, while Emilia was at Yale.

By eight, the rest of the team had assembled in the kitchen and filled their plates. While they were eating, Stuart reviewed the day's itinerary. "Our first stop is the Troy Museum in Tevfikiye. It's a wonderful resource, housing an enormous collection of artifacts from a hundred and fifty years of excavation. After that, we'll walk through the site. We'll have lunch back here, take a few hours to rest, then discuss the schedule and the logistics before dinner. Does that sound all right?"

Dusty gave him a thumbs-up. "You got it, boss."

"Thanks for going easy on us," one of the students said. "I'm still on Chicago time." The others nodded.

Though the students asked a few more questions, no one brought up Dr. Hughes' absence or acted disappointed that he hadn't shown up. Since only three of them were from the University of Boston—the rest were from universities like Brown, Michigan, and Penn—Stuart wondered whether they were fully aware of the professor's tainted reputation.

At ten, everyone crammed into the two Land Rovers and met up with Mort at the Troy Museum. Located half a mile from the ruins, the stunning, cube-like building stood out in stark contrast to the flat farm fields surrounding it. Inside, the museum was well-lit and beautifully curated, with four floors of material surrounding a large central atrium. The team appeared enthralled by the quality of the displays, especially Mort, who used his phone to take a lengthy video of his visit, complete with a running commentary.

Their next stop was the ruins of ancient Troy, located on a hilltop site known as Hisarlik. After parking their vehicles in a lot filled with rental cars and tour buses, their group passed through the main gate onto a wide, paved courtyard containing a gift shop and an outdoor café.

The star attraction was the giant model of the Trojan horse, which stood forty feet high. Stuart had seen it in countless photos, but the wooden structure was more impressive up close. Kids of all ages swarmed around it, waiting to clamber up the ladder to go inside the horse's belly. Without a hint of shame, the entire crew joined in, taking selfies and group shots next to the horse and posing with a band of reenactors dressed like Greek gods and Trojan soldiers.

Naturally, Dr. Özgen showed up during their impromptu photo session. Stuart cringed inwardly, anticipating a snide remark, but the professor merely smiled and waited for them to finish. With his muscular build, olive-toned complexion, and dark beard, he looked more like a Trojan warrior than any of the young reenactors.

His warm laugh put Stuart at ease. "Splendid horse, no? I brought my nephews here last month, and they loved it." Stuart motioned for the others to gather around. "Folks, this is Dr. Kerim Özgen, from the university at Çanakkale. He's been the lead Turkish archaeologist on the site for years, so we're lucky to have him as part of our team."

Dusty and Emilia were the last to join them since they'd been flirting with a performer dressed like the Greek god Apollo. When Dusty saw Dr. Özgen, she beamed at him. "Kerim. It's so good to see you."

How was it that Dusty was on a first-name basis with him? Then again, she was on a first-name basis with a lot of prominent archaeologists, thanks to her parents. But the way Kerim drew her into a hug made Stuart suspect their connection was personal rather than professional.

"Miss Danforth," he said. "Always a pleasure."

After hugging him for a long beat, she turned to the others. "Kerim is friends with the director of the Institute of Nautical Archaeology in Bodrum. When I was working there, Kerim sailed down to Bodrum and spent a few weeks helping us with the project."

*Sailed?* The guy owned a boat?

As the students introduced themselves, Stuart grappled with an unexpected surge of jealousy. Had Dusty hooked up with Kerim when she'd been in Bodrum? Though the Turkish professor was in his late thirties, she'd gotten involved with older men before.

*Don't dwell on it. You can't lose focus now.*

"Are you all ready to walk through the ruins?" Kerim asked. "I'd be happy to lead you, unless Dr. Carlson would like that honor."

His gracious tone made Stuart feel like a dick for letting envy cloud his emotions. "Call me Stuart, please. You're welcome to lead us. I'll gladly defer to your expertise."

A wide wooden boardwalk stretched around the perimeter of the seventy-four-acre site, making for an easy stroll. Though the sun was out in full force, a brisk breeze eased the heat, and the abundance of oak and olive trees provided ample shade. At each stopping point, tourists clumped together in groups, listening to their guides.

As they walked, Kerim pointed out the parts of the site Stuart had read about—the massive stone walls, the remains of fortified towers, the paved ramp near the eastern entrance, and the northeast bastion of the citadel. Based on the archaeological record, the citadel would have housed Troy's palatial complex.

They paused at a giant trench gouged into the hilltop. Over fifty feet deep, it revealed seven layers of occupation, going back over five thousand years. Known as "Schliemann's trench," it was named after Heinrich Schliemann, the amateur archaeologist credited with discovering Troy in the 1870s.

Kerim turned to Stuart. "Why don't you take it from here? I don't want to dominate our tour."

Before Stuart could launch into his spiel, Mort whipped out his phone. "Hang on. I'd like to record this, if I may."

Stuart straightened up and smiled at the older man. "Go ahead. Given your fascination with archaeology, I assume you've heard of Schliemann's exploits?"

"But of course," Mort said. "Even if his practices were somewhat questionable, he's the one who put this site on the map."

"True, although the term 'questionable' might be a little generous." Stuart began with an overview, but just when he was about to share the story of "Priam's Treasure"—a priceless cache of gold and silver artifacts unearthed by Schliemann—a hand clapped him on the back. Hard.

"I'll take it from here," a gravelly voice said.

Fighting back his trepidation, Stuart turned to face his boss, Dr. Rutherford Hughes. Up close, the man was intimidating, tall and barrel-chested, with a bushy gray beard and a face weathered by decades spent outdoors. At the sight of him, Mort lit up with a jubilant smile, as though in the presence of a celebrity.

"Rutherford," Kerim acknowledged him with a terse nod. "Welcome back."

Dr. Hughes' lip curled up in a sneer. "Kerim. You're not working with the Germans anymore? I hope we can trust you."

Kerim folded his arms across his chest. "As long as you behave professionally, there should be nothing to worry about."

"Are you telling me how to behave? I've got at least twenty years of experience on you. I was digging here when you were still a schoolboy."

As the two men stared each other down, Stuart sought to defuse the tension. "Isn't it great that we're all together? Finally getting to work at Troy? I was just telling the group about Schliemann's discoveries, but if you want—"

"What I want is to highlight the important parts of the site, like the areas *I* excavated back when I was in charge of this entire operation." With a sweeping motion, Dr. Hughes gestured for the group to join him. "Let's go."

As he led the way, followed by Kerim and the students, unease crawled up Stuart's spine. Should he have waited for his boss before leaving this morning? Had the professor arrived at the field house and erupted in a rage when he found it empty?

Dusty sidled up to him and spoke in a hushed tone. "Hey. You have your stressed face on. Don't worry about Hughes."

"I think I screwed up. He looked pissed that I started without him, but I emailed him the itinerary four days ago. He's the one that showed up three hours late."

"He's probably more pissed at Kerim than at anyone else. Like, he regards him as a traitor because he's been working with the Germans. Which is ridiculous because Kerim is one of the nicest, most courteous professionals I've ever met." She tugged on Stuart's arm, pulling him forward. "Come on, let's see what pearls of wisdom old Hughes has to dispense."

Though Dusty's words eased a little of his insecurity, Stuart couldn't regain his earlier enthusiasm. Nor could he ignore the glowing way Dusty had described Kerim.

*Focus, damn it.* Even if he couldn't stave off the jealousy simmering inside him, he couldn't allow it to affect his professionalism. He had too much at stake.

# CHAPTER SIX

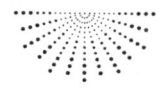

As Dr. Hughes led the group along the boardwalk, Dusty stopped to tie her hiking boots. She needed a minute to herself since Kerim's appearance had thrown her off-kilter. When she'd met him in Bodrum two years ago, she'd swooned over his warm, approachable manner and his smoldering good looks. Though all she'd done with him was exchange flirtatious banter, she'd been tempted to take things further.

But now? As desirable as he was, she didn't feel the same spark of attraction. Nor did she have any interest in pursuing him—not if she still had a chance with Stuart.

When she hustled to catch up with the others, Emilia stopped her. She'd lingered behind, clearly waiting to talk to her.

Dusty raised her eyebrows. "Yes? Something you wanted to ask me?"

Emilia gave her a sly smile. "That was quite the hug between you and Kerim. He's, like, an eight on the archaeological hotness scale. Maybe even a nine."

Dusty didn't believe in objectifying anyone—male or female—but whenever she was around Em, she tended to revert to her teenage self. "I've seen him in a swimsuit. Definitely a nine. He's like a cross between a hot lumberjack and a sexy professor."

"Nice. Did you and he ever...?"

She shook her head quickly. "He was only in Bodrum for a couple of weeks."

"That's more than enough time." Like Dusty, Emilia preferred short-term flings to lengthy relationships, and she'd experienced her share of shenanigans in the field.

"Honestly? I was seriously lusting after him until I found out he's a Louisa Danforth fanboy. He *idolizes* my mother. So, sex with him might have been weird. But he took us out on his boat a few times, and we had a blast. If you want to go after him, you won't have any competition from me."

"Nope. After last year's debacle, I've sworn off dig romances."

Dusty nodded in sympathy. Last summer, while excavating in Italy, Emilia had gotten involved with a guy who'd claimed to be single. Once the season had ended, she'd learned he was engaged and had been using the dig as his "free pass" before settling down.

Seeing that Dr. Hughes had led the group to the ruins of a Roman amphitheater, she and Emilia hurried to catch up with them. They stood at the back, listening while he described his first few seasons at the site. Dusty had to give him credit—he was a fount of knowledge about Troy. But any trace of the charming speaker who'd once commanded the academic lecture circuit had vanished. Instead, he came across as boastful and arrogant.

Emilia leaned down and hissed in Dusty's ear. "Speaking of archaeological hotness, Stuart's looking good. A little more jacked than I remember. And that beard? *Yes, please.* Are you finally going to climb that tree?"

Dusty flushed. One night during their dig in Greece, she and Em had gotten drunk on ouzo and shared their deepest secrets. "We're still just friends. Now that he's single, I thought I had a chance, but he's already got his eye on Clarissa."

"Well, shit. Anyone else worth considering? How about TJ?"

"No, thank you. Although..." She snuck a peek at him. "Stuart's not the only one who's been lifting. TJ's filled out nicely since I saw him last year."

"He's kind of cute, I'll grant you that. Too bad he never shuts up." Emilia rolled her eyes. "Did I tell you *why* we had to share a room in Istanbul? Because the idiot didn't think to reserve two rooms."

Dusty grinned. "Was there only one bed? If so, were you tempted?"

"Shut up. There were two beds, and no. Even if I've been feeling a little deprived in that aspect of my life, I'd never consider it. He never stops boasting. He'd probably claim that his last experience was somewhere hard-core, like the ruins of an ancient site."

The thought made Dusty laugh. "Speaking of ruins..."

"Ladies!"

She froze in horror, suddenly aware everyone was staring at them. Kerim looked as though he was holding back his laughter, but Dr. Hughes nailed her with a murderous scowl. And Stuart had those grumpy frown lines on his forehead. Had all of them heard what she and Emilia had been talking about?

"Um...sorry," she said. "We got sidetracked."

"I certainly hope the two of you will behave professionally," Dr. Hughes said. "Especially you, Miss Danforth. I know who your mother is."

*Yeah, and she hates you.* But Dusty felt firmly chastised. "Sorry."

She kept quiet, listening as he went on and on—not just about the site itself or the recent excavations, but also about his own triumphs, reminding them he'd once been a big name in the field. He'd published numerous books and articles about Troy, and he'd starred in a 2010 documentary entitled *Ancient Troy: Myth, Legend, and Reality*. Not once did he mention anyone else on his team unless it was to disparage them for trying to steal his glory.

No wonder her mom couldn't stand him. More than ever,

Dusty was glad she'd come to Troy to support Stuart. Considering what a jerk his boss was, he needed all the help he could get.

～

Dr. Hughes' behavior was even more unbearable than Stuart had expected. Boasting, talking over people, pushing their questions aside. But for all his braggadocio, his behavior reeked of desperation. Like he didn't want anyone to forget how important he was, despite his ten-year exile from Troy.

Had Dr. Fiorelli not realized how low Dr. Hughes had sunk? Or had she and the rest of the department been too easily swayed by Mort's donation?

To compound Stuart's anxiety, Dusty and Emilia had been gossiping and giggling like a couple of tweens. Emilia had been a part of the crew during that disastrous summer in Greece when Shelby had left him feeling miserable. After he'd retreated into himself, Dusty had bonded with Emilia, and they'd stayed in touch ever since. Though Dusty had gotten up to plenty of shenanigans on her own, she was more likely to embrace her wild side when Emilia was around.

Was that what Emilia was doing now? Telling Dusty to go after Kerim?

Stuart cleared the thought from his head. Now wasn't the time to get distracted, not after he'd offended his boss by starting the site tour without him.

As they rounded the boardwalk, they passed the South Gate, which had once served as the southern entranceway into the Trojan citadel. Below the walkway were four trenches cut into the earth, currently under excavation by a large team of German archaeologists from the University of Tübingen. Stuart had reviewed their site reports before coming to Turkey, only to learn that their lead archaeologist, Dr. Friedrich

Wagner, was the professor Hughes had clashed with ten years ago.

Though the area was roped off and displayed signs forbidding public access, Dr. Hughes stepped off the boardwalk, pushed past the ropes, and motioned for the others to follow. As they clambered down to join him, Dr. Wagner walked over to them. Tall, blond, and muscular, with high cheekbones and piercing blue eyes, he gave off an unquestionable air of authority.

Frowning, he addressed Dr. Hughes in English. "So, they finally let you back here, did they?"

"It's where I belong," Dr. Hughes said. "If it weren't for you, I could have been working here for the last ten years. You had to go crying to the Turks."

"For good reason. You're lucky you didn't end up in prison."

Dr. Hughes stiffened. "How dare you? My offense was hardly worth the fuss you caused."

Stuart wished he could find out what his boss had done to merit expulsion. Maybe if he could get on Dr. Wagner's good side, the German dig director would fill him in.

Kerim placed his hands out, as though trying to placate a couple of children. "No quarreling, please. We're starting a new chapter this season."

"Just stay away from our excavation," Dr. Hughes said to his German rival. "We're going to find the lost cemetery of Troy, and when we do, you'll wish you were a part of it."

"Good luck with that," Dr. Wagner said. "No one's found any evidence yet, other than a few skeletons."

"Enough," Kerim said. "We're working toward a common goal, for the good of Turkish history."

Stuart had to admire the guy. It couldn't be easy coming between two academics with giant egos.

After scowling at his nemesis for another minute, Dr. Hughes gave a dismissive wave of his hand and instructed the group to return to the boardwalk.

While Stuart didn't want to overstep his position, he didn't like the thought of antagonizing the Germans. Once the others had gone on ahead, he addressed his boss quietly. "Sir? Should I instruct our team to steer clear of the Germans' site? Since we're not digging near each other, there's no need for us to cross paths."

It was to their advantage that the boardwalk surrounding Troy made a complete circle. Though both teams would head out in the morning from the north end, where the café and parking lot were located, the Americans could reach their site by heading west along the boardwalk. This way, they could avoid the Germans, who were digging near the southeast perimeter.

Dr. Hughes regarded him with contempt. "Where's your backbone? Do you think I'd ever let a man like Wagner intimidate me?"

"I just thought—"

"We have the full run of Troy. Understand? The only reason to bypass the Germans is because their excavations are unlikely to produce anything of significance."

With that, he strode on ahead. Feeling dejected, Stuart trailed behind, suddenly overcome by a wave of fatigue. Clarissa hung back to wait for him. When he caught up to her, she placed her hand on his arm. "Sorry about Dr. Hughes. My dad's admired him for years, but I wasn't impressed with his behavior."

"Thanks, but I should have waited for him before starting the site tour."

"And make us sit around the field house for hours? You did the right thing. I'll bet everyone's wishing *you* were the dig director."

Up close, he caught the faint hint of lavender. Her shampoo? Whatever it was, the scent had a calming effect. When she squeezed his arm, he wondered if she was trying to convey more than sympathy, but he dismissed the thought. In all likelihood, she was just being nice.

After they'd viewed the ruins situated along the boardwalk, Kerim suggested they check out the area they'd be excavating, which was known as the lower city of Troy. Unlike the rest of the site, it wasn't visible from the boardwalk and was closed to tourists.

"Let's wait," Dr. Hughes said. "We'll get to see the lower city tomorrow when we start digging. For now, we could all use a break."

No one seemed disappointed by his announcement. If anything, Stuart caught a few relieved expressions. Most of the students were probably still adjusting to the heat and the jet lag.

When they returned to the field house, the crew went to wash up for the midday meal. Before joining them, Stuart ambled outside to check on lunch. The two women from Güzelyali had already arrived and were setting out the food. His stomach growled as he took in the generous spread—a large platter of lamb shish kabobs, bowls of pearled couscous, baskets of pita bread, and a hearty village salad made with cucumbers, tomatoes, and olives.

As he was eying the food, Kerim approached him. "How are you doing?"

Stuart's shoulders sagged. "I've been better. That site tour was rough."

"I would agree. After today's altercation, I suggest we keep Dr. Hughes as far from the Germans as possible."

"Good plan." Though Stuart didn't want to pry, his curiosity got the better of him. "If you don't mind me asking—wouldn't you rather dig with them?"

Kerim let out a long breath. "That was what I'd hoped for. Their team is larger and better equipped than ours. They have ten specialists on their staff and full access to the lab at the Troy Museum. Unfortunately, the Ministry of Culture wants me to keep an eye on Dr. Hughes. I agreed, but with certain limitations."

"What kind of limitations?"

"I'm willing to work with all of you on-site, then return here in the afternoon for lab work and dinner, but I'll head home at night to sleep."

Stuart's throat tightened. Another wrench he hadn't expected. "Are you sure? You and Hughes are the only ones with private rooms."

"You take it. I'd just as soon sleep in my air-conditioned apartment."

"I understand. Thanks for letting me know." At least he didn't have to worry about Kerim abandoning them in favor of the Germans.

After lunch, when the others retreated to their rooms to rest, Stuart was once again pulled aside—this time by Dr. Hughes. He led Stuart to the research library and gestured for him to have a seat at one of the study tables.

With his boss looming over him, Stuart felt lower than ever. "Is everything all right?"

"I wasn't pleased you started without me, but I'm willing to forgive a first offense. You need to remember you're merely the assistant director. I'm not about to engage in a power struggle with a young whelp who's barely gotten his feet wet."

A young whelp? Seriously? But Stuart nodded quickly. "No power struggles from me. I'm just doing my job. I apologize for jumping the gun on the site tour, but you hadn't told me when you were arriving and—"

"I don't answer to you. Understand? The only one calling the shots here is me. Are you aware of what transpired ten years ago, when I was exiled from Troy?"

*Trust me, I'd love to know.* "No, sir, but—"

"The Germans betrayed me, and the Turks took their side. All over a minor infraction. I was cast out like a pariah, my academic reputation in tatters. Now that I'm back, I fully intend to reclaim my good name, and I won't have anyone stand in my way."

Could this guy have a bigger ego? "Not planning on it, sir. I'm here to help."

"Good. With my connections, knowing me could be advantageous to your career, but you need to play by my rules. Your job is to make sure everything runs smoothly—the vehicles, the kitchen, the supplies, the students' needs, and whatnot. Is that understood?"

"Absolutely." Here was an area where Stuart could shine. If there was one thing he loved, it was spreadsheets and checklists.

"Glad to hear it." Dr. Hughes turned as if to leave but stopped short. "Are you the one who invited the Danforth girl on this dig?"

"Yes. Dr. Fiorelli said you were too busy to deal with logistics, so she authorized me to hire an illustrator. Dusty will do a great job. She's worked on dozens of projects."

Even if she hadn't been his closest friend, he'd still have wanted her on board. Not only was she an incredibly talented artist, but she also had a wealth of archaeological experience.

Dr. Hughes grunted. "I worked with her mother once, on a tour for Ancient Excursions. She was a complete pill. If Dusty's anything like that old crow, I don't want her around. Mort told me his daughter's an artist. We could use her instead. She's a lot easier on the eyes than Dusty, if you know what I mean."

Stuart choked back a wave of disgust. He wanted to chastise his boss for speaking so inappropriately, but he couldn't risk antagonizing him again. "Since Clarissa doesn't have any formal training, I think we should stick with Dusty. I'm sure she won't be any trouble."

"See to it. Otherwise, I'll have no qualms about shipping her out of here."

# CHAPTER SEVEN

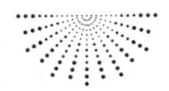

During the afternoon break, the field house was blissfully quiet. With most of the crew sleeping off their jet lag, Dusty had the lab to herself. She scrounged the supply cabinet for measuring equipment and set it up at a table next to the window. This would serve as her illustration table and give her a little space from the rest of the students, who'd be using the lab to sort, label, and analyze their finds. Whenever she worked on a project, she always liked to carve out her own domain.

By dinnertime, everyone seemed to have recovered from the day's outing except Stuart, who was oddly subdued. Dusty suspected the site tour had ramped up his anxiety. He'd started out with such confidence, only to be put in his place by Dr. Hughes. While the others might regard the professor as little more than a blustering egomaniac, Stuart had to follow his orders without question. And once the dig ended, he'd be teaching with him at the University of Boston.

Rather than retreat to their rooms after dinner, the crew gathered in the common room to play cards. But Stuart's absence was notable. Hoping that he'd gone outside, Dusty grabbed her flip-flops and went to look for him. If nothing else, she could give him a pep talk.

When she peered around the side of the field house, Stuart wasn't alone. Seated beside him on a patio chair, with her hand resting on his arm, was Clarissa. From the way her head was bent close to his, she appeared to be consoling him.

Taking a deep, shuddering breath, Dusty bottled up her emotions and went back inside. Maybe this was a sign she should focus on something else. Like her dissertation. She went into her room and grabbed a handful of Jolly Ranchers from her backpack, along with a couple of pencils and a brand-new notebook.

After retreating to the research library at the back of the field house, she flicked on the lights and plunked down at one of the study tables. Setting a timer on her phone for fifteen minutes, she tried brainstorming a list of topics centered on the site of Troy, only to end up doodling in the margins of her notebook. But her doodles inspired her in a completely different way. Grabbing a few pieces of blank paper from the printer, she started sketching characters from *The Iliad*: Helen of Troy, Odysseus, Agamemnon, and Achilles.

Until now, her Etsy store had featured Egyptian-themed artwork. But what if she expanded her repertoire? She could do a series of pieces based on *The Iliad* and *The Odyssey*.

Damn it. This wasn't helping.

Emilia opened the door and stepped into the library. "Want to play cards with us? TJ's been bragging about his prowess as a poker player, so we're thinking of challenging him, tournament-style."

Dusty laughed. "Been there, done that, last year in Cyprus. He's not lying about his ability. He knows how to read people, like one of those savants in Vegas."

"Maybe I should bow out. If he wins, he's going to be

insufferable." Emilia plopped down across from Dusty. "Nice drawing. Achilles looks just like Brad Pitt."

"Can you blame me? That movie was very formative." Laughing, she pushed the sketches aside. "But I'm letting myself get distracted. Long story short, I promised my mom I'd get serious about my dissertation this fall. Which means I should start thinking about it now."

"Fair enough. What's your topic? Didn't it have something to do with that Bronze Age shipwreck you worked on the last time you were in Turkey?"

"Nah. I ended up scrapping it. Same with my last topic—the impact of colonialism on the nineteenth-century excavations at Carthage in Tunisia. Every time I work at a new dig site, I think, 'This is it, I'm going to be inspired,' but I spend all my time drawing."

Emilia reached for the sketches and leafed through them. "You're so talented. How long did you spend on these—fifteen minutes? Twenty? You could put them on merch and sell them. Everyone's into Greek myths these days."

"Not helping, Em." Though Dusty had to admit she loved the idea. Suddenly, she was itching to draw the Trojan horse.

"Okay, so why do you think you haven't found a decent topic yet? You've worked at a lot of sites. Did you have a favorite? Did something ever call out to you? Like, an issue you wanted to *dig* into? No pun intended."

"Maybe? Sometimes? I'm fine with doing research, but with writing, I get hopelessly stuck. I was thinking I could write about Troy. Considering all the archaeologists who've worked at the site, there must be loads of material."

"Right, but you'd need to narrow it down to a specific topic."

TJ poked his head in the open doorway. "We're ready to start. You coming, Em, or are you afraid I'll kick your ass?"

"Afraid? I don't know the meaning of the word." Emilia stood up. "Sorry, Dusty, I need to defend my honor. You sure you won't join us?"

"I'm good, thanks."

After TJ and Emilia left, shutting the door behind them, Dusty drew a cartoon version of the Trojan horse. She included a tiny cluster of faces peeking out from the slats in the horse's side and, beneath it, a group of Trojan soldiers peering up in curiosity. Though she did most of her professional work using her tablet, she loved sketching freehand, using nothing but a sheet of paper, her drafting pencils, and her imagination.

When the door opened again, she didn't look up. "I'm not playing poker, so forget it."

"I wasn't asking." Stuart came into the room and sat across from her.

Pleased at the sight of him, she set down her pencil. "You doing okay? I was going to check on you earlier, but…" She let the words trail off, not wanting him to know that she'd backed down after seeing him with Clarissa.

"I was outside taking a breather. Today was a lot."

"Sorry Em and I were naughty. She always brings out the worst in me." Dusty offered an apologetic grin. "When we're together, we act like hormonal teenagers."

"What were you so hormonal about? Kerim, perhaps?"

Was it her imagination, or did he sound jealous? "We were just being immature. But I promise I'll rein in my behavior."

She slid a Jolly Rancher across the table. Since the watermelon ones were his favorite, she always saved them for him. When his fingers brushed against hers, she shivered. She wished he'd come in here to catch her alone for entirely nonplatonic reasons.

What if she stood up, went to his side of the table, and sat in his lap? Ran her fingers through his thick blond hair and whispered in his ear, "Forget about Kerim. All I want is you."

*Are you serious? He was just cozying up to Clarissa.*

She shook off her lustful thoughts and focused on boosting his morale. "For what it's worth, you rocked the first day. We got a great overview of the site and the museum and still had time to rest. Not gonna lie, the site tour would have been more bearable if it hadn't turned into 'The Dr. Hughes Show,' but that's not your fault."

Stuart let out a pained breath. "I wish he didn't have so much riding on this summer. He's so obsessed with restoring his former glory. Like, if he doesn't find something newsworthy, he'll have wasted an entire season. Which is such bullshit. The goal of our excavation is to learn more about daily life at Troy during the Late Bronze Age."

She grinned. "I love it when you go into professor mode, Dr. Carlson."

*Oops*. Had she just used the word "love"? But Stuart didn't seem to notice.

After popping the Jolly Rancher in his mouth, he peeked at her drawing. "Did you come in here to sketch or to research your dissertation topic?"

"Research. But I ended up doodling because I didn't have you to kick my butt." She passed him her picture of the Trojan horse. "Like it?"

"It's brilliant. I love all the details. Can I keep it? I'll add it to my Dusty Danforth collection."

Her heart swelled with affection. Over the years, he'd accumulated dozens of her sketches, including ones for every dig they'd been on. "Of course. I'm thinking of doing a whole series based on *The Iliad*."

"Sounds great. But Dusty..." He twisted the candy wrapper in his hands. "You told me to kick your butt. Can you think of what you'd like to write about?"

"I was just talking it over with Emilia. Maybe something to do with the site of Troy? I'm not sure what yet. There are almost too many possibilities."

He brightened. "That's still a great starting point. Your topic wouldn't have to be based on this year's dig—the library here is full of site reports and research materials from decades of excavation."

"I guess." In theory, the idea was solid. But in reality? She'd rather spend her free time drawing and hanging out with the crew than holing up in the library with a stack of dry-as-dust site reports.

"No pressure. Just think about it. Maybe you could ask Kerim for suggestions. He's worked at Troy for years, so I bet he's loaded with ideas." Stuart paused a minute, then spoke in a less confident tone. "I didn't realize you knew him so well. It took me by surprise."

*Was that what made you uneasy? Or the thought that I might have slept with him?* Dusty gnawed on her lip, choosing to keep Stuart in suspense a little longer. "We had a lot of fun when he was in Bodrum. He's an amazing sailor."

Stuart gave a terse smile. "I can imagine. Listen, since there's nothing for you to draw yet, are you okay digging with us for now? Obviously, we'll need you to sketch the architectural features of the site, but it might take a while before we find any artifacts worth illustrating."

"No problem. I'd just as soon spend my mornings on-site with everyone else and do my illustrations when we come back here in the afternoons for lab work."

"Thanks. And…" He sighed. "Can you try not to piss off Hughes? He's already got a grudge against you. Not because of anything *you* did, but…"

"Because of my mom. She made it sound like they're bitter enemies. I'm sure he'd love to kick me off the dig in retaliation." Though she kept her voice light, the thought unsettled her stomach. She couldn't risk losing her summer with Stuart.

"You're not going anywhere. Not if I can help it. But I thought I should warn you to play nice."

She flashed him a cheeky grin. "Are you aware this is the second time you've asked me to be nice? I'm not a terrible ogre."

"I know. But you're not afraid to assert yourself, either. Just like your mom. Speaking of which, let's spend a half hour brainstorming ideas for your thesis, okay?"

She groaned. "Why don't we go play poker instead? Losing to TJ sounds less painful."

"Nope. I made you a promise, and I intend to keep it. I'd rather hang out with you than get my ass kicked at cards."

"Really?" She caught his eyes.

He nodded, holding her gaze for a beat. She could have sworn something sparked between them. A tiny current. A flicker of attraction. Like he wanted more but didn't know how to ask for it. But maybe she was just projecting her own feelings. For now, her safest bet was to focus on her dissertation.

Brainstorming a thesis topic was as unromantic an evening as she could imagine.

But it was time alone with Stuart, and that counted for a lot.

# CHAPTER EIGHT

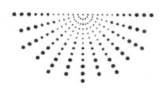

Stuart hadn't intended to get up at 5:00 a.m. Like everyone else in the crew, he'd set his alarm for six. But once he was awake, he couldn't fall back to sleep. It didn't help that he'd woken with a bad case of morning wood, brought about by a steamy dream. He'd been with Dusty at her parents' condo in Boston, and they'd been on her couch, naked, their bodies entwined. But before they could do the deed, he'd jolted awake, as if his conscience had shaken some sense into him and said, "What's wrong with you?"

Clearly, he'd been affected by his chat last night with Dusty. Even if he'd intended to help her with her dissertation, they hadn't spent much time discussing it. Instead, they'd talked for hours, in a way they hadn't since last summer. Teasing and sharing stories and reestablishing their friendship after months spent in different cities. Amid all the joking, he'd felt a stronger connection with her than usual. A feeling that she wanted something more. That if he made a move, she'd be receptive to it.

But he couldn't dwell on that now, not when he needed to focus on his responsibilities. After yesterday's problematic site tour, he was plagued with insecurity over the first day of excavation.

He dragged his tired butt out of bed and sequestered himself in the research library, where he spent the next hour reviewing the logistics of the dig. Switching to organization mode was a surefire way to tame his troubled thoughts. By the time he'd created a series of spreadsheets, a little of his self-confidence had returned. He went into the kitchen to make the coffee, only to find Dusty had already brewed the first pot.

She lifted her coffee mug in a friendly greeting. "Morning, bud."

"Morning, Dusty."

She looked as cute as ever in a faded Wonder Woman T-shirt that hugged her curves. When she raised her arms to reach for the mugs in the cupboard and revealed a sliver of pale skin just above the waistband of her shorts, he pulled his eyes away, not wanting to ogle her. Instead, he laid out his spreadsheets on the breakfast bar and admired them. Why couldn't everything in life be this tidy?

She raised her eyebrows. "Look at you, trying to organize every facet of the dig."

"Too much?" He'd compiled an inventory of all the tools in the shed, itemized the food in the pantry, made a schedule for their grocery runs, and arranged the crew into two excavation teams.

"Not at all. It's admirable." She peered at the crew list. "Though I notice you put me in the same trench as TJ."

"I couldn't put him with Em because I was afraid they'd kill each other. I also separated you and Em to avoid any mischief."

"Spoilsport." She poured the contents of the coffeepot into the large urn. "Just kidding. I'm fine with TJ as long as I don't have to listen to him rehash all his adventures in Jordan."

By six thirty, the entire crew had assembled in the kitchen, dressed and ready to go. Dr. Hughes was the last to arrive, looking far less cheerful than the others. He filled his mug from the urn, took a sip, and sputtered in anger. "Who made this swill? It's too strong."

Stuart spoke up. "Sorry about that. I'm still getting used to the pot." When Dusty caught his eye, he gave a quick shake of his head, hoping she wouldn't correct him. She already had enough strikes against her. He handed his boss a spreadsheet. "I went ahead and assigned the teams, but you can make adjustments if you want."

"Should be fine." Dr. Hughes set it down. "Who's driving us to the site?"

"I'll take one of the Land Rovers. Dusty can take the other, or —if you'd rather drive—she can handle the truck."

"One of the Turkish students can take the truck. How are we supplied for tools?"

Stuart gave him another print-out. "Here's our inventory. We should be all right for now, but we'll need to do a supply run at some point."

"More paperwork?" Dr. Hughes gave a snort. "Are you always this organized, Carlson?"

The guy made it sound like it was a character flaw. Maybe he was the type who flew by the seat of his pants, but Stuart couldn't work that way. In his mind, the only thing standing between him and chaos was his passion for Excel spreadsheets.

Once Dr. Hughes had finished his coffee, he ordered everyone to pack up and head out. With three vehicles at their disposal, there was more than enough room for all of them, along with their tools and equipment.

When they arrived at the site, Kerim and Mort were waiting for them by the café. Standing beside them were a group of men who looked to be in their twenties or thirties carrying shovels, picks, and buckets. These were the local laborers who'd be helping them excavate the site. As Dusty started chatting with them in Turkish, a surge of guilt rushed through Stuart. He'd planned to brush up on the language before he left, but his frantic schedule hadn't left him enough time.

He turned to greet Mort, who was clad in his khaki outfit, complete with matching safari hat. "How are you doing? You look like you're prepared for a day in the field."

"I'm more than ready. But it's a hot one."

*Oh no.* If Mort thought it was hot now, he'd be miserable by noon. Stuart made a mental note to check up on him every few hours, just to make sure the older man didn't overexert himself.

With the help of the workmen, they gathered up everything they'd need for a day in the field and loaded it into four wheelbarrows. Not just their tools, but two large coolers filled with food for the morning break and jugs of water for drinking and washing up. After trekking to the western edge of the site, they left the boardwalk and followed Kerim until they came to the area designated as the lower city of Troy.

Stuart walked with Dusty, Emilia, and TJ to check out the section where they'd be digging, which was already roped off and marked with "No Trespassing" signs. Over the past thirty years, this part of Troy had been excavated intermittently, revealing stone foundations of densely packed houses laid out in rectangular city blocks.

"What do you think?" Dusty asked the others. "Looks like it has potential."

"Agreed," TJ said. "I'm glad we're off the beaten path. Less chance for nosy tourists."

Stuart scanned the site. "I wish there was more tree cover, though. This area's a lot more exposed than the rest of Troy, and it's going to be in the nineties today."

"The nineties?" TJ gave a dismissive wave of his hand. "When I worked in the Jordanian desert, it got up to a hundred and ten."

Dusty poked him in the shoulder. "No more desert stories. You promised."

"Besides, that was probably a dry heat," Emilia said. "Try

digging in a jungle with ninety-five percent humidity, vicious snakes, and giant bugs."

"Hey, we had scorpions," TJ snapped. "Deadly ones."

"I'll take a scorpion over a venomous spider any day."

Stuart frowned at them. "Both of you might be used to working under harsh conditions, but I'm concerned about Mort and Clarissa."

Emilia gave him a sheepish look. "Sorry. Maybe you could ask the workers to set up a few canopies once we get the trenches laid out."

He nodded. "That's a great suggestion." Even if most of the crew could handle the heat, they'd all benefit from less sun exposure.

Before he could propose the idea, Kerim called everyone to attention. "If you'll all gather around, I'll give you a quick overview. This is where we'll be working this summer. If you've done your background reading, you'll know that archaeologists initially claimed that Bronze Age Troy was confined to the citadel. But in the 1980s, remote sensing revealed a series of structures in this area, which we refer to as the lower city since it's below the citadel walls. This would have served as the residential part of the city, occupied by the working-class citizens. By contrast, the citadel would have housed the royal family and upper-class occupants.

"Since only a small percentage of the lower city has been dug up so far, we have a large area to work with. By excavating here, we're hoping to reveal more of the residential structures, storage buildings, and other architectural features dating to the Late Bronze Age, also known as Troy VI or VII. Since all of you have some archaeological training, we can start by taking ground levels and staking out a couple of trenches."

Clarissa raised her hand. "Dr. Özgen? Sorry, but I've never been on a dig, and neither has my dad."

"No need to apologize," Kerim said. "We'll get you up to speed soon enough. Stuart, could you help them?"

"Of course. I already assigned them to my trench." Stuart cast a reassuring smile at Clarissa, who beamed at him in response.

Mort wiped his forehead. "Any chance for some shade? It's going to be damn hot if we're out in the sun all day."

"We'll erect some canopies soon, I promise," Kerim said. "But Mort, if you need to take a rest, feel free to head back to the café, relax in the shade, and have a cold drink. We can't have you getting heatstroke."

The thought made Stuart's stomach churn. The last thing he wanted to do was put one of the university's most valuable donors at risk. He was glad Kerim was on board with the canopy idea.

At the pause, Dr. Hughes spoke up, his voice laced with frustration. "If you've quite finished, Kerim? It's all very well to be digging up bits of broken pottery, but that won't impress my peers when I give my talk in Amsterdam. It's vital that I—I mean *we*—uncover something groundbreaking this season. Something that proves without a doubt that the Trojan War took place thousands of years ago."

It was a bold claim, and one Stuart wasn't entirely comfortable with. Even if most archaeologists agreed that this site—Hisarlik—fit the description for the legendary city of Troy, they weren't convinced the Trojan War had been a real event.

But Stuart knew better than to contradict his boss.

TJ, however, had no such qualms. "Sir? Are you implying the Trojan War was more than just a story? That there was an actual ten-year siege, like *The Iliad* described? Because that hasn't been accepted by most of the scholarly community."

"TJ," Stuart hissed. "Be quiet."

But TJ was on a roll. "A lot of archaeologists think there might have been a series of smaller wars. Or that the city was destroyed by an earthquake, but—"

"Enough!" Dr. Hughes snapped. "Are you—a mere grad student—calling *my* theories into question?"

"I...no. Sorry, sir." Firmly chastised, TJ stepped back a pace.

"As I was saying," Dr. Hughes continued. "What we're really after is a cemetery—the spot where all the soldiers ended up after the Trojan War. There must be loads of skeletons, complete with Bronze Age weapons. Perhaps even the remains of chariots." He pointed off in the distance. "I suggest we strike out further west, past the defensive ditch ringing the lower city. We might have more luck there."

"The Ministry of Culture asked us to focus on this area first, and I'm not about to go against their wishes," Kerim stated. "Is that clear?"

Dr. Hughes turned to Stuart. "I think my assistant director would agree that my goals could yield more important results. Isn't that right, Dr. Carlson?"

Stuart stood frozen in place, pinned in the laser beam of his boss's scrutiny, until Dusty caught his eye. She gave him a quick nod, as if to say, "You've got this."

He straightened up, keeping his voice firm. "Since we'd like to stay on the Turkish government's good side, let's comply with their wishes. Depending on what we uncover, we can always expand our efforts later. For now, why don't I divide us into teams, and we can start clearing the site?"

He held his breath, hoping his boss wouldn't lash out in anger, but Dr. Hughes gave a grudging nod. "I'm not about to sacrifice my chance to make history because of a few shortsighted bureaucrats. But since this is the first week, I'll let it go."

Crisis averted. But for how long?

∽

Dusty had been on so many digs that she'd lost count, but one thing never changed. The first day in the field always sucked.

Before they could even think of lifting a shovel, they needed to take measurements and set up the trenches. Then they had to dig through the layers of modern dirt covering the site. Even with the Turkish laborers assisting them, the work was hot, filthy, and exhausting. While the breeze provided some respite from the heat, it also blew the dirt into their faces, forcing most of them to cover up with face masks or bandannas.

Rather than troop back to the café to take their morning break, they stayed at the site to save time. A few of the laborers erected a makeshift canopy and set out a patchwork of large striped blankets underneath it. This would serve as the crew's breakfast area and a place to rest if they got overheated during the day.

Dusty joined the others in washing up, using one of the large water jugs they'd brought from the field house. She was about to sit with TJ and Emilia until she noticed Clarissa seated by herself. Why wasn't Stuart hovering over her the way he had all morning?

She bit back her resentment. *Stop judging him. He's just doing his job.*

If anything, she was the one who should make an effort with Clarissa. She loaded her plate with breakfast fixings: a hard-boiled egg, some cheese, three slices of tomato, a cluster of grapes, and two pieces of flatbread. After refilling her water bottle, she went to sit beside Clarissa.

Only then did she notice Clarissa wasn't eating. "Are you okay? You should grab some food while you have the chance."

Clarissa closed her eyes and let out a sigh. "The heat has sapped my appetite and my energy. Not like the rest of you." She glanced at a group of students. Crowded together on one of the blankets, they were laughing over a shared joke.

"In a few days, you'll be used to the heat. Give yourself time to adjust." Dusty piled the cheese and tomato on top of the bread and took a bite. Delicious.

"I didn't realize you were an archaeologist, too," Clarissa said.

"Stuart said you were the site illustrator."

"I'm both. My mom trained me to work in the field since I was a kid, so I can do either, though I prefer drawing." She popped a few grapes in her mouth, then held out a handful to Clarissa. "Try some. They're so good."

Clarissa took the grapes and ate them. "Thanks. They're really sweet." She cleared her throat. "Um...can I ask you something?"

*As long as it's not about Stuart.* "Sure."

"Do you think I could help you illustrate the finds? It would be nice to feel useful. Right now, I feel anything but."

Though Dusty didn't appreciate Clarissa edging onto her turf, she could sympathize with her for feeling out of place. "Don't be so hard on yourself. This is only the first day. But if you'd like to help, I'd need to train you. When you illustrate artifacts, you have to use certain conventions so that they can be included in our site reports."

"Do you draw everything freehand or use a tablet? I'm totally comfortable with graphic design software like Adobe Illustrator and Procreate."

"That's great. I usually start with pencil sketches, then transfer them to my tablet to fill in the detail, like the shading and the stippling. I can walk you through the whole process."

"Thanks. How'd you learn? From your mom?"

"Hardly. She doesn't have an artistic bone in her body. Stuart's mom taught me. When his dad worked with my parents in Egypt, he used to drag his whole family along. Since Stuart's mom didn't have much interest in helping in the field, she kept busy with her artwork. If she wasn't drawing our finds, she was painting watercolors of Egypt. She also made the time to take me under her wing."

Under Judy Carlson's gentle guidance, Dusty's talent had flourished. Though she and Stuart had spent a chunk of each day studying with their tutors, once they were done, they could help on-site however they chose. Stuart always wanted to jump in and get his hands dirty, but Dusty was happiest when she was drawing or painting.

"You were lucky to have her," Clarissa said.

"I really was. She was like my second mom." And a lot more compassionate than her own mother had been.

"Stuart told me you grew up together, and now I see what he meant. You really are like a brother and sister."

*Ouch.* Dusty swallowed back the pain with a swig from her water bottle. "As kids, sure. Now he's one of my best friends."

*And the object of my dreams.*

But she wouldn't reveal *that* tidbit anytime soon.

# CHAPTER NINE

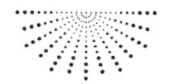

No matter how many places Dusty had worked, she always took a solid week to adjust to the conditions. A new project meant a new crop of people, a new set of expectations, and a new boss. While she had no problem taking orders from Stuart or Kerim, Dr. Hughes was another story. With every imperious command he issued, she battled the urge to snap at him in response. But after the warning Stuart had given her, she'd kept her temper under control.

By the second week of excavation, the crew had dug down to the Late Bronze Age settlement, which was dated between the fourteenth and the twelfth century BC. Now that they'd reached the layer of history they wanted to study, their next step was to expand their trenches horizontally, to reveal as much of the lower city as possible.

Though Dusty had initially been disappointed not to be assigned to Stuart's trench, she enjoyed working with Kerim. Rather than dismiss her rudimentary knowledge of Turkish, he encouraged her to practice with the laborers. He also enjoyed sharing anecdotes from his previous seasons at Troy. With fifteen years of experience, he knew the site better than most people. But unlike Dr. Hughes, he wasn't the type to boast about it.

When it came to boasting, Dusty had expected TJ to behave the same way he had in Cyprus the previous summer—braggy and full of himself. But he only acted like that around Emilia. Otherwise, he was easy to work with, which was why Dusty had agreed to pair up with him.

At the moment, he was outlining a row of stones with his trowel, while she stood at the side of their trench and used a wooden sieve to sift through the dirt he'd unearthed. With each bucket she sifted, she picked out the broken pottery, tool fragments, and animal bones.

Setting down the sieve, she hopped into the trench and held up a few pieces of a broken pot. "Look at how big these are. I'll bet they're pithoi fragments." Previous excavations had revealed rooms filled with pithoi—enormous ceramic jars used for storing food.

TJ stood up and stretched out his back. Taking a piece from her, he rubbed it against his shirt. "Yep. That means Kerim's assessment was right. This building was probably used for storage. Disappointing."

Placing her hands on her hips, she gave him a mock glare. "What's wrong with a storage facility? I didn't take you for a treasure hunter."

"A treasure hunter? Me? That's the lowest form of insult. Well, that and 'tomb raider.' But don't get me started on that one. I hate the way the media sensationalizes archaeology instead of regarding it as a science."

She couldn't help but laugh. More than once, TJ had expressed disgust at Hollywood's version of archaeology, including the Indiana Jones movies. "Then why are you so eager to find something newsworthy? Are you trying to score points with our evil overlord, Dr. Hughes?"

TJ's lip curled. "No. The guy's a has-been, living off his former glory. It's so disappointing. Remember when he bragged about that documentary he was in? I saw it when I was fifteen, and it totally inspired me. I wanted to be as famous as he was. But so far, he's barely gotten his hands dirty. He expects everyone else to do the work while he hangs out with Mort and regales him with stories."

Dusty peered across the site. Sure enough, Mort and Dr. Hughes were sitting in a couple of camp chairs in the shade next to Stuart's trench. Per Mort's request, the Turkish laborers had set up canopies over each work area.

TJ pointed to Emilia, who was on sieving duty at the other trench. "She's the reason I'm on this mission, so to speak. When we found out Stuart put us on different teams, we made a bet to see which of us would uncover the most significant find. Before you judge me, the idea was one hundred percent hers."

Dusty took a swig from her water bottle. "What's up with you two? You met less than two weeks ago, and you're already rivals?"

"We might have just met, but she was on my radar long before that. Like me, she's a Bronze Age archaeologist, focused on the Mediterranean region. Once we get our PhDs, we'll be competing for the exact same jobs."

"But you have different specialties. You're a lithics expert, and she's into paleoethnobotany."

He snorted. "Yeah. She studies ancient seeds. Talk about dull. But we're both writing dissertations about the collapse of Bronze Age civilization during the late twelfth century BC."

What was it with academics and their petty rivalries? "Then you should be working together, not competing."

"Hard pass. First of all, we have totally different theories. And second? She's a huge pain."

"How so?"

He let out a huff of frustration. "This thing with the hotel room in Istanbul? I'll admit I should have read the reviews before I booked it. Or I should have asked her if she wanted her own room. But you know me—I can handle any conditions. You give me four walls, a bed, and running water, and I'm in the lap of luxury."

Dusty bit back a laugh. "Yes, we all know how hard-core you are."

"Right? I've slept on the ground in the desert, I've dug my own shitter, I've gone for a week without showering."

She wrinkled her nose. "Maybe don't brag about that one."

"But you know what I mean, right? When I realized Em wasn't happy with the room, I assumed she hadn't worked under the same grueling conditions I had. But before I could apologize, she laid into me for not vetting the hotel on Yelp. Like I care what some tourist thinks? And when I accused her of acting like a diva, she blew up and started bragging about her dig in Mexico. As though she'd dealt with worse shit than I have. Hardly." He wiped his forehead with the back of his hand and crouched down to resume digging.

"So now you're trying to one-up her?" Dusty clambered out of the trench and grabbed another bucket of dirt. Before dumping it into her sieve, she removed the bigger pieces of pottery and set them into the finds bucket.

"She's the one who suggested it. I still think the Trojan War was just a legend. But what if Hughes is onto something? What if our team could find the cemetery he's looking for, filled with fallen warriors and Bronze Age weapons?" He punched his hand into his fist. "If we found it first, Em would have to admit defeat."

"I'd be up for anything that would put Hughes in a better mood. He's such a grouch."

"Did you notice he left for the site super early this morning?" TJ asked. "Mort must have swung by the field house and picked him up. They were already here when we arrived."

"Yeah, I thought that was kind of weird. Hughes is always the last one up, and he never stops bitching about the coffee." After the first time he'd grumbled about it, she hadn't made it again.

"I know, right? Like, he was expecting a Starbucks?"

"Maybe that's why Mort came and got him so early—so they could grab coffee in Güzelyali."

After another hour of sieving, Dusty took a breather. Settling herself next to the finds bucket, she brought out her field notebook so she could jot down a few observations about the pithoi fragments. TJ joined her. They'd only been writing for a few minutes when he pointed to the break area, where Emilia and Clarissa were setting out the food for the morning meal.

"What are they doing over there already?" he said. "It's not break time yet."

Dusty brushed the dirt off her watch. "Yeah, it is. It's already ten past. Kerim should have let us go by now." She scanned the area, intending to catch his eye, but he was standing on the other side of the trench, his attention focused on someone approaching their site.

She watched in shock as Dr. Wagner, the director of the German excavations, tromped over to Stuart's trench. She turned to TJ. "What's the German dude doing here?"

"Dunno. But this can't be good."

She strained to listen to the conversation. Clearly, she and TJ weren't the only ones intrigued by their unexpected visitor because the entire site had gone quiet.

Dr. Wagner stood over Mort and Dr. Hughes, who hadn't moved from their camp chairs. "Are you two having a relaxing morning?"

"What of it?" Dr. Hughes snapped. "Is there a reason you're barging onto my site?"

"One of my students arrived early this morning and saw the two of you prowling around our trenches, taking photos. You have no right to snoop on us."

"I was not prowling," Dr. Hughes said. "Mort and I were out for a walk this morning, and our route took us past the South Gate. Stop being so paranoid."

TJ leaned closer and whispered in Dusty's ear. "No wonder he left the field house before the rest of us. Do you think he's planning some espionage?"

"Shh. Keep quiet." She didn't want to miss anything.

"Don't lie to me," Dr. Wagner said to Dr. Hughes. "My student saw you go past our barriers and poke your nose around. Whatever you're looking for, you won't find it."

Dr. Hughes stood to face him, his cheeks mottled scarlet with rage. "I'm not looking for anything. How dare you make such accusations?"

Kerim walked over to them and held up his hands. "Gentlemen, let's take this down a notch." He turned to Mort. "What happened this morning? Why did you two get here so early?"

"We...ah...we were taking a morning constitutional," Mort said. "For...exercise."

Dr. Wagner's mouth set in a grim line. "So you didn't push past the ropes, as my student claimed, and take photos of our excavation?"

"N...not at all," Mort said. "While I'll admit we were curious about your project, I can assure you there was no foul play."

His uneasy expression made Dusty suspect he was lying to protect Dr. Hughes. Even if he was doing it willingly, he shouldn't have been placed in this position.

"Since nothing happened, there's no need for anyone to lose their temper," Kerim said. "Dr. Wagner, now that you're here, you're welcome to have a look around."

"No, thank you. I've got too much work to do. Just stay away from our site." With that, he turned and left, striding off so fast he stirred up a cloud of dust.

For a moment, no one spoke until Kerim clapped his hands together. "Break time, everyone. Yes? We've earned it."

Dusty pushed all thoughts of breakfast aside. Her top priority was to talk to Stuart.

Earlier that morning, Stuart had been surprised to see Dr. Hughes heading out to the site a half hour early. Rather than question his boss's motives, he'd appreciated the chance to enjoy his coffee in peace. Once they'd gotten to the site, he hadn't even minded that Dr. Hughes had done little but sit in the shade. At least this way, he wasn't constantly asserting his authority.

But the altercation with Dr. Wagner had put Stuart on high alert. What had Dr. Hughes been up to? Had he and Mort been taking pictures, like a couple of spies? Since Stuart was loath to confront his boss outright, he'd have to confer with Kerim later. Before he could join the others for their morning break, Dusty approached him and tugged on his arm.

"I need to talk to you," she hissed.

What now? He walked with her until they were out of earshot of the crew. "Everything okay?"

She let out a huffy breath. "No. What Hughes did was totally *not* okay."

"You mean poking around the Germans' site? I agree, it wasn't professional."

"Not that. If Hughes wants to act like a spy, that's on him. But he used Mort as his shield. Probably puffed up the guy's ego by treating him like a friend and telling him he needed him for his 'secret mission' or whatever." She shook her head. "That's a terrible way to treat a volunteer. Someone needs to tell Hughes he can't pull shit like that."

From Dusty's tone, Stuart suspected she wanted to do it. He needed to derail that train right away. "Calm down. By the looks of it, they're becoming real friends. Hughes has spent more time hanging out with Mort than actually working, which is a huge blessing for me and Kerim. I agree, we need to keep Hughes away from the Germans, but I can't tell him what to do. So, let it go, all right?"

She crossed her arms. "Do you realize how dismissive you sound?"

Swallowing back his frustration, Stuart locked eyes with her. He couldn't fault her motivation since she was speaking on Mort's behalf. But sometimes her temper got her into trouble. "I'm sorry I came across that way, but you *have* to stay on Hughes' good side."

"You told me that already. I've been playing nice with him, even when he's been a total prick."

Stuart blew out a long breath. Over the past week, he hadn't missed the way Dr. Hughes had treated her, especially during the afternoon lab sessions. More than once, he'd demanded she redo a drawing, even when she'd done a flawless job. Each time he criticized her, she let it slide without a word of protest. "I know how hard you've been trying, but…"

"But what?"

Should he warn her about Dr. Hughes' threats? Tell her that his boss was eager to replace her with Clarissa? *No.* He didn't need her getting more riled up than she already was. But before he could speak, Dusty's expression softened.

She placed her hand on his arm. "Sorry, bud. You're under enough stress already. I'm making this harder for you, aren't I?"

He leaned in closer, suddenly noticing how the dirt had blended in with her adorable freckles—something he shouldn't be fixating on right now. "Maybe a little. But your heart's in the right place. I didn't even know you liked Mort."

She smiled. "I've been warming up to him. The guy loves archaeology stories, so I've been telling him about our adventures in Egypt. He couldn't believe all the shit we got up to when we were kids. Do you remember when our parents were feuding with that nasty team of treasure hunters?"

He chuckled, grateful her burst of anger had passed. "How could I forget? You volunteered to sneak into their camp in the middle of the night to gather information. I was terrified you'd get caught."

"I figured if I got pinched, I'd pull the 'innocent kid' act. But I nailed it."

"Yeah, you were gutsy as hell."

She gave his shoulder a gentle poke. "Partly because I wanted to impress *you*, Dr. Carlson."

He'd always been impressed by her. Still was. Staring into her hazel eyes, he longed to break the boundaries he'd set in place. He wanted to reach over and wipe the dirt from her cheek, then cup her face in his hands and kiss her tenderly.

But he had to stay focused. As much as he admired her feisty spirit and her willingness to take risks, that wasn't what he needed from her right now. He needed her to play by the rules, even if it ran counter to her nature.

"Are you okay not saying anything to Hughes?" he asked.

All at once, the gleam vanished from her eyes. Whatever connection they'd shared evaporated into the warm summer air. "I'll keep quiet, but I'll be watching him." She cast a wary glance toward the professor. "He's definitely not to be trusted."

Stuart couldn't argue with that. But there wasn't much else he could do except hope his boss would behave himself.

## CHAPTER TEN

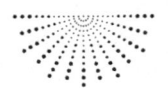

Cradling two bottles of beer in one hand and a bowl of roasted chickpeas in the other, Dusty kicked the door to the field house shut. She joined Emilia on the patio and passed her a beer. "Your beverage, madam."

"Thanks." Emilia unscrewed the top and took a long drink. "And thanks for joining me when you could be out carousing with the others."

Dusty settled herself in a patio chair and looked up at the evening sky, now speckled with stars. Summer nights in Turkey were so pleasant compared to the blistering heat of the day. "I'd rather be outside than in a crowded bar." She held up her beer. "Here's to surviving another week of excavation."

Emilia clinked her bottle against Dusty's. "I'll drink to that. I'm beat."

"Is that why you wanted to stay in tonight? Usually, you're first in line for a bar crawl."

"Don't tell anyone, but I needed some space from TJ."

Rather than tease her, Dusty softened her tone, aware of the vulnerability in her friend's voice. "Why? What did he do now?"

"It's not really his fault. But there's an archaeology conference coming up in October that I wanted to attend. I applied to speak on a panel session but found out today I got rejected."

"Sorry, Em. That sucks." Dusty held out the bowl of chickpeas, and Emilia grabbed a handful.

She popped them in her mouth and coughed. After washing them down with a swig of beer, she glared at Dusty. "What did you put on those? They're so spicy."

"Salt, pepper, paprika, cumin. And a dash of cayenne. Sorry."

Emilia grabbed another handful. "No, they're good. I just wasn't expecting that kick. Just like I wasn't expecting today's shitty rejection. If that wasn't bad enough, TJ's paper was accepted. He was bragging about it during our lab session this afternoon. There was no way I could deal with him tonight."

"I totally get it. At least we have tomorrow off. That'll be a nice break. Plus, we get to spend the day on Kerim's boat."

Emilia grinned. "I bet that'll bring back some sweet memories."

Dusty rolled her eyes. "I told you before, we didn't have sex on his boat. We're just friends. No, we're *colleagues*."

"Colleagues," Emilia snorted. "You know damn well you could take things further. I've seen the way he checks out your ass when you're bent down in your trench."

"Not going to happen. He's hot and all, but he's not the one I want." This unrequited love business was frustrating as hell. Here she was, turning down a potential hookup with a sexy Turkish archaeologist, all because she was so fixated on Stuart. But even after three weeks together at Troy, nothing had changed between them.

"Are you still lusting after Stuart? You need to stop messing around and tell him before—" Emilia paused as Mort's car pulled onto the gravel driveway. Dr. Hughes emerged from the front passenger side, followed by Clarissa, who got out of the back. She stood and waved as her father drove off.

As Dr. Hughes leaned in to talk to Clarissa, Dusty tensed up, worried he was saying something inappropriate. But he only spoke to her for a few seconds before going inside the field house. When Clarissa didn't follow him, Dusty called out to her.

"Hey, Clarissa. Come join us."

She looked as beautiful as ever, clad in a pale pink sundress and sandals, her long blond hair cascading around her shoulders. But her hands trembled as she lowered herself into one of the patio chairs.

"Are you okay?" Dusty asked.

Clarissa shook her head. With a shuddering breath, she spoke softly. "I'm not. Um...I'm kind of freaking out, actually."

"What happened?" Emilia said. "Weren't you just at dinner with your dad?"

"And Dr. Hughes. Dad invited him to join us."

"You want a beer?" Dusty asked. "I can get you one from the fridge."

"No, I'm good. I had a lot of wine. It was the only way to get through dinner. Dr. Hughes was awful. He kept making lewd remarks about our waitress, even though she was my age."

Dusty recoiled. Didn't he realize how messed up his behavior was? Back in the day, he might have had a way with women, but now he was just a creepy old guy leering at someone young enough to be his daughter.

Emilia made a face. "What a dick. Sorry you had to put up with him."

"That's not the worst of it," Clarissa said. "He wouldn't stop talking about the German archaeologists. Like, he's totally obsessed with them. I'm not sure where he got his information, but he found out that half their team started excavating in a different part of Troy. He's dying to know what they're after, but he can't risk poking his nose around again."

Emilia grunted in frustration. "What does he think he's going to find? Even if they make an incredible discovery, they won't leave it at the site. They'll take it back to their field house or to the lab at the Troy Museum."

"He's aware of that," Clarissa said. "He just wants to make sure they're not going to one-up him. Have either of you heard of the Troy symposium in Amsterdam?"

"Stu told me about it," Dusty said. "It's taking place in November. A big symposium with scholars from all over the world."

"Dr. Hughes is giving a talk there. Trying to restore his former glory or whatever. But he doesn't want to be blindsided if Dr. Wagner's team makes a better find than us, so…he asked me to spy on them."

"No!" Emilia said. "That's a terrible idea. What did your dad say?"

Clarissa twisted her hands together. "He went along with it. You have to understand—he idolizes Dr. Hughes. He's read all his books and watched that documentary three times. Now Hughes is acting like they're best friends, and my dad's eating it up."

Dusty clenched her fists, fighting off a wave of fury. Her earlier suspicion had been right. Dr. Hughes hadn't befriended Mort because he enjoyed the older man's company. Instead, he was taking advantage of his trusting nature. What an asshole.

"What does Hughes want you to do?" Emilia asked.

"He suggested I show up at the Germans' new dig site dressed like a tourist and ask a few questions," Clarissa said. "He told me to use my 'feminine wiles' to win them over."

"Nope. Hard pass." Emilia pounded her fist into her palm. "Tell him you won't do it."

"That's awful," Dusty said. "I can't believe your dad would agree to it."

"It's just that…" Clarissa's voice broke. "When my dad was growing up, he wanted to be an archaeologist more than anything. But his dad was a total hard-ass who forced him to go into the family business. This dig is the closest my dad's ever gotten to living out his dream, and Hughes...he..." She blinked back tears.

"What?" Dusty growled.

"He promised my dad that if I did this 'secret mission,' he'd include Dad's name in his next publication about Troy. He'd make him sound like a fellow archaeologist rather than just a rich volunteer. Dad was so excited. I'd love to do this for him, but I... I'm scared."

*That's it. I'm done playing nice.* Dusty set down the bowl of chickpeas and got to her feet, propelled by a burst of righteous anger. "I'm going to talk to Hughes right now."

"Don't do it," Emilia said. "He already hates you."

"I don't care." Last week, when Stuart had asked her not to confront him, Dusty had held her tongue. Now she wished she'd spoken up. "He needs to understand this isn't okay."

Clarissa wiped her eyes. "You don't have to do this for me." But from the way she was watching Dusty, almost in expectation, it was clear she was hoping *someone* would speak up on her behalf.

"Do you know if he's in his room?" Dusty asked.

"I think he was going to the lab to look over a few things," Clarissa said.

Emilia held up her hand. "Wait—"

But Dusty was already on her way, wrenching open the back door and marching down to the lab. Dr. Hughes sat at *her* illustration table, perusing the sketches she'd done earlier. She let herself in and closed the door, her heart thudding furiously.

Dr. Hughes regarded her with a condescending smile. "Miss Danforth. You look upset. Is something wrong?"

Her anger rose to the surface, like boiling water overflowing a pot. "I was just talking to Clarissa. I can't believe you asked her to spy for you. What kind of bullshit is that?"

He gestured to the chair across from him. "Why don't you have a seat so we can discuss this like rational adults."

"I don't need to sit down. I need you to back off and leave Clarissa alone. She's here as a volunteer. You have no right to ask her to do something so slimy and underhanded."

"There was no coercion on my part. I merely asked her a small favor."

Dusty's jaw tightened. After three weeks of putting up with his shit, she was sick of it. "When Clarissa talked to me tonight, she wasn't okay with it. She was *crying*. This is way out of her comfort zone."

"Really? Her father thought she'd be able to accomplish this task with little trouble."

"If you're that keen on collecting intel, why don't you ask the Germans yourself? Or ask Stuart to talk to them?"

For that, she got a derisive snort. "As if they'd tell him anything."

"Does Stuart know you're planning this? He'd never approve."

Dr. Hughes regarded her with a glint in his eye. "You and Stuart are quite close, aren't you? Is that the reason he hired you?"

Was he implying something sordid? She scowled. "We've been friends for years, but that's not why he invited me to join the dig. I've served as an illustrator on dozens of projects for lots of different universities. I have years of experience."

"So you have. And from what I understand, you've been training Clarissa to help you." He picked up two drawings from the table. Both showed cross-sections of a ceramic pot incised with a series of wavy lines. "Which is yours, and which is hers?"

What the hell did this have to do with anything? She stared at the sketches for a few seconds before picking the left one. "That's mine."

"True, but you could barely tell the difference." He set them back down. "At dinner tonight, Clarissa couldn't stop raving about you. She was thrilled at how much you'd taught her in such a short time. But now that she's at your level, I wonder if I need you at all."

His words hit her with the force of a gut punch. Was this the thanks she got for playing nice? She'd been trying to help Clarissa, not screw herself out of a job. She spoke clearly, hoping to hide the tremor in her voice. "But I was hired for the whole season."

"If it were up to me, you wouldn't have been hired at all. You're no better than your obnoxious mother—always poking your nose where you don't belong." He gave a nasty laugh. "I don't see any reason to keep you here. Clarissa can do your job. Since she's a volunteer, we don't even have to pay her."

Dusty's breath caught. Why hadn't she heeded Em's advice and kept her mouth shut? Now she'd put herself at risk. "You can't fire me. I haven't done anything wrong."

"I disagree. Your behavior tonight—barreling in here, swearing at me, calling me slimy—has been completely unprofessional. I can't afford such a loose cannon on my team."

*Fuck.* In all her years of digging, she'd never been kicked off a job. She couldn't get fired. Not when she hadn't accomplished any of her goals. She had yet to make inroads on her dissertation *or* her relationship with Stuart. If she got sent home now, she wouldn't see him again until September. By then, he would have spent the entire summer with Clarissa. More than enough time for him to fall in love with her and decide she was the one.

She'd have to suck it up and apologize. "I'm sorry about my outburst. I promise it won't happen again."

"Too late. The damage has been done." Dr. Hughes leaned back in his chair. "Unless…"

"What?" Her heart was pounding, her mouth dry. She licked her lips, tasting cayenne, and longed for a drink of water.

"Unless you'd be willing to do me a huge favor."

With a shudder, she shrunk back toward the door. "What kind of favor?"

"If Clarissa is so anxious, why don't you lend a hand? Go with her and help her gather the information I need." When Dusty hesitated, he gave an arrogant laugh. "What are you afraid of? Mort told me about your exploits in Egypt. Clearly, this type of subterfuge is right up your alley. Do this for me, and we'll be good."

"You won't fire me?" She hated that she was putting herself at his mercy. Hated that she was bargaining with such a loathsome, immoral asshole. But she didn't want to leave Troy.

"If you pull this off, you can stay. But no betraying me, understand?"

"I understand." She relaxed her stance but was unable to dispel the tension coiled in her belly. "What about Stuart? He'd never agree to this." Few people she knew had a moral compass like his.

"I'd rather keep him and Kerim out of this. But if you do a good job, I might throw Stuart a bone. I could email Dr. Fiorelli and tell her what a splendid job he's been doing. You'd like that, wouldn't you?"

Dusty let out a long breath. She didn't want to do Dr. Hughes any favors. But if she went along with his scheme, she wouldn't have to worry about losing her spot on the dig. If she could help Stuart, all the better. "Okay, but we'll need a foolproof plan."

He smirked. "That's just what I was thinking."

∽

WHEN DUSTY RETURNED OUTSIDE, CLARISSA AND EMILIA WERE still sitting on the patio. Emilia had started on her second beer while Clarissa was drinking from her water bottle.

"Finally!" Emilia said. "Did you give him hell?"

"Um..." Dusty plopped down on a chair. "I tried to, but he had serious leverage over me, and..." She didn't want to reveal that he'd threatened to replace her with Clarissa. No sense making the other woman feel guilty. "I caved and said I'd help him out."

"What kind of leverage are we talking about?" Emilia asked.

Dusty raked her hand through her hair. "I'd rather not say, but we came up with a plan. Clarissa, if you're game, I'll go with you. We'll need to wear disguises and pretend we're visiting students from the University of Cologne."

Emilia's jaw dropped. "Are you out of your mind?"

"I know it sounds risky, but it could benefit all of us. If Hughes finds out what the Germans are up to, he might stop obsessing over them. Kerim and Stuart would love it if they didn't have to worry about him causing any more trouble."

*And I won't get fired.* But she didn't say it. Better to have them think she was doing this mission for the good of the dig than reveal how much she feared being replaced.

Clarissa gave her a beatific smile. "Thank you so much. I think I could handle this if we did it together. I used to spend my summers in Berlin with my mom's relatives, so my German's decent. What about you?"

Dusty's shoulders loosened in relief. She hadn't expected Clarissa to agree so readily. Then again, she got the sense Clarissa would do almost anything for her dad. "I'm fluent in German. Learned it as a kid from one of my tutors. It's also a requirement for a PhD in Classical Archaeology."

"Humblebrag," Emilia muttered.

"Seriously, Em? You and TJ had a brag-off two days ago about your linguistic fluency."

"For the record, I won. He only speaks three languages. What a lightweight."

"If I may continue?" Dusty said. "Not only do I speak German, but I also know Professor Schultz from the University of Cologne. He's an Egyptologist who worked with my mom ten years ago, so I could easily pretend to be one of his students. You want to come with, Em? German's one of your languages."

Emilia's mouth quirked up in a crooked smile. "Yeah. I'm in. I can't resist a good con."

Dusty couldn't deny the frisson of excitement surging through her. She loved it when a plan fell into place. "I still need to figure out the logistics. Clarissa, we'll need your dad's help."

"No problem. He loves spy movies. He'll be thrilled if we include him."

"Perfect. And we'll call this…" Dusty thought for a moment. "Operation Odysseus. Because we're being sneaky, the same way he was when he pulled the Trojan horse trick."

Emilia frowned. "Before you get too ahead of yourself, *Odysseus*, I need to know if this mission is top secret or if you plan to tell Stuart about it."

Dusty cringed. As much as she hated keeping Stuart in the dark, Dr. Hughes didn't want him involved. "Nope. Hughes asked me not to tell him or Kerim."

"You sure that's how you want to play it?" Emilia gave her a knowing look. As if to say, "Do you really want to keep a secret from the guy you've been crushing on for years?"

For an agonizing moment, Dusty considered the possible fallout. What if they screwed up and got Dr. Hughes in trouble? What if Stuart found out and was furious at her for plotting espionage behind his back? But then she imagined how bereft she'd feel if Dr. Hughes sent her home. Hiding this plan from Stuart was better than losing the next five weeks with him.

"We're doing this," she said to Emilia. "On Monday, during our morning break, we'll put Operation Odysseus into action."

If she succeeded, she'd keep her job. Mort would get a shout-out in Dr. Hughes' next publication, and Stuart might even benefit. It could be a win for all of them.

As long as she didn't get caught.

## CHAPTER ELEVEN

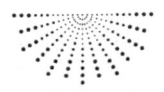

After a long, exhausting week, Stuart was eager for his day off. All he'd wanted was a nice, quiet beach day where he could relax, swim, and reconnect with Dusty. They'd been working at Troy for three weeks now, and he had yet to reveal his feelings. If he didn't take action soon, he might lose her to Kerim, who was growing closer to her with each passing day.

But Stuart's dream vanished in a puff of smoke when Kerim suggested everyone drive up to the marina in Çanakkale so he could take them sailing. He'd even promised to dock in a protected cove so they could go swimming.

In theory, a great idea. What better way to spend a sweltering July afternoon than lazing on a boat on the Aegean Sea?

Unfortunately, Stuart was having a hard time controlling his jealousy whenever he imagined Dusty and Kerim together. What made it worse was that he genuinely liked Kerim. So far, he'd been an ideal colleague—smart, even-tempered, a true professional in the field. But he was obviously attracted to Dusty, who'd responded enthusiastically when he suggested sailing.

At least it wasn't a romantic trip for two. Since Kerim had

extended the offer to everyone, most of the crew was going, other than Mort and Dr. Hughes.

Now that they'd been at sea for an hour, Stuart should have been able to unwind. Kerim's boat was the perfect size for a daylong outing—a forty-two-foot Fisher sailboat with ample deck space and a couple of cozy cabins below. Beneath them, the sea glimmered turquoise in the sunlight, inviting them to jump right in. But Stuart's nerves were on edge. How could he possibly relax when Dusty stood only a few feet away, clad in nothing but a tiny black bikini?

When she caught him staring, his cheeks heated in shame. He averted his gaze but was too late. As she strolled over to him, he tried not to ogle her breasts, barely covered by the thin strips of fabric. Instead, he focused on the familiar tattoos that graced her arms and shoulders. One shoulder bore the image of a stylized pyramid; the other, two crossed shovels. But a new one, along her upper arm, displayed an old-school compass, like the kind seen in vintage maps.

She grinned at him. "You're staring. What is it? Is my boob slipping out of this bikini? I forgot how small it is."

*Please don't talk about your boobs.* He swallowed, painfully aware of the dryness in his throat. "Just noticing your new tattoo. I like it."

"Thanks. I got it after Cyprus. Something to commemorate my incessant wanderlust." She held out a bottle of sunscreen. "You want me to do the usual?"

"What?"

"Your back. Right? I know how easily you get fried in the sun. Isn't that why you caught my eye earlier?"

*No, I was staring at your body in that bikini. Like a hormonal thirteen-year-old.*

"We've barely left the dock and you're already turning red," she said. "Let me do your back before it's too late."

"Right." No need to reveal that his reddened face wasn't from the sun. As Dusty spread the warm lotion over his skin, her touch sent ripples of desire through him. She took her time, kneading his back and shoulders, skimming her hands just above the waistband of his shorts. Forget swimming. He wanted to stand here all afternoon while Dusty massaged suntan lotion onto his skin.

But she pulled away with another grin. "All done. Don't forget to reapply it after we go swimming."

"Do...do you need me to do you? I mean, do your *back?*" Clearly, today he'd be playing the part of a tongue-tied middle schooler with a giant crush.

"Nope, I'm good. Kerim already got me. But thanks." She set the bottle down on the padded bench next to the railing and sauntered across the boat, her hips swaying enticingly as she approached Kerim.

When she leaned in to tell him something, Stuart battled a wave of frustration. He flipped the lid on the cooler near his feet and pulled out a bottle of water. He drained half of it in a few swallows, hoping the icy liquid would cool his overheated emotions. Against his better judgment, he peered over at Dusty again. Now she was standing so close to Kerim that their bodies were almost touching. Was he going to kiss her? Right here, in front of everyone? Stuart clenched the water bottle so tight it crumpled.

"Hey." Clarissa's soft voice startled him into dropping the bottle. When he retrieved it and stood to face her, she placed a gentle hand on his arm. "Don't look so worried. Kerim seems like a decent guy. I'm sure you can trust him around Dusty."

"What?"

She laughed. "You're giving off a protective older brother vibe right now. Like you're worried he's going to mess with your little sister. It's cute the way you look out for her. The other day, when she told me you two grew up like a brother and sister, I couldn't quite envision it. But I totally see it now."

*Like a brother and sister?* Was that how Dusty viewed them? As kids, they'd treated each other like siblings, but once he hit puberty, he'd never thought of her that way again. A friend? Yes. But definitely not a sister. "Is that what she told you?"

"I think it's nice. When I was younger, I used to wish I had an older brother or sister."

"You don't have any siblings?" Though he'd spent a lot of time teaching Clarissa the basics of field and lab work, she hadn't shared much about her personal life other than her love of ancient history and her passion for teaching.

"I'm an only child." Her voice carried a slight wobble, as though speaking about it pained her. "My mom died right after I was born."

"I'm sorry. I...I had no idea. Since your dad never mentioned her, I thought maybe he was divorced." Either way, Stuart felt like an idiot for not knowing about it sooner.

"It's fine. I don't remember her, but Dad was devastated. He never remarried, just threw himself into his work. By the time I was five, he'd made his first million, but he was hardly ever home. I was raised by a series of nannies." She took off her sunglasses and wiped her eyes.

"That must have been hard."

"It wasn't that bad. But two years ago, he had a serious heart attack. Too much stress and too little self-care. He decided to sell the business and enjoy all the things he'd never made time for." A gentle smile crossed her lips. "Like travel. I told him I'd go with him whenever I could. That's one benefit of being a teacher—summer vacations guaranteed. When he said he'd gotten a chance to dig at Troy, I couldn't resist coming along."

"I'm glad he went for it." Over the past three weeks, Stuart had come to appreciate Mort's eager attitude and his colorful stories. The guy wasn't just an entitled millionaire trying to live out his Indiana Jones fantasy but someone whose brush with death had given him the courage to try new opportunities. "I also think it's admirable that you joined him. I know you've been out of your comfort zone."

Her soft laughter was like the tinkling of bells. "Thanks to your help, I'm slowly getting the hang of things. Dusty's also teaching me the basics of archaeological illustration so I can contribute even more."

Once again, his gaze was drawn to Dusty, whose hand was resting on Kerim's shoulder. Any minute now, they'd be in each other's arms. It was too much.

Clarissa gave his arm a gentle squeeze. "Stop checking on her. She'll be fine."

He had to get over it. If he couldn't accept them as a couple, he'd spend the next five weeks wallowing in misery.

Unless they weren't a couple yet. Maybe he still had a chance. But he had to let Dusty know he was interested. Above all, he needed to make sure she didn't think of him as a big brother. Anything but that.

∽

WHILE DUSTY APPRECIATED KERIM'S ATTENTIVENESS, THE MORE she flirted with him, the guiltier she felt. When she and Clarissa had first boarded the boat, she hadn't missed the way Stuart's eyes lit up, no doubt admiring Clarissa's figure. In response, Dusty had behaved like a petty teen. At first, she'd teased Stuart by applying sunscreen longer than necessary; then, she'd left him abruptly, directing all her attention to Kerim.

Which wasn't like her. As much as she delighted in flirty banter, she wasn't the type to play games. If she met someone who sparked her interest, she was always up-front about what she wanted: a little fun in the field, but no promises once it was over. When she met Kerim two years ago, she'd suspected he would have been up for a short-term arrangement of that nature. And now, she was getting those vibes from him again—that if she wanted a steamy, no-strings hookup, he'd be willing to go for it.

But despite all Kerim had to offer, he wasn't the one who'd occupied her dreams over the past three weeks. At night, when she drifted off to sleep, it was always Stuart who played a starring role in her fantasies. His body, his hands, his kisses.

"Dusty?" Kerim's voice brought her back to the moment.

"Sorry, I was just daydreaming."

"Last week, when we were working in the lab, you asked me for help with your dissertation topic. I've been thinking about it."

She gave his shoulder a playful shove. "This is our day off. You don't need to think about archaeology."

He chuckled. "I'm always thinking about archaeology. I'd be glad to help."

"How about we spend an afternoon looking over some of the material in the research library? Would that be okay?"

"I have a better idea. After we're done on the boat, why not have dinner with me here in Çanakkale? We could talk about your topic for as long as you like. Then I could bring you back to the field house later tonight."

Maybe all he wanted was a quiet dinner between two professionals. But his smile and his nearness made her suspect otherwise. If she accepted his offer, she'd be signaling her interest. Which wasn't fair to him. Or to herself.

"I'd love to, except I'm having dinner with Stuart tonight. When I first arrived in Çanakkale, he promised to treat me to a decent meal in exchange for my coming out early." She gave a quick laugh. "I need to hold him to his promise."

"Oh. I didn't realize you two were close that way. I apologize."

Her cheeks prickled with heat. "No, it's not like that. We're friends, but, um..." Shit, she sounded like an idiot. Felt like one, too.

Kerim merely graced her with another of those indulgent smiles. "It's fine, Dusty. Another time, perhaps?"

"Sure. That would be great."

"In the meantime, I can still help you out. Monday afternoon, we'll discuss ideas in the library. As colleagues."

Maybe she was making a huge mistake. Kerim wasn't just a hot guy with a boat; he was also a thoughtful, accomplished archaeologist who genuinely liked her. But before she left Cairo, she'd told herself this was her summer to seize the moment with Stuart. To tell him how she felt, no matter what it cost her. If she wasn't brave enough to admit her feelings, she could lose him to Clarissa.

When Kerim docked the boat at the cove, she joined the others in jumping in. The water was cool and delicious, the perfect remedy for a hot summer's day. She floated on her back and closed her eyes, letting the sun warm her. Try as she might, she couldn't stop thinking about Stuart. Though she'd taken a long time lathering him up with sunscreen, she hadn't wanted to stop. She'd yearned to keep going, to touch him until he begged for more.

First things first. Now that she'd concocted an excuse to get out of dinner with Kerim, she needed to follow through with Stuart.

When she opened her eyes, he was swimming toward her, moving through the water with powerful strokes. Perfect. A few minutes alone with him were all she needed.

"Having fun?" he asked.

She treaded water next to him. "The best. This boat is incredible. I'd love to spend a week sailing around the Aegean."

"Well, if you ask Kerim, I'm sure he'd be thrilled to take you on a private excursion. Just the two of you."

His snarky tone struck a nerve. He'd never passed judgment on her sex life before. Or was that the jealousy talking? Either way, she was calling him on it. "Wow, you went there."

"I did. From where I was standing, it looked obvious. Or was I off base?"

Again with the tone. Not hostile but verging on possessive. Still, if he wanted honesty, she'd give it to him. No more games. "No, your instincts were correct. He asked me if I'd like to have dinner with him tonight."

"Are you going to?"

She almost laughed because Stuart wasn't even trying to play it cool. "I was tempted, but you know who owes me dinner? You." Heart pounding, she waited for his reaction.

From the gleam in his eye, she knew she'd made the right call. "Come to think of it, I did promise you, didn't I?"

"You sure as hell did." With a sassy grin, she splashed water at him. "A nice dinner, with two desserts."

He rubbed his eyes. "Brat. I seem to remember one dessert."

"Your promise has accrued interest over the past three weeks. I'm also ordering wine with dinner. Maybe a meze platter."

His eyes were dancing with amusement now, water droplets sparkling in his beard. "You're going to bleed me dry."

He looked so irresistible that it took all her willpower not to touch him. Instead, she kept her voice light and flirty. "Would you rather I dine with Kerim?"

"Nope. Tonight, after we get back, I'm taking you to dinner in Güzelyali."

"Alone?"

"Alone."

*Yes.* Maybe it would just be a dinner between friends. But she wasn't ready to concede yet.

# CHAPTER TWELVE

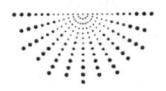

Dinner started off exactly as Stuart had hoped. He'd chosen a seaside restaurant where they could dine outside on a shaded patio. Their candlelit table provided a perfect view of the Aegean. Above them, a veranda adorned with twinkling fairy lights added to the ambiance. They'd ordered a bottle of dry red wine and a meze platter, heaped with toasted pita wedges, green olives, grilled vegetables, flaky slices of cheese borek made of filo pastry, and four different dips.

But the best part about dinner was spending time alone with Dusty. She looked radiant in the flickering candlelight, her face flushed from their day in the sun, a fresh crop of freckles scattered across her nose. She'd swapped out her bikini and cover-up for a pale blue sundress that set off her tan. Even clad in her filthiest dig clothes, she was hard to resist. But dressed like this? Unbelievably tempting.

Her infectious smile and attentiveness suggested this was more to her than a dinner between friends. But so far, they'd kept the conversation light, talking about the dig and its quirky crew members. Though Stuart was hoping they'd reach a deeper level of intimacy, he enjoyed having time to build up to it.

Until Dusty refilled her wineglass, took a sip, and nailed him with a flinty glare. "So...honest answer. Why were you asking me about Kerim earlier?"

Caught off guard, he swallowed abruptly, almost choking on a piece of pita bread. As he cleared his throat, he struggled to explain, only to come up with a pathetic apology. "Sorry. It wasn't any of my business."

Her furrowed brow implied she wasn't letting him off that easily. "We've been friends for too long to bullshit each other. You've never gotten judgy about my partners before. But today, you sounded accusatory. Why?"

*Because I was jealous.* But he couldn't admit it until he knew whether she planned to hook up with Kerim. Otherwise, he'd be setting himself up for a mega dose of humiliation. "I...I guess I was surprised. You talked about the Bodrum project a lot when you got back but never mentioned him."

"Would you care if we'd been together?"

Rattled by her answer, he blurted out the first thing he could think of. "He's at least ten years older than you. I wouldn't want you getting hurt."

As soon as the words were out of his mouth, he wanted to take them back. He was now fulfilling the exact role Clarissa had cast him in—that of Dusty's protective older brother. A role he didn't want.

And one she didn't appreciate, from the scowl she gave him. "He's twelve years older, to be exact. That's hardly an issue. My dad's fourteen years older than my mom."

"Didn't their affair cause a huge scandal?"

"Only because she was his grad student at Harvard. Plus, she was supposed to be marrying some rich British aristocrat. But I'm not one of Kerim's students. No one would care if we got involved. Except maybe you, now that you're acting like my big brother."

Her accusation sent his pulse racing. "I don't know why you're so surprised. You're the one who told Clarissa you think of me that way."

"What?" Her mouth gaped open, but before she could respond, their server came by to ask if they needed anything. She answered with a quick "no, thanks," then focused on Stuart again. "All I told her was that we grew up together like a brother and sister. I didn't imply I felt that way *now*."

His frustration boiled over, eclipsing all rational thought. "Yet, somehow, that was what she inferred."

Her hazel eyes flashed with anger. "Who cares what she thinks? What matters is how *you* feel about me. Do you think of me as a sister?"

How had this conversation gone so badly off the rails? He had to stop dancing around the subject and answer truthfully, no matter what it cost him. If he went all out and confessed his love for her, he might spook her, but at least he could admit how much he wanted her.

He topped up his wineglass and took a long drink. "No. I don't think of you that way. Because it would be totally messed up to have erotic fantasies about your little sister."

The silence that followed was sudden and shocking. Like he'd thrown a hand grenade onto the table and was waiting for the explosion. Around them, the world carried on like normal. Servers bustled about, glasses clinked, and laughter carried over from the other tables. But nothing would ever be normal again, now that he'd told his best friend how he felt about her.

She drained her wine in one quick swallow. "Did you just admit you had dreams about banging me?"

He rubbed his hands across his face. *Shit.* He'd blown it, bigtime. "Yes. I'm sorry if that was horribly inappropriate."

"Why the fuck didn't you lead with that? Why ask me all these questions about Kerim?"

So, she wasn't mad about the fantasies? Or was she? His head was spinning in confusion. "Because I...wasn't about to confess my feelings if you and he were..." He made a sweeping motion, too flustered to continue talking.

"If we were fucking? Is that what you're trying to say?"

"Yes, but in a less blunt way."

A hint of a smile played at her lips. "We're not. We weren't together in Bodrum, and I had no intention of jumping into bed with him tonight. Or any night, for that matter."

The tension eased from his shoulders. He set down his wineglass, suddenly aware he'd been clutching it in a death grip. "Then why did you tell me he asked you to dinner?"

"I wanted to make you jealous." All traces of anger vanished from her face. "You think you're the only one harboring erotic fantasies about your best friend? Think again. I've been dreaming about you for years."

He stared at her, unable to form a coherent sentence. A mixture of shock and delight coursed through him as her words registered. He didn't care that she'd been flirting with Kerim to get a rise out of him. Or that her confession—like his—was more about their physical desires than their emotional connection.

What mattered was that they were *finally* on the same page.

∽

DUSTY'S HEART WAS BEATING SO LOUDLY SHE WAS CERTAIN STUART could hear it. With a shaky hand, she set down her wineglass before she dropped it. Though she wished he'd admitted he was secretly in love with her, this was a damn fine start.

As she looked into his eyes, the warmth in those ocean-blue depths filled her with a heady glow. She was torn between vaulting across the table and kissing him, and barraging him with questions. How long had he felt this way? Had he dreamed of her when he was with Shelby? Did he want more than just a few nights of passion? But right now, only one issue needed resolving. "What about Clarissa? I thought you were into her."

"Nope. She's sweet and smart, and I like working with her, but there's no spark." He gave her a sly grin. "Never once have I imagined her naked, underneath me, moaning while I do unspeakable things to her body."

A flush of heat rose in Dusty's cheeks. "Unspeakable, huh? You'll have to give me more details."

She wished he knew the truth—that he'd done a *lot* of those things to her during that one evening of drunken passion—but she hesitated to bring it up. What if he was upset she'd never told him about their botched hookup? Since he didn't remember any of it, maybe it was better if they started fresh.

Aware her face was still prickling with warmth, she tried to focus on the half-empty meze platter, spearing a piece of grilled eggplant with her fork, but she was too conscious of Stuart's eyes on her. "What?"

"You're cute when you blush like that. It's not easy getting you to blush."

"Stop it. We need to finish dinner. And even then..." She gnawed on her lip as she considered the logistics of their situation. "I don't think we can have sex in the field house. The walls are paper-thin, and..."

And going from best friends to fuck buddies was a huge leap. Though she'd never had any qualms about jumping into flings before, she'd never felt this strongly about any of her romantic partners. Stuart wasn't just a hot guy she wanted to nail. She was in love with him. If all he wanted was a romp in bed, she could get her heart broken.

As if sensing her unease, he reached across the table and took her hand, lacing his fingers with hers. "Maybe it's better if we don't rush. This is all pretty new."

She released a tight breath. "Right. It's kind of overwhelming. But in a good way."

"In the best way. I'm glad you weren't upset. I wasn't sure how you'd react." His lips quirked up in a smile. "For all I knew, you might throw your wine in my face."

"And waste perfectly good wine? Never." She squeezed his hand. "Thanks for being honest. I didn't say anything before because I didn't want to mess up our friendship."

"We won't mess it up. I promise."

His earnestness was so sweet that her eyes misted over. She blinked quickly, trying to get her emotions under control. But their server interrupted the tender moment by asking if they wanted more wine. Somehow, they'd drained the entire bottle.

"I think we're okay," she said. "Let's get the check. Could we also get a few pieces of baklava to go?"

"Dusty, I promised you a whole dinner," Stuart said. "All we've had is wine and appetizers." But he was fishing his wallet out of his pocket, like he couldn't wait to get going.

Sure, they could take it slow. And sex wasn't an option until they could find somewhere private to do the deed.

But that didn't mean they had to rush back to the field house yet.

# CHAPTER THIRTEEN

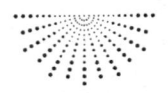

After Stuart paid the bill, Dusty grabbed the box of baklava and followed him out of the restaurant. When he took her hand and led her along the gravel path leading to the beach, butterflies spiraled through her. This was real. Not a dream, not a fantasy, but real life.

Stuart *wanted* her.

Upon reaching the sand, she kicked off her flip-flops and basked in the feel of the cool, damp grains beneath her feet. The wind tugged at her hair, brushing it across her face. Pushing it away, she looked up at him. Without saying a word, he pulled her toward him, stroked his fingers across her cheek, and kissed her gently. Just the faintest brush of his lips across hers. She opened her mouth a little wider and swept her tongue against his, tasting red wine. The sensation filled her with a delightful, fizzy happiness.

It wasn't their first kiss, but it felt like it. The promise of a brand-new relationship with someone she'd loved for years. As his mouth claimed hers again, she pressed her body closer, her toes curling in the sand. He wove his hands through her hair, sending tingles of desire through her. Around them, gulls wheeled overhead, and waves broke against the shore. She couldn't have asked for a more romantic setting.

When he pulled away, he sighed and smoothed a strand of hair from her face. "I wish we could keep going."

"Me, too." She leaned her head against his chest, taking comfort in his nearness. Even with the surf crashing in the background, the faint thump of his heartbeat was audible.

"I hate to ruin our delightful buzz, but we should probably figure out how public we want this to be," he said.

She hadn't even considered the optics. "I don't want to get you in trouble. Technically, you're a professor and I'm a grad student, so this isn't a good look, but..." Her heart constricted with uncertainty. "I still want to be with you."

"I do, too. But we don't have to worry about the professor-student thing since you're not one of *my* students."

"Right." She smiled up at him. "I'm from Harvard, and don't you forget it."

He chuckled. "As if I could. But it works in our favor. Plus, you're not here to earn a grade or get course credit. You were hired on as an independent illustrator."

"What about Hughes? Do you think he'll have a problem with us being together?"

"Given his reputation? I doubt it. Even so, we should behave like professionals when we're at the dig site. Would that be okay?"

She kept her tone light. "You mean no kissing while we're working? I can live with that."

Even if she wanted more, she'd take whatever she could get. Knowing that she wouldn't lose him to Clarissa or anyone else was an enormous relief.

By the time they headed back to the Land Rover, she was still floating on a blissful cloud. Not only had they revealed their feelings for each other, but they also had five weeks left at Troy. Five weeks to work together, enjoy their free time, and find some way to sneak off and have sex. The thought of intimacy with Stuart—when they were both sober enough to know what they were doing—sent shivers through her.

But now that they were together, she couldn't give Dr. Hughes any excuse to fire her. Come Monday, she'd need to pull off Operation Odysseus without a hitch. She wished she didn't have to hide it from Stuart, but if she told him the truth, he'd never approve. If anything, he'd insist on confronting Dr. Hughes about it, who'd then retaliate by booting her off the dig. Better to keep her plan under wraps and hope it all worked out.

As they pulled up to the field house, Stuart shut off the engine and killed the lights. When he placed his hand on her thigh, she inched closer. Cupping her hands around his beard, she reveled in the feel of his whiskers before kissing him passionately. His hand caressed the back of her neck, sending delicious tremors along her spine. She wanted to run her hands under his shirt and stroke his bare chest, but she restrained herself. One touch could lead to another, and before she knew it, she'd end up straddling his lap, grinding against him until they both got off.

She'd definitely fantasized about *that* before.

When their kisses grew more frantic, he broke away and pressed his forehead to hers. He drove out a ragged sigh. "I don't want to stop. But we probably should. Right?"

She loved how torn he sounded. How she'd made sensible, buttoned-up Stuart react in a way that ran counter to his rules and propriety. She smoothed her hand against his cheek, letting it linger in the bristles of his beard. "Yeah. Someone could come out at any minute. But we could carve out some alone time tomorrow night. Maybe after dinner?"

He threaded his fingers through her hair. "I'd like that."

"Me, too." She picked up the box of baklava. "If you don't mind, I'll take this to my room. I'm going to dream about you all night. What a combination—baklava and sex dreams." Giving a little shimmy, she unlatched her door and hopped out. "Coming?"

"Uh...in a minute. I need to get things under control here."

She laughed. "I'll leave so you won't be tempted. Good night, Stu. Thanks for dinner."

"My pleasure. Night, Dusty."

She hustled through the common area, hoping to dodge questions about her evening out. The crew was so engrossed in an elaborate tabletop game that they barely looked her way. Good. She needed time to process everything. To savor the euphoric feelings coursing through her, now that she knew exactly how Stuart felt about her.

As she opened the door to her room, she stopped short at the sight of Clarissa and Emilia, sitting on their beds and chatting. Pinned in the spotlight, she wished she'd taken a moment to brush her hair or adjust her clothing.

Emilia regarded her with a shit-eating grin. "Ooh. Someone got laid."

"Did not. I was at dinner with Stuart. That's all." She raised her eyebrows, trying to signal that she didn't want to discuss this in front of Clarissa, but Em was oblivious.

"That's all, my ass," Emilia said. "You're glowing, and it's not just because we spent eight hours on a boat today. Something happened tonight."

To Dusty's surprise, Clarissa started laughing. "Oh, my God. No wonder Stuart was glaring at you and Kerim earlier. I thought he was being protective, but he was *jealous*."

Flustered by her friends' scrutiny, Dusty set the box of baklava on her nightstand. "Do either of you want some dessert?"

"I don't want baklava, you bitch. I want details. Though now that you mention it..." Emilia eased off her bed. "Got any forks?"

"Yep." Dusty opened the box and brought out a handful of plastic forks. After passing one to each of them, she took a bite, groaning at the sweet, sticky goodness. "Mmm. This is incredible."

Emilia joined her, digging into a piece with her fork. "It's totally delicious, but you still owe us some answers. When we were on the boat, you were cozying up to Kerim. Then you had dinner with Stuart. Is this a legit love triangle? Do I need to decide if I'm Team Kerim or Team Stuart?"

"I'm firmly Team Stuart. And as it happens, he's Team Dusty." She grinned as she recalled the way he'd bared his soul at dinner. "Apparently, he's been fantasizing about me for some time."

Clarissa's eyes gleamed with amusement. "Here I thought you were more like siblings. I was so off base."

"Sorry if I implied that before, but—"

"But you were carrying a torch for him." Clarissa placed her hand over her heart. "A secret, burning love that was eating you up from the inside. It's so romantic."

Dusty stared at her. Could anyone truly be that good-natured? "You're okay with it?"

"Of course. I mean, he's a total snack. Hot, smart, sensitive. But I didn't feel any sparks from him. Probably because he's so obsessed with *you*." Clarissa inched over to the nightstand, dug into the baklava, and took a bite. She let out a groan of satisfaction. "Oh, that's good."

Emilia grinned at Dusty. "If you and Stuart need our room for a private session, just let us know. We'll be sure to give you some space."

Dusty snickered as she imagined draping one of her bandannas over the doorknob as a signal. "Thanks for the offer, but Stuart has his own room. For now, we're going to hold off."

"Why?" Emilia sounded even more disappointed than Dusty felt.

"The walls here are paper-thin. Remember last night when we heard someone snoring? It was like he was in the same room with us."

Clarissa wrinkled her nose. "Whoever it was, he was so loud I had to wear earplugs."

"I'm pretty sure it was TJ," Emilia said. "But, yeah, it might be stressful trying to keep things quiet while in the throes of passion. Unless you could find somewhere else to go?"

"We'll figure it out. This is all kind of new and..." Dusty hesitated, unsure of whether to say any more. It was one thing to confess that she wanted to drag Stuart off to bed but another to admit how deeply she cared for him.

"What?" Emilia demanded.

Feeling self-conscious, Dusty covered her face. "I might want more than just a hookup? Like an actual relationship? I don't know."

Emilia waved her fork at her. "Slow down. You can worry about the future later."

"True." There was no sense getting ahead of herself, not when they still had over a month left at Troy. "Speaking of the future, are we all set for Operation Odysseus tomorrow?"

Clarissa gave her a thumbs-up. "I called Dad tonight, and he's all in. Tomorrow morning, he's going to swing by at six thirty and give me a ride to the site. That way, I can give him the bag with our disguises. He'll work with us until nine thirty and then leave for the café. At ten, the three of us will walk down there for our morning break."

"Good plan," Dusty said. "After we change at the café, we can head over to Dr. Wagner's dig site. I'm not sure how much he'll tell us, but we'll do our best to charm him."

"I'm kind of excited. And scared. Definitely scared," Clarissa said. "I've never done anything like this before."

"Me neither," Emilia said.

"We should be okay as long as Wagner doesn't recognize us," Dusty said. "After that, we'll have to make sure we don't walk past his site on our way to the café or the parking lot."

"Now that you and Stuart are together, are you okay not telling him?" Clarissa asked.

Dusty released a drawn-out breath. "I hate keeping secrets,

but Hughes didn't want him to know. At least this way, if something goes wrong, he won't be implicated."

"But nothing's going to go wrong," Clarissa said. "Right? It's a good plan."

That still didn't mean it wouldn't go sideways. Or that Stuart wouldn't somehow find out. But Dusty couldn't focus on failure. If she had any hope of staying at Troy, Operation Odysseus *had* to work.

## CHAPTER FOURTEEN

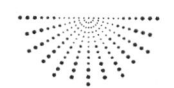

Whenever Stuart worked on a dig, his favorite time of day was early morning, just around sunrise. Evenings were fun, when the crew could unwind together, playing cards, sharing stories, relaxing with a beer. But waking up before everyone else gave him time to think. To enjoy the cool morning air before the sweltering heat became oppressive.

After firing up the coffeepot, he wandered outside and sat on the patio. The breeze ruffled his hair and brought with it the scent of dried grass. Unlike most mornings, he wasn't thinking about the dig. Instead of reviewing his mental checklist, he let his mind wander back to his romantic dinner with Dusty. Last night, when he opened up to her, he hadn't known how she'd react. She could have been offended. Or uncomfortable. Or pitied him, which would have been the worst reaction of all. But she'd felt the same way he had.

She *wanted* him.

But for how long? In all the years he'd known her, he'd never seen her in a serious relationship. Most of her flings lasted two or three months at most. He couldn't recall a time when she'd ever committed to anything for longer than a dig season.

Except for their friendship.

They'd been friends for twenty years, and she'd never let him down. Even when they'd been thousands of miles apart, separated by ten time zones, she'd always answered his texts. If he wanted to talk face-to-face, she'd jump on a call via FaceTime or Zoom. She might show up on his screen with her hair dyed crimson, teal, or fuchsia, but he could always count on her encouraging smile and snarky sense of humor. When she said, "ride or die," she meant it.

Did that mean he might get more than just a summer with her? With all his heart, he hoped so.

By the time he went back inside the field house, the coffee was done. He grabbed a box of Ülker tea biscuits from the cupboard but dropped them in shock when someone clasped him around the waist. A soft pair of lips grazed the back of his neck, and a singsong voice woke up a different part of his anatomy. "Good morning, Dr. Carlson."

He leaned against her, taking a moment to savor her nearness and the feel of her soft curves pressing against his back. "Good morning, Dusty. You're awfully chipper."

"Thanks to my delightful dreams. Which will hopefully soon become reality." She trailed kisses up his neck, then tugged on his earlobe with her teeth.

Damn, he really liked Dusty this way. But he froze at the sound of an irritated groan.

"Can you not?" Emilia said as she strolled into the kitchen. "Waking up at six is hard enough without you two going at it."

Dusty released Stuart from her grip and grinned at her friend. "You're just jealous."

"Damn right. But it's still annoying as hell. Keep it in your pants until after dinner."

Stuart's cheeks blazed. Maybe Dusty could be nonchalant

about getting caught, but if he wanted the others to respect him, he needed to show more restraint. After picking up the box of biscuits, he turned to face Emilia. "Sorry, Em. We'll keep it G-rated in the morning."

She grabbed a mug from the counter. "You'd better. Bad enough that I was kept up last night by TJ's snoring. I could hear it clear through the walls."

TJ ambled into the room and glared at her. "That wasn't me."

"Bullshit," Emilia said. "I recognize your snores from Istanbul."

"Not Istanbul again. For the love of God, will you get over it?"

~

ONCE THE CREW HAD ASSEMBLED AND HEADED OUT TO THE SITE, Stuart forced himself to push Dusty from his thoughts. The only way to succeed at his job was to switch his brain into organization mode and maintain strict boundaries between his personal and professional life. If he wanted to be alone with Dusty, he could seek her out after the day's work was done.

But when Kerim approached him and asked if they could talk in private, Stuart's stomach clenched up. As far as he knew, Dusty hadn't told anyone about them except Emilia. While he had no problem owning up to their relationship, he didn't want to discuss it while supervising the students. He followed Kerim until they were clear of the trenches, standing beside a weedy patch of grass. Without the protection of the canopy, the sun beat down with a blistering intensity.

He adjusted his hat and wiped his forehead. "Is everything all right?"

"Something's come up, and I thought we should discuss it."

Better to apologize now than act like a coward. "If this is about Dusty, I'm sorry if you felt blindsided. I'm not sure what she told you, but we didn't expect to end up together."

Kerim raised his eyebrows. "You two are together? That's not what she said yesterday."

"It…um…happened last night. At dinner. When I told her how I felt." The words came out in a messy jumble, making him more self-conscious than ever. Unlike him, Kerim didn't seem like the type to lose his cool over a woman.

But Kerim merely chuckled. "Good for you. I take it she shared your feelings?" When Stuart nodded, Kerim glanced at the trench where Dusty was crouched down, scraping at the dirt with her trowel. "Can't say I blame you for going after her. She's truly a delight. But there are plenty of fish in the sea, so to speak. No harm done."

Stuart blew out a relieved breath. "Thanks. I'm glad that's out of the way."

Kerim gave him a wry smile. "Though I appreciate the honesty, that's not why I wanted to talk to you."

So his awkward confession was for nothing? *Ouch.* "What was it, then?"

"It's our friend, Dr. Hughes. He's not satisfied with our progress."

Stuart scanned the site until he located the professor. As usual, Dr. Hughes was sitting in a camp chair talking to Mort. "Not satisfied? He's barely lifted a finger to help us."

"Believe me, I feel the same way. It's not so much our pace as our discoveries that are upsetting him. Or, rather, our lack of spectacular finds. He's convinced we'll unearth the lost cemetery if we expand our efforts beyond the lower city."

That damn cemetery. Why couldn't Dr. Hughes take pride in what they'd already accomplished? In the three weeks since they started digging, they'd uncovered a large storage building and two residential dwellings. Their finds included pottery, stone tools, animal bones, carnelian beads, and fragments of jewelry. Some of the potsherds and beads were from places like

Mycenaean Greece and Egypt, confirming Troy's reliance on international trade.

"Last night, Dr. Hughes called me at home," Kerim said. "He found out the Germans started digging in another section of Troy last week. They're working near the ruins of the ancient Temple of Athena. He's convinced they're onto something, and he assumed I'd know what it is."

"Do you?"

"No, and I haven't asked, either. I agreed to extend the parameters of our excavation, but only after he promised he wouldn't venture onto the Germans' site again."

Would that mean they could get through the next five weeks with no hostilities between the two teams? If so, Stuart was on board. "Perhaps it's worth it if we can avoid another confrontation with Dr. Wagner. What's the plan?"

"Dr. Hughes is going to stake out a new trench and wants three of the Turkish laborers to help him, plus Mort and Clarissa."

Losing the workmen was a minor inconvenience, but Stuart disliked the thought of Clarissa toiling under Dr. Hughes' lecherous gaze. More than once, the older man had commented on her looks. Even if he'd done it in a complimentary way, his behavior made Stuart uncomfortable. "Is that what Clarissa wants?"

"She wants to make her dad happy, so she's in. They'll start digging there this morning. I'd rather keep the other students here. If Hughes finds something important, we can switch things up. Does that work?"

"Fine with me." If Kerim was willing to go along with the plan, then he would, too. Besides, if by some miracle they found the cemetery, Dr. Hughes might be so pleased that he'd ease up on all of them.

"Then it's settled." Kerim made as if to leave but stopped. "One more thing. Dusty asked for help with her dissertation topic, so I said I'd work with her sometime this week." He smirked. "Platonically, of course."

After his awkward confession, Stuart suspected he'd be on the receiving end of many smirks whenever Dusty's name came up. He'd gladly put up with them, knowing he was in no danger of losing her to Kerim.

∽

AN HOUR LATER, DR. HUGHES HAD STAKED OUT A NEW TRENCH IN A location fifty meters west of the large defensive ditch that ringed the lower city. Besides recruiting Mort, Clarissa, and three of the laborers as his excavation crew, he insisted on adding a graduate student to his team. With some reluctance, Stuart relinquished one of his students. Anything to keep his boss happy.

A half hour before the morning break, Mort left for the café, claiming he needed a cold drink. Dr. Hughes waited until the older man was out of earshot before striding over to Stuart's trench and demanding more "muscle" for his site. This time, Stuart lost one of his best workers, a Turkish laborer with years of experience in the field.

Once Dr. Hughes had returned to his trench, Stuart focused on supervising his own crew, hoping he wouldn't have to give up anyone else. At ten, just as he was about to announce that it was break time, Dusty sidled up to him. When she brushed her fingers against his bare arm, he relished the contact, however slight.

She tilted her head toward Dr. Hughes' trench. "Our esteemed director seems to have carved out his own kingdom."

Stuart nodded. "Kerim and I weren't thrilled about it, but if it keeps him out of trouble, we'll all benefit."

"Agreed. It's best to let him play in his own sandbox. Maybe if we're lucky, he'll uncover his army of skeletons." She brushed the dirt off her shorts. "I should have mentioned this sooner, but

Mort offered to treat me and Emilia this morning. During our break, he wants us to come to the café with Clarissa so he can buy us cake. Who am I to say no to cake?"

"Sure. No problem." He gestured toward Clarissa, who was setting down her sieve. "Have you said anything to her about us?"

Dusty laughed. "I didn't have much of a choice. When I went inside last night after our date, she and Em were hanging out together. Before I could tell Em to play it cool, she started grilling me, and I revealed everything."

"That's fine." He was relieved Dusty had done the job for him. Telling Kerim had been awkward enough. "How'd she take it?"

"She wasn't upset at all. If anything, she thought it was romantic." She turned to leave. "Anyway, I'm off to enjoy copious amounts of cake. See you later."

"Have fun, but don't be too long. If Mort has his way, he'll keep you at the café all morning, and we have work to do. What with Hughes' side project, we're spread a little thin."

She gave him a cheeky salute. "Duly noted, Dr. Carlson. I promise we'll work extra hard when we come back."

He watched as she walked away, taking a moment to savor the view. As she headed toward the boardwalk with Clarissa and Emilia, he allowed himself to relax. Now that he and Dusty had confessed their feelings, he didn't have to worry about losing her to Kerim. And if Dr. Hughes could keep his focus on his own trench, they could avoid any run-ins with the German contingent.

Then the next five weeks could proceed without a hitch.

Or was that too much to hope for?

# CHAPTER FIFTEEN

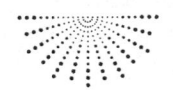

After talking with Stuart, Dusty walked with Clarissa and Emilia to the café, where Mort was waiting. He sat at his favorite table—the one shaded by an expansive olive tree with a view of the giant Trojan horse. As planned, he'd brought the bag Clarissa had put together, containing makeup and a change of clothes for all of them. After they scrubbed their faces in the café's tiny restroom, put on makeup, and donned sundresses, sandals, and sunglasses, they looked like a trio of tourists. Clarissa had also loaned each of them a floppy sunhat since she'd packed four for her trip to Turkey.

Upon leaving the café, they approached the Germans' new dig site located at the eastern curve of the circular boardwalk. As they drew nearer, Dusty's pulse raced in a mix of fear and anticipation. So far, they'd only encountered Dr. Wagner twice—during their initial site tour and on the day he'd stormed over to the lower city to confront Dr. Hughes. Both times, he'd focused his attention on his rival rather than on the women.

As with the other site, this one was roped off and marked with "No Trespassing" signs. Dusty walked up to the ropes and gave a cheerful wave. "Yoo-hoo!"

A student approached the ropes warily. Tall and muscular, with floppy white-blond hair, he shared Dr. Wagner's high cheekbones and piercing blue eyes. Were they related? Either way, he was a total hottie.

"Ja?" he said.

She addressed him in German. "Good morning. My name is Hilde. I'm visiting from the University of Cologne, where I'm a student of Dr. Anselm Schultz." She gestured to the other two. "We're all archaeology students, out doing a little sightseeing."

The German student put out his hand, then took it back sheepishly. "I'm Leopold, but everyone calls me Leo. I'd shake your hand if I wasn't covered in dirt. You know how it is."

"Do I ever." Clarissa giggled. "Though I'm sure you clean up *very* nicely, Leo."

Dusty refrained from rolling her eyes at Clarissa's flirtatious tone. "Is Dr. Wagner around by chance? We went looking for him over by the South Gate excavations, but a student told me he was working here with a small crew. Dr. Schultz has spoken of him so highly that I had to meet him."

"Of course. Give me a minute."

When he left, Emilia nudged her. "Hilde? That's the best you can come up with?"

"Shut it, Gerta."

"Gerta? That sounds like someone's grandma."

"Shhh," Clarissa said. "No talking in English. We need to stay in character. I'm Liesel. *The Sound of Music* is one of my favorite movies."

Dusty stifled the urge to laugh out loud. Even if their mission was risky, she was enjoying the role-play aspect of it. Was Stuart into role-play? A tantalizing thought to set aside for later. For now, she needed to be on point as Hilde.

When Leo returned with Dr. Wagner, Dusty beamed at him, hoping he wouldn't remember her. He was no less intimidating than before—tall, blond, and aloof, with a firm jaw and cheekbones that could cut glass. "Can I help you?" he asked in German.

Dusty gave a silent thank-you for her stern-as-hell German tutor, Frau Huber, as she answered him in his own language. "Are you Dr. Wagner? Anselm—I mean Dr. Schultz—told me all about you. He said I should look you up while I was visiting Troy."

Dr. Wagner nodded. "How is Anselm? Still working on that project in Luxor?"

In preparation for Operation Odysseus, Dusty had contacted her mom for an update. Good thing, since the professor had stopped digging in Egypt two seasons ago. "No, he hasn't worked there for a couple of years. He's too far behind on his publication schedule."

"Understandable. I've been there myself. How may I help you?"

"Could we have a peek around your site? Naturally, we won't take any photos, but we'd love to know more. These are my fellow students, Gerta and Liesel."

Both women greeted him in German. Dusty waited as he assessed them, anxious that the sight of them might jog his memory. But he showed no sign of recognition. Instead, he graced them with a benevolent smile that transformed his entire face. "Well…we normally don't allow tourists, but since you're Anselm's students, I'll make an exception."

"Thank you so much," Clarissa gushed. "We appreciate it."

As a gust of wind blew toward them, Dusty clamped her hat firmly on her head and followed the others past the ropes. Unlike the Germans' site near the South Gate, this was a smaller operation, with just two trenches and a handful of students and laborers. Near the trenches was the limestone foundation of an ancient Greek altar, built to honor the goddess Athena; around it lay scattered fragments of marble capitals.

Dr. Wagner stopped at the edge of the first trench. "Last month, we started excavating near the South Gate of the citadel at the southeast section of the boardwalk. However, our team is large enough that we could expand our efforts to include this area. You may wonder why we're digging near the ruins of a Hellenistic temple built five hundred years after the Bronze Age ended. It's because of the construction methods favored by the ancient Greeks. Do any of you know what I'm referring to?"

Clarissa raised her hand, as if eager to show off her knowledge. "I do. When the Greeks occupied Troy, they razed the former Bronze Age citadel to make way for their own buildings. They leveled the ruins of that citadel to create a flat mound where they could erect the temple."

*Someone's been doing their homework.* Dusty shot Clarissa a quick grin, glad that one of them had done a little background research.

"Correct," Dr. Wagner said. "It's always been thought that if a team were to excavate some of the backfill created by the Greeks, they'd uncover more artifacts from the citadel. Scholars have assumed the Trojan citadel, or palace, housed a royal archive, presumably written on clay tablets, but no one has ever found any evidence."

Dusty sucked in a breath. Dr. Hughes had been right in his assessment. The Germans *were* onto something. Finding written evidence from this era would be incredibly newsworthy. "A find like that could change history."

"It could indeed," Dr. Wagner said. "No one's ever found any tablets at Troy dating back to the Bronze Age. Can you imagine what they might contain?"

Emilia spoke up. "They could hold palace records. Or treaties containing the names of different rulers."

"That's what we're hoping for," Dr. Wagner said. "This is the first time the government has allowed us access to this area, so it's a huge opportunity. But no matter what we uncover, we'll analyze all our findings before making any announcements. We're scientists, not treasure hunters, like the Americans."

"The Americans?" Clarissa said, all wide-eyed. "We haven't met them yet."

"Don't bother. They're a rude bunch, digging in the lower city." He shook his head in disgust. "Did you know their director was kicked out of Troy ten years ago? It was a huge scandal."

"No!" Clarissa clapped her hand over her mouth. "That's terrible."

"Very unprofessional. The Turkish government revoked the university's permit. I suspect they're only here because they paid off the right people, but it wouldn't take much for them to lose this privilege."

Dusty felt a twinge of foreboding. All the more reason Dr. Hughes needed to behave himself. If he messed up again, he could place their entire project in jeopardy.

After talking with Dr. Wagner a little longer, she grew uneasy. By now, Stuart and Kerim might be questioning their lengthy absence. What if the two men came looking for them? She caught the others' eyes, then graced Dr. Wagner with a grateful smile. "Thank you for taking the time to show us around. We should let you get back to work."

"You're very welcome. Tell Anselm hello from me. And tell him to visit Turkey sometime. The climate here is much more reasonable than Egypt."

As they made their goodbyes, smiling, waving, and backing away, Dusty's heart rate ratcheted up a notch. Only a few more steps and they'd be on their way.

Until a familiar voice stopped them in their tracks. "Em? Dusty? What are you doing?"

Dusty froze. TJ stood at the edge of the rope barricade, staring at them.

With lightning reflexes, Emilia whirled around and yelled at him in English. "Stop following us, you American pig! We're not interested." Still fuming, she turned to face Dr. Wagner. "I apologize, but this *boy* has been trailing us all over the site, trying to pick us up, if you can believe it."

Did he believe it? Dusty held her breath, waiting for Dr. Wagner's reaction. To her immense relief, he glared at TJ and spoke to him in English. "I suggest you leave these women alone. Clearly, they are not interested in you."

Dusty clenched her hands as she waited for TJ's response. Rather than challenge their blatant lie, he gave the women a humble smile. "Sorry, ladies. I didn't mean to bother you."

Once he had skulked away, Emilia apologized to Dr. Wagner in German. "I'm so sorry for my outburst, but he kept bothering us earlier. I think he mistook us for someone else."

"Not to worry," Dr. Wagner said. "It looks as though we've scared him off. Anyway, we must resume our work. It was a pleasure."

"The pleasure was ours," Dusty said. She motioned for the others to follow, and they left the site quickly. As if by unspoken agreement, they remained silent until they came to the paved courtyard where the Trojan horse stood. TJ waited beside it, arms crossed, with a stormy look on his face.

"What the hell was that?" he asked. "Why are you dressed like tourists? And why did you act like I was a stalker?"

Emilia held up her hand. "Forget about it, okay? The less you know, the better."

"Are you working with the Germans? Betraying us?"

She rolled her eyes. "Of course not. We're on a covert mission for Dr. Hughes. Trying to learn more about the Germans' project without implicating him."

"Are you insane?" TJ said. "What if Dr. Wagner had recognized you?"

"He didn't," Emilia said. "None of them did because we weren't dressed as archaeologists, and unlike you, we all speak German." She beckoned to the others. "Let's get going."

TJ insisted on following them, still muttering under his breath about the insanity of their plan.

"What were you doing there, anyway?" Emilia asked him. "The morning break should be over by now."

"It ended ages ago. When Stuart grumbled that all of you were taking too long, I volunteered to go look for you and took the long way around." He gave a petulant shrug. "I figured if you were still in the café, I'd grab a Coke. I could use the caffeine."

"Fine, you can join us at the café," Dusty said. "But keep your mouth shut about our visit with the Germans. Got it?"

He scowled. "I can't believe you're doing Hughes any favors. I thought you hated him."

Clarissa spoke up. "They were doing it for me. Or rather, for my dad. That's all you need to know."

They found Mort seated outside at his familiar table. After greeting him, the three women went into the restroom to change into their dig clothes. Once they were done, they joined him and TJ. As they recapped their conversation with Dr. Wagner, Mort jotted down the details in a little notebook he produced from the pocket of his vest. Dusty had seen him pull it out before, often when Dr. Hughes was speaking. Clearly, Mort was the kind of guy who liked to document everything.

He waved the notebook at Dusty. "Don't worry, my dear. If we're captured, I'll eat this. No one will ever get any information out of me."

She laughed. "Good to know. I'm hoping it won't come to that."

"I'm sure Dr. Hughes will be pleased by your work," he said. "You ladies can order anything you want. My treat."

"We should get back," Dusty said. "We don't want to piss off Stuart and Kerim."

"No way," Emilia said. "We already missed our break. If we go back to the site without eating, we'll have to wait until lunch, and I'm starving."

Dusty conceded. After ordering tea and three types of cake, they sat in the shade with Mort and enjoyed his company. Emilia and TJ took turns regaling him with dig stories, each more hardcore than the next.

When Dusty peeked at her watch and saw it was eleven thirty, she told them to finish up quickly. As she cleared her teacup and plate from the table, she spied Dr. Hughes walking toward the café. By now, he must be dying to know how their mission had gone.

Telling the others she was going on ahead, she raced out to intercept him. At the sight of her, he stopped and waited in a shaded area free from the crush of tourists.

He frowned at her. "About time. What took you so long?"

"Sorry, but..." *Wait.* Why was she apologizing after she'd just put herself at risk? Clearing her throat, she infused her voice with confidence. "Once Dr. Wagner agreed to talk to us, we didn't want to rush him. The more we let him talk, the more we learned about his goals for this new site."

"He didn't suspect anything?"

"Nope. We pulled it off perfectly."

Dr. Hughes chuckled. "That idiot."

She winced at his words. Now that she'd spent time with Dr. Wagner, she no longer viewed him as an imperious jerk. Despite the stern image he projected, he'd treated her respectfully. He was a true professional, which was more than she could say for Dr. Hughes.

Still, she had to play along. "I'll say. He told us everything." Suddenly afraid the German dig director might materialize out of nowhere, she moved in closer. In a hushed voice, she told Dr. Hughes what she'd learned.

After she was done, he bristled with indignation. "A royal archive? That's impossible. No one's ever found evidence of anything like that at Troy."

"I know. I suspect he was just trying to impress us." She took a step back, wanting to put an end to the conversation. "Anyway, it's done. Are we all good?'

"We're good. If you behave yourself for the rest of the dig, I see no reason you should leave any earlier than you'd planned."

*If I behave myself? What the fuck does that mean?* But she knew better than to voice her irritation. "Will you include Mort in your publication like you promised? Or give him some kind of credit?"

"Of course. I'm a man of my word." He cast a glance toward the café, where Emilia and Clarissa were clearing their table. "I suggest the lot of you get back to the site as soon as possible. Wouldn't want Stuart to get more anxious than he already is."

"Yep. Right." Wiping the sweat from her brow, she hustled over to the café to urge the others along.

As they walked back to the site together, she pushed her lingering guilt aside.

She'd done what she had to. And if luck was with her, she'd never have to worry about it again.

## CHAPTER SIXTEEN

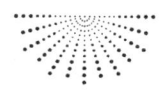

On their next day off, Stuart was once again denied a relaxing day at the beach. Rather than allow the crew to "squander" their free time, Dr. Hughes had insisted they embark upon a field trip. So, instead of lazing in the sun, they were driving to Bergama, a city near the ruins of Pergamon, a well-preserved site that had risen to fame during the Greco-Roman era. While Stuart agreed Pergamon was worth a visit, the drive was a grueling three hours each way.

In anticipation of the long day ahead, they'd all risen at 6:00 a.m. and shared a quick breakfast. Stuart assumed he'd be driving one of the Land Rovers, as he did during their workdays, but Kerim volunteered to take his place. "That way, you and Dusty can ride together."

Stuart could have done without Kerim's knowing smirk, but he accepted the offer gratefully. When he hopped into the front of Dusty's vehicle, she was already in the driver's seat.

She flashed him a cheeky grin. "You're here. What say we ditch this road trip, check into a hotel in Güzelyali, and spend all day fucking like bunnies?"

He chuckled at her candidness. "Behave yourself."

"Oh, please. Are you telling me the thought didn't cross your mind?"

Of course it had. Though he was glad they weren't rushing into things, his fantasies about her had ramped up considerably. He placed his hand on her thigh, inching up past the hem of her shorts to caress the bare skin underneath. As he imagined touching her everywhere without inhibition, he craved her even more.

He tried to clear the tempting visions from his head. This wasn't the time for lewd daydreams. "As much as I'd love to whisk you off to a hotel room, it wouldn't be a good look."

"I guess we'll have to wait for the right moment. Such a shame."

The back door of the Land Rover opened, and the two Turkish students settled in behind them. Hayat and Tufan were in their midtwenties; both were graduate students at the university in Çanakkale, studying under Kerim.

Stuart removed his hand from Dusty's thigh and turned back to greet them. "Welcome aboard."

"Thanks," Hayat said, securing her long, dark hair into a ponytail. "I'm glad we got a spot in your vehicle. TJ and Emilia are in the other one and…" She let out an exasperated breath. "They never stop fighting."

"Sitting with them for three hours could be painful," Tufan added.

"They're in the same vehicle?" Dusty said. "Not good. Never fear, Stuart and I get along just fine. But anyone who rides with me has to listen to music. Without it, I go a little stir-crazy."

Once the rest of the crew had assembled, the two Land Rovers headed out, followed by Mort's car. Stuart fiddled with the radio until he landed on a Turkish pop station with decent reception. He wasn't a fan of pop music in any language, but the ancient Land Rover didn't have a USB port or a spot to plug in an auxiliary cord. Hayat seemed to enjoy it, though, singing along in Turkish whenever she recognized a song.

After a half hour on the road, Stuart grabbed a Ziploc bag filled with Petit Beurre tea biscuits and offered it to the others. "Biscuit?"

Tufan made a face. "No, thanks. We need to talk about the snacks. On your next grocery run, I'm coming with you."

"Same here," Hayat said. "We can help you find something better."

"I'm all for it." Stuart didn't like the dry, tasteless biscuits, either, but that didn't stop him from eating two of them.

"No one actually *likes* Petit Beurre biscuits," Dusty said, "but somehow, they've been the default snack on a bunch of my digs."

"You've worked in a lot of places, right?" Hayat asked. "How do you like Troy so far?"

"I'm really enjoying it. Working with Kerim—I mean Dr. Özgen—has been a treat. He's so knowledgeable about Turkish archaeology."

Two weeks ago, Dusty's words might have plagued Stuart with jealousy. Not anymore. Kerim might be an accomplished archaeologist, but he wasn't the one who'd spent an hour with Dusty last night, locked in a passionate embrace on the patio.

"I wish I was still in his trench," Hayat said, bristling with irritation. "Working with Dr. Hughes has not been pleasant. His behavior is very unprofessional."

Guilt prickled Stuart's conscience. Over the last week, Dr. Hughes' attitude had improved markedly. Though he was still hellbent on finding his lost cemetery, he'd stopped snapping at the students. He'd even praised one of Dusty's drawings in full view of everyone. Because he'd eased up on the crew, Stuart hadn't offered any objections when he'd asked if Hayat could join his team.

"I'm sorry," Stuart said. "I didn't realize there was a problem. Has Dr. Hughes said anything offensive to you?"

"Not about me," Hayat said, "but he's made inappropriate comments about Clarissa."

Dusty turned to face Hayat. Stuart clutched onto his seat as they barely missed hitting a car that had slowed to turn off the highway. "What kind of comments?" she demanded.

Hayat drove out a harsh sigh. "Yesterday, when Clarissa was bent over, he nudged one of the workmen and said in Turkish, 'Quite a view, isn't it? If only I were twenty years younger.' And that's just one example."

"What the fuck?" Dusty said. "Why hasn't her dad said anything?"

"How could he? He doesn't understand Turkish, and half the time, he's not even at the site. The sun is hard for him to handle, so he spends more time drinking tea at the café than working with us."

Dusty's grip tightened on the steering wheel. "You shouldn't have to put up with Hughes' sexism. Do you want me to say something? Because—"

"No." Stuart placed a hand on her arm. Not only was she driving too close to the car in front of them, but she also had that fiery look in her eyes. A look that could get her into hot water. "It's not your place."

She let out her breath in a huff. "Then will you talk to him?"

He paused, trying to sort out the best course of action. He didn't want Hayat to be miserable, but he wasn't the one in charge. "I'll mention it to Kerim. If he thinks it's an issue, he can bring it up with Dr. Hughes."

Hayat sighed. "Good luck with that. I doubt he'll want to cause trouble."

As they moved on to other topics, Stuart mulled over Dusty's request, feeling the weight of her judgment. But he was in a precarious position. Unlike Kerim, who'd been teaching in Çanakkale for over a decade, Stuart was a brand-new hire who had yet to prove himself. Right now, he had everything to lose.

DUSTY WAS DISAPPOINTED IN STUART, BUT SHE HELD HER TONGUE. Her last altercation with Dr. Hughes had taught her a painful lesson. No matter how much she wanted to call him out on his insufferable behavior, she needed to keep her mouth shut. Otherwise, she could end up with another target on her back.

*Nope. Not going that route again.*

Besides, work was so much easier now that Dr. Hughes didn't actively hate her. While she still didn't trust him, she could do her job without being subjected to his constant criticism. And he'd stopped bitching about the Germans, probably because he'd convinced himself Dr. Wagner's search for a royal archive was a "wild goose chase." More than once, he'd taken Dusty aside to ask her opinion, whereupon she'd agreed that the German director was wasting his summer digging through an ancient Greek garbage heap.

Did she believe that? Hell, no. Dr. Wagner was *definitely* onto something. But she'd never admit it to her boss.

As they drove through an area thick with pine nut trees, Hayat suggested they stop at a local stand selling honey, nuts, and fruit. They bought a few bags of nuts for their snack arsenal and a large jar of honey for their morning tea breaks. When they reached Bergama, they parked in the older part of the city, which looked like a delightful place to explore, filled with narrow, cobbled streets, colorful houses, and small restaurants.

Though the ruins of Pergamon were spread out around the city, the main attraction was the ancient Acropolis, located on a hilltop site that could be reached by car or gondola. Dusty lobbied for the gondola since she loved rides—everything from slow-moving cable cars to death-defying roller coasters. Crowded together in their gondola, Dusty pressed her body close to Stuart's. The mere act of sitting beside him with their shoulders touching filled her with an unexpected burst of happiness. In the past, she'd always jumped into flings with little buildup. But she loved this feeling of anticipation as their desire for each other grew stronger each day.

Once they reached the Acropolis, they had a breathtaking view of the city below. Even better, Dr. Hughes had opted not to join them due to his aversion to heights. Kerim led them around the major attractions: the Temple of Trajan, with its perfectly preserved columns, the Temple of Athena, and the massive remnants of the city walls. The best feature was the stunning Roman theater, built right into the hillside.

"This is the steepest theater in the ancient world," Kerim said. "Back when the Romans used it for performances, it could hold over fifteen thousand people. Be careful walking around because it's easy to get vertigo."

Case in point, Mort had plunked down on one of the carved stone seats and was wiping his brow. Since Clarissa was busy taking photos of the valley below, Dusty went and sat beside him. "You doing okay?"

"I'm a little dizzy. Not used to heights like this, especially in the heat."

"The view's worth it, though. Want me to take your picture?" When he handed Dusty his phone, she backed up and tried to capture the shot but almost careened over a row of seats.

Stuart grabbed her elbow. "Watch your step. It's a long way down."

She took a moment to catch her breath. "Thanks. You'd better take it."

After Stuart handed the phone back to Mort, he gave them an indulgent smile. "You two make a cute couple. Let me take a photo of you."

Dusty had posed for plenty of pictures with Stuart, but she didn't have one where they were an actual couple. She placed her arm around his waist and leaned into him. To her surprise, he didn't check to see if anyone was watching but rested his arm on her shoulders. After Mort sent her the photo, she let out a cry of delight. "This is perfect. Thanks, Mort."

When they'd finished their tour of the Acropolis, they took the gondola back into the city, where they visited the ruins of the Red Basilica, a monumental building with tall, red-brick walls and arched doorways. Since it had once served as a temple for the worship of Egyptian gods, Dusty took a few photos to send to her mother.

During the last hour of their visit, Kerim suggested they explore the town of Bergama. While most of the group went in search of a coffeehouse, Dusty and Stuart wandered off on their own. Older homes with crumbling facades lined the narrow streets, bringing to mind a bygone era. Dusty loved old neighborhoods like these. Even if archaeology was in her blood, sometimes she preferred exploring cities to tromping through another set of ruins.

When they came upon a quiet side street, she pulled Stuart into the shade and kissed him. All the week's tension faded away as he wrapped his arms around her waist and kissed her back with equal passion. She tasted watermelon on his tongue—from the Jolly Rancher she'd given him on the gondola ride down. For the moment, she wanted to forget the dig and pretend they were nothing more than two lovers enjoying a few stolen moments while on vacation together.

At the sight of an elderly couple, Stuart pulled away but kept hold of her hand. "You okay to drive back? If you're tired, I can take over."

"Are you saying that to be nice or because you're terrified I'll get into a wreck? I saw you clutching your seat a few times."

"Only when you got riled up about Hughes. You lost focus there for a minute."

"Sorry, but he needs to stop with those sexist comments. There's no excuse for shit like that." She tugged on his hand.

"Come on. Let's grab some Turkish coffee before we go back. I could use a little caffeine for the drive."

Stuart nodded but stopped when they passed a store displaying tourist trinkets. "Wait. I have to ask. Were you disappointed in me?"

Dusty picked up a key chain bearing a large blue glass bead, meant to ward off the evil eye. She'd seen different versions of these beads all over Turkey. "What do you mean?"

"During the drive, when Hayat asked me to talk to Hughes, I felt like I let you down."

"It doesn't matter what I think." She set the key chain back on the spinner rack. "I'm not the one with all the responsibility."

"Don't bullshit me. I saw the way your hands tensed around the steering wheel."

Trust Stuart to see right through her. "Only because that asshole ahead of me was barely going the speed limit. But yeah, I was a little disappointed. I get that Kerim doesn't want to rock the boat, and I know you're trying to be careful, but Hayat shouldn't be stuck with Hughes for the rest of the season. Can't all of us rotate through his trench?"

Stuart did that pensive thing where his brow furrowed, but he wasn't angry. Just thinking. Then he smiled. "That's a good idea. I could ask Hughes to rotate all the students but frame it positively. Like everyone should get the chance to dig in this new trench in case it leads us to the cemetery. Then it wouldn't look like I was playing favorites."

"You see? That's better than doing nothing, and you can suggest it in a way that flatters his ego."

He grinned at her. "How are you so smart?"

"I'm just used to archaeologists with big egos." She poked him in the shoulder. "Don't turn out like that, okay? I like you just the way you are." She'd almost said the word "love" but caught herself in time. "It's usually easier to solve someone else's problems than your own."

"Speaking of which, I haven't had a chance to ask. How'd it go with Kerim the other night when you worked on your dissertation topic?"

When a stray cat brushed against her ankles, she bent down to pet it, hoping Stuart would change the subject. Now that they were alone, the last thing she wanted to talk about was her thesis.

He didn't let it go. "What are you hiding? Was your meeting that bad?"

She stood to face him. "It was fine. Just very academic. We spent hours poring over excavation reports from past seasons at Troy. Then we scoured a bunch of academic databases so I could find out what's been covered before. I decided to write about the advance in archaeological methodologies used at Troy over the past century, from the 1930s up to the present day. I'll be examining how they've affected our interpretation of the site."

"Sounds like you're off to a good start."

His response wasn't as enthusiastic as she'd expected, but she hadn't exactly been leaping for joy about it, either. She tried to inject some excitement into her voice. "If I can squeeze in enough research while I'm at Troy, I'll make good headway. I could even whip up an outline and a few chapters."

The thought of *writing* her thesis still daunted her, but Kerim had been an encouraging mentor.

Stuart leaned over and kissed the top of her head. "As long as that's what you want."

Again, he didn't sound entirely convinced. But he'd seen her go through this phase of planning before, only to have it fizzle out.

This time, it was different. She'd show her mother and everyone else who doubted her that she could pull it off.

# CHAPTER SEVENTEEN

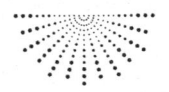

Two days after their field trip, Dusty's enthusiasm for her new dissertation topic had faded a little.

No, it had faded a *lot*.

After settling on her idea, she'd emailed her graduate adviser with the message, "This is the one!"

To which her adviser had replied, "I'll believe it when you've written over two chapters."

Fair, given that Dusty's last three attempts had stalled out within the first twenty pages. But this time, she wasn't daunted. Even if Stuart had responded with less enthusiasm than she'd hoped, she still felt certain she was on the right track.

But on Tuesday, after the day's work was done, she sat in the library, surrounded by piles of books and articles, and literally wished she were anywhere else. Though she enjoyed delving into research, she didn't want to do it now. Not when the crew were gathered in the common room, playing cards together.

And to think—this was only the research phase. A walk in the park compared to the gut-wrenching prospect of writing hundreds of pages of dry academic material.

*Why not set it aside until Boston? You can start working on it when you get back.*

Who was she kidding? If she wanted to write about Troy, she should do it now, when the site was close at hand, and she had access to scads of excavation reports. Besides, once she got home, she'd get distracted by her artwork, her friends, and her life in Boston.

In a fit of frustration, she threw her notebook across the room. As it made its arc, the door opened, and Stuart poked his head in. He ducked as the notebook hit the wall above him, then reached down and grabbed it off the floor. "That bad, huh?"

She scowled at him. "Go away. I don't need you mocking me. I'm working."

He strode over to her and placed the notebook on the table. "Are you? Or are you stewing in misery, ready to snap at anyone who comes to help you?"

Guilt swamped over her. She placed her head in her hands. "Sorry. I'm a beast right now."

He gestured for her to stand up. "Come on. Let's go outside."

"That's your solution? To kiss me until I forget about my thesis?"

"Who said anything about kissing?" He laughed. "I'm not here to corrupt you. I'm offering you a change of scenery. You've been here for two hours and haven't made any progress. Right?" When she nodded, he came around to her chair and took her hand. "Let's go."

Even if he'd promised to kick her butt when she needed it, she hadn't asked him to do it tonight. But she appreciated that he'd come to help her.

Grumbling, she stood and followed him out of the research library, then out the back door of the field house. The night sky here was much darker than in Boston or Cairo. She could easily make out the Big Dipper and the North Star. Taking a deep, cleansing breath, she allowed the cool night air to wash over her.

She hadn't realized how tight her shoulders were or how much tension had been coiled inside her body.

Without a word, Stuart went behind her and massaged her back and shoulders. As his firm hands kneaded her muscles, she groaned with relief. She'd spent too many hours sitting hunched over. When she leaned back into him, he kissed the top of her head. "Let's walk a bit. All right?"

"You led me on with that massage, and now we're just going to walk?" But when he pointed to the road, she took his hand and went with him.

As they strolled along the side of the road, he kept quiet. Was he waiting for her to speak first? To explain why she'd succumbed to a tantrum like a little kid? "Sorry. I don't know why this is so hard for me."

His voice was gentle. "Can I ask you something? Why get a PhD? Is it because you've invested five years at Harvard? You already have a master's degree, which is a huge accomplishment."

"Funny how my mom never seems to acknowledge that," Dusty muttered. "But I don't regret any of the time I've put into grad school. I've taken some great classes and gotten to work at a lot of amazing sites." She'd always enjoyed the learning aspect of academia. It was the writing that killed her. And a dissertation involved a ton of writing. Best-case scenario, she'd have to crank out at least two hundred pages.

"Then is it because you want to teach? Or work in the curatorial department of a museum? Or do you want the honor of calling yourself Dr. Danforth?"

She let out a huff of exasperation. "You know I don't care about titles or academic rank. It's because of my parents."

"I didn't ask about them. I asked about you, Dulcinea Francesca Danforth. Do you want any of those things?"

Using her full name was a low blow. When a car sped by, she inched over. Walking along a country road at night wasn't the safest move, but she liked the forward motion. It was easier to open up to Stuart when she wasn't looking him in the eye. "No. But my mom threatened to cut me off if I didn't get serious about my future. Which means the PhD thing matters a lot to her. I'm the only shot she and my dad have at carrying on our family's legacy."

Not only were her parents noted archaeologists, but her maternal grandfather was a professor who had excavated in Egypt for years. Her dad's parents were academics as well. Everywhere she went, she was surrounded by brilliant people with PhDs.

"Don't you think your folks would prefer it if you did something you loved?" Stuart asked. "You're a talented artist—why not follow that path and see where it leads? I've known you for almost twenty years, and you're always happiest when you're drawing."

As they continued walking, she mulled over his words. Though she loved archaeology, loved the act of discovery and the camaraderie of the crew, her happy place was at her illustration table, drawing the finds from the day's work. When she was back at home, be it Boston or Cairo or London, she could easily spend hours lost in her art. Not so with writing. Even if she removed all other distractions, she found it a struggle to arrange her thoughts into coherent paragraphs. It was a wonder she'd made it this far in academia.

After another ten minutes, they turned around and headed back to the field house. Stuart led her over to one of the picnic tables and sat beside her with his hand resting on her thigh. "I'd never tell you what to do, but you've always stood up for everyone else. Why not stand up for yourself?"

She imagined calling her mother to confess she was dropping out of grad school. Or worse yet, telling her in person. She rubbed her hands over her arms, suddenly chilled at the prospect of a confrontation. "I don't want my mom to hate me."

"She wouldn't hate you. Maybe she'd be disappointed, but she'd learn to live with it."

As much as Dusty loved Stuart, he could be so oblivious. "Easy for you to say. You've done everything right—played by the rules, gotten perfect grades, finished your doctorate in record time, and landed a great job. Your parents must be proud as hell."

"They are, but it still hasn't been easy, and..." When his voice caught, she stared at him, surprised by the vulnerability in his eyes.

"What do you mean?"

"I mean, yes, I've played by the rules, and I've gotten everything I wanted, and—let's face it—I'm a straight white male, which comes with a ton of privilege. But academia is still a huge crapshoot. Do you know how lucky I was to land a teaching job? A tenure-track job at a great university? Of all the PhD students in my field, only a handful of us got jobs right away. The others? Working in contract archaeology, from project to project. Or taking an adjunct position that might not be renewed. Or doing *anything* to pay off student loans in the hopes of finding a real job next year."

She hadn't considered how fortunate he'd been. Last summer, when he'd admitted he was worried about finding a job, she'd assumed he'd land one with little difficulty. But she also remembered that he'd applied everywhere he might have a chance, even if it meant he could end up in a city where he didn't know a soul.

"I'm sorry it was such an ordeal. Is that why you've been so careful around Hughes?"

"Partly. I don't want to screw up, not when there are dozens of recent graduates who'd gladly take my place." He stroked her hair. "Anyway, this isn't about me. It's about you. I know your mom is intimidating, but think about what I said. No sense making yourself miserable, especially since a PhD won't guarantee you a job."

For the first time ever, she allowed herself to envision a different path. Making a living as an artist was risky as hell, but she'd built up a lot of connections in the archaeological community with her academic commissions. She'd also be willing to work in graphic design if need be. She'd rather produce commercial artwork than write a bunch of scholarly articles.

"Thanks," she said. "I appreciate the support."

"Anytime. Like you said when we were in Bergama, it's easier to solve someone else's problems than your own. Maybe that's why I was so clueless about my relationship with Shelby. I kept trying to make it work, even when it was obvious she was totally wrong for me."

After Dusty's first night at the field house, when she'd argued with Stuart about Shelby, she hadn't brought up his ex again. It was just too painful to talk about. But with Stuart giving her an opening, she seized the chance to ask the question that had plagued her for years. "Since we're being honest, why'd you stay with her for so long? I know she was rich and athletic and stunningly beautiful, but she put you through so much grief."

He let out a lengthy sigh. "My parents asked me that, too. When I first started dating her, I thought I'd found my match since she wanted the same things I did. But the longer we were together, the more critical she got. Like the way she'd mock me for being a 'perpetual grad student.' I put up with it because…she really messed with my head. So much that I was afraid if I ended things, I'd never find someone who felt the same way she did. Someone who loved me enough to want to spend their whole life with me."

Dusty clenched her teeth, fighting the urge to hurl curses at Shelby. She wanted to jump back in time and smack her sideways for messing with Stuart's psyche. "Are you serious? You're an amazing guy. You're kind, thoughtful, and so smart it makes my head hurt."

"I'm also a giant ancient history nerd."

She snorted. "Being a nerd is sexy these days. Plus, you've got a great body, and you're rocking an incredibly hot beard."

His warm chuckle sent a bolt of heat spiraling through her. "You like the beard, don't you?"

"Hell, yes. I can't wait to feel it grazing the inside of my thighs when you finally have your way with me." She shivered at the thought.

"Are you trying to torture me? Now I'm going to be thinking about that all night."

"Good." She leaned in closer and whispered in his ear. "I want you to dream about everything you're going to do to me."

"Trust me, I've been dreaming about it a lot." He gave her thigh a gentle squeeze. "But I'm sure the reality will be even better."

The low timbre of his voice filled her with a powerful yearning. She wanted more than just furtive kisses on the back patio. She wanted—no *needed*—to touch him everywhere, to brush her lips over his bare skin and make him groan with pleasure.

"I can't wait until we can finally be alone," she said. "But for now, I'll take a kiss."

With that, all thoughts of Shelby and academia were forgotten as he took her in his arms and kissed her under a sky filled with stars.

# CHAPTER EIGHTEEN

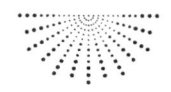

In the three weeks he'd been working at Troy, Stuart had never visited the café. Though Mort had offered to treat him to a cold drink or a spot of tea, Stuart had always turned him down. Unlike the others, he needed to be present onsite as much as possible. So it was ironic that the one time he popped into the café, Mort wasn't around to make good on his promise. He and Clarissa had taken a few days off to go on a bus tour that included Ephesus, Aphrodisias, and Hierapolis—ancient sites that were worth a visit but too far from Troy for a day trip.

Fighting back a yawn, Stuart cursed himself for sleeping through his alarm. Normally, he didn't need one, but he always set it just in case. Today, he'd woken so late that he'd missed the chance for a quick cup of coffee. He'd thought he could last until the morning break, but no such luck. By eight, he was battling a wicked caffeine headache.

When the barista set down Stuart's cappuccino, he inhaled the scent gratefully. He went to add a packet of sugar and almost bumped into Dr. Wagner. Stuart hadn't seen him in over two weeks—not since the stone-faced director had barged onto the site to accuse Dr. Hughes of spying. Since then, there hadn't been any interaction between the two groups.

What harm could there be in extending an offer of friendship? Stuart smiled at Dr. Wagner. "Good morning. I'm Stuart Carlson from the University of Boston."

Dr. Wagner gave a curt nod. "One of the Americans."

"We're not that bad. I know you and Dr. Hughes have a troubled history, but the rest of us are just trying to do our jobs."

"I take it you're still searching for that cemetery?"

"Dr. Hughes is. But the real focus of our project is the Late Bronze Age settlement in the lower city. We're hoping to learn more about the population and add to our knowledge of Troy's history. Isn't that what these excavations are about?"

Dr. Wagner sniffed. "For us, definitely. And for you, maybe. But not so for your boss. All he cares about is making headlines, hoping everyone forgets his past sins."

Stuart couldn't argue with a statement like that. He backed away. "Sorry. I was just trying to be friendly. Anytime you want to visit our site, feel free. We've got nothing to hide."

Feeling awkward, he turned to leave, only to have the older man stop him with a question. "You wouldn't be related to Dr. Samuel Carlson, would you?"

Though Stuart's father was nowhere near as important as Dusty's parents, he'd made a name for himself as an archaeologist before retiring from fieldwork and moving to Southern California to work for the Getty Villa. "He's my father. Do you know him?"

"I heard him speak at a conference in Berlin years ago with Dr. Louisa Danforth. Their project in Egypt was impressive."

"It was. I was fortunate to spend a lot of my childhood there." Stuart waited, curious to see where the conversation would lead.

"When would be a good time to visit your site?" Dr. Wagner asked.

Stuart was so taken aback he took a second to respond. "Why don't you join us for our morning break at ten?"

"Very well. I'll stop by then."

After Dr. Wagner left, Stuart sipped his cappuccino slowly, glowing with pleasure. Though he hadn't cleared this impromptu invitation with Dr. Hughes, he was pleased to be making inroads with the Germans. Wasn't it better to get along with them than regard them as enemies? Maybe they could work together at some point or do a joint presentation at that fall symposium in Amsterdam.

After finishing his cappuccino, he walked back to the site, called Kerim over, and told him the news.

"I'm surprised Wagner responded to your efforts," Kerim said. "He's barely spoken to me all summer. But I'm not sure how Hughes will react to the idea of him visiting our site. You should go warn him."

Stuart's enthusiasm faded as he made his way toward Dr. Hughes' trench. Maybe he'd been a tad hasty in making this offer without asking his boss's permission. He'd just have to convince him that this overture would benefit both groups.

Today, Emilia, Dusty, and Hayat were digging in Dr. Hughes' trench, aided by a few of the Turkish workmen. As Stuart got closer, he stopped abruptly when Emilia let out a loud cry. She stood and waved her trowel in the air. "We found a skeleton!"

Everyone stopped working, dropped their tools, and rushed over to peer down at Emilia. She pointed to the area where she'd been digging. Poking out of the dirt, the slightest hint of human bone was visible. Stuart stared in amazement. Was his boss right? Or was it a lone skeleton, like those found on past excavations?

Dr. Hughes dropped down next to Emilia and rubbed his hands together. "Aha! It's just as I told you. We'll need to work carefully. I'll start by taking a few photos of it in situ."

As the others crowded around to watch, Stuart gestured for

them to return to their trenches. "Let's get back to work. We can talk about the skeleton during the break."

Only when his watch beeped, alerting him it was ten, did he remember he was supposed to tell Dr. Hughes about their visitor. *Damn.* He'd been so distracted by the skeleton that he'd totally forgotten. He hustled over to his boss's trench, joining him at the edge where he stood, observing Dusty and Emilia as they slowly uncovered the skeleton. It was painstaking, delicate work involving dental picks and toothbrushes.

Dr. Hughes waved him off. "Start break without us. I don't want to lose momentum."

"It's not that. I invited Dr. Wagner to stop by. He'll be here soon." At his boss's shocked look, Stuart forced a note of optimism into his voice. "Think of it as a good thing. Now you can show him you were right about the cemetery."

Dr. Hughes puffed up with pride. "Indeed. Your timing couldn't be better." But his smile vanished as he looked down at Dusty and Emilia. Both had stopped working and were staring at him in wide-eyed terror. "Why don't you two ladies head to the café and take a break? *Now,*" he said. "You've earned it."

Dusty scrambled to her feet. "You're right. I'd love a cold drink. Coming, Em?"

Emilia jumped up and brushed the dirt off her knees. "You bet. Let's roll."

Stuart frowned, unable to comprehend why they were so keen to leave. "Don't go. We're trying to make nice. Dusty, Dr. Wagner knows your mother. He heard her give a lecture in Berlin." He pointed to the weedy path leading to their trenches. "Here he comes now. At least stay and introduce yourself."

~

Dusty wanted to bolt, but it was too late. Instead, she could only stand like a deer caught in the headlights as Dr.

Wagner advanced toward the site. Maybe if she was lucky, he'd focus his attention on the other two trenches. But he headed straight for Dr. Hughes, as if drawn by a magnet.

As he reached the edge of the pit, he sized up her and Emilia. "What is the meaning of this?"

*Shit.* They were totally busted. It wasn't Stuart's fault. But if Dusty had told him *anything* about Operation Odysseus, he wouldn't have made such a catastrophic mistake. As the rest of the crew drew closer, she braced herself for the inevitable humiliation.

Still oblivious, Stuart regarded the German professor with curiosity. "Dr. Wagner? Are you referring to our recent find? I didn't know about the skeleton when I talked to you this morning. We uncovered it less than two hours ago."

"I'm talking about them." He pointed to Dusty and Emilia, his body radiating fury. "Hilde, was it? And Gertrude?"

"Gerta," Emilia muttered. Even beneath a layer of dirt, her face had flushed a deep red.

"What are you talking about?" Stuart asked.

But Dr. Wagner wasn't looking at him. He kept his gaze laser-focused on Dusty. "I should have known your visit was a ruse. Did you think I wouldn't find out?"

By now, Kerim had reached the edge of the trench. "What visit? We haven't gone near your site since that first incident. We've tried to respect your boundaries."

"You might have, but not these two," Dr. Wagner said. "Their behavior was very unprofessional."

Dusty's face was flaming, her heart pounding in fear. Right about now, a powerful earthquake would have been welcome. Or a sinkhole opening up and swallowing her whole. But no such luck.

Stuart caught her eye. "Dusty? What did you do?"

Before she could answer him, Dr. Wagner spoke up, his voice thick with anger. "These two and the blond girl, wherever she is, came over to our site dressed like...tourists. They claimed they were students from the University of Cologne, working with Dr. Schultz." He scowled at Dusty. "None of that was true, was it?"

She swallowed, tasting dust and grit. Licking her lips, she tried to moisten them enough to get the words out. "No. It was a ruse. I'm sorry."

Dr. Wagner leveled a furious gaze at Dr. Hughes. "This was your doing, wasn't it? Sending your women to spy on us? Pathetic."

Dr. Hughes crossed his arms. "I had nothing to do with it. By the looks of it, they pulled this prank for a lark, like a bunch of immature schoolgirls. I would never condone such an unprofessional act."

Dusty gasped. She couldn't speak, couldn't move, couldn't do anything but stare at her boss. She had expected him to go on the defensive, to argue that his decision to send them had been justified, given the rivalry between the two groups. Instead, he'd thrown them under the bus. Beside her, Emilia drew in a sharp breath.

Before her friend could incriminate herself, Dusty took control. She wanted to place the blame squarely on Dr. Hughes, but she couldn't risk it. No telling how he would retaliate if she implicated him. She'd just have to take the fall. "It was all my fault. I..."

"Dusty has a history of pulling pranks in the field, don't you?" Dr. Hughes said. "But this time, you took it too far."

She nodded miserably, but Emilia wasn't as complacent. "How can you let Dusty take the blame when—"

"Don't," Dusty said. "You don't have to cover up for me. I'm sorry."

"You're sorry?" Dr. Wagner demanded. "That's all you have to say? I wasted a lot of time talking to you and your friends."

"I know, and I apologize. But please don't blame them. I'm the one who convinced them to go along with it." As excruciating as it was, she kept her focus on him. If she looked at Dr. Hughes, she'd want to kill him, and she couldn't face the disappointment in Stuart's eyes.

"If it would make you feel better, I'd be willing to banish her from the site for the rest of the dig," Dr. Hughes said. "I could send her back to the lab so that she won't cross your path again."

Kick her off the site? For helping pull off his stupid spy mission? Dusty waited, hands clenched, hoping Stuart would defend her, but Kerim spoke up first. "That's a little harsh. If we've really found a cemetery, we're going to need everyone's help to finish the season."

"Fine. Two weeks, then." Dr. Hughes glared at Dusty. "Some time alone in the lab might give you a chance to reflect on your reckless behavior. If you weren't so useful, I'd send you home, but I want you off the dig site immediately."

Stuart addressed Dr. Wagner. "I apologize, sir. I didn't know about any of this."

"That much is obvious," Dr. Wagner said. "But after what I just witnessed, I have no interest in joining you for your morning break. We've got work to do."

Dusty fought back tears as she stuffed her things into her daypack. She peeked over at Stuart, hoping he'd offer to take her back to the field house, but all his attention was focused on Dr. Wagner. Shoulders slumped, he stared at the professor's retreating figure, no doubt cursing himself for offering an olive branch to the Germans.

When Kerim came up to her, the kindness in his voice almost sent her over the edge. "Dusty? I can drive you to the field house."

"Thanks." She could barely get the words out for fear Dr. Hughes would notice how much her voice was shaking. Under no circumstances could she cry in front of him. She followed Kerim away from the site, walking past the others with her head held high.

When they reached the boardwalk, the tour groups were out

in droves. She pushed past an unwieldy crowd listening to a guide speaking in Italian and another one filled with Russian tourists. Try as she might to stem the angry flow of tears, her eyes welled up. She blinked quickly, hoping to regain a little self-control.

Kerim stopped when they got to the paved courtyard that held the giant Trojan horse. A rowdy line of kids waited to climb into the horse's belly. He placed his hand on her shoulder. "Dusty?"

"What?"

"Please tell me this 'ruse,' or whatever you want to call it, wasn't your idea."

She kept her tone light. "Sure it was. You know how much I love shenanigans."

"I do, but not when they could lead to serious repercussions. Dr. Hughes asked you to do this, didn't he?"

She sniffed and nodded. While she'd lied to protect her boss from the wrath of his German rival, she wanted to be honest with Kerim. "At first, he just asked Clarissa, but she felt so uncomfortable that she came to me and Em for help. When I confronted Hughes about it, he threatened to fire me unless I went along with it."

"Oh, Dusty. You should have come to me first. Or talked to Stuart."

"I know that now," she muttered. "I put myself in a terrible position. I only agreed to do this so I could keep my job. I didn't think Dr. Wagner would find out since we've been steering clear of his site. And I never intended to humiliate him." Guilt surged through her as she imagined how he must have felt, learning that he'd been the victim of an elaborate con.

Kerim frowned. "I'm going to talk to Dr. Hughes when I get back. He can't treat you this way."

"Don't. I'm just glad he didn't fire me. That's what he wants. He had the perfect excuse to send me home. Maybe he assumed that if he let me stay, I wouldn't implicate him in this stupid scheme."

That had to be it. By offering herself up as the guilty party, she'd saved Dr. Hughes' ass. If Dr. Wagner had known who was truly responsible for her "prank," he might have done more than just yell. He might have taken further action, like trying to get the Americans expelled from Troy. Better to think this ruse was the whim of an impetuous young woman than a scheming academic.

"Even so, it's wrong what he did," Kerim said. "You shouldn't have to suffer for it."

"I'll be fine. I'm pretty tough." She walked with him toward the parking lot, which was packed with cars and tour buses.

He squeezed her shoulder. "I know you are, Dusty. Or should I say, Hilde?"

A burst of laughter tumbled out. When she reflected on the ludicrous nature of their mission, it was borderline hilarious, even if Dr. Wagner didn't think so. Maybe one day, he'd look back on it and laugh. He could use a little lightening up.

"If you think that's bad, Emilia was Gerta." Dusty laughed even harder. "And Clarissa was Liesel, like in *The Sound of Music*."

Kerim chuckled. "Did your mission have a code name?"

"Of course it did. Operation Odysseus. Because good old Odysseus was a cunning bastard. Gotta give him props for that."

"I like it." When they reached Kerim's car, he unlocked it and opened the front passenger door for her. "Will you be all right back in the lab by yourself?"

She got in and set her daypack on her lap. "It won't be the first time I've done lab work on my own. I've got enough material to illustrate. But I'll miss digging with everyone. Other than Hughes, this is a great crew."

"You're a true gem," he said. "I hope Stuart appreciates what he's got."

She hoped so, too. Right now, it sure didn't seem like it.

## CHAPTER NINETEEN

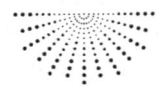

A full ten minutes after Dusty had left, Stuart was still processing everything. Not only had she pulled off this elaborate scheme, but she'd also hidden it from him. What had she been thinking? Sure, she was always up for a clever prank or a night of drunken fun, but to the best of his recollection, she'd never behaved so recklessly.

"Stuart!" Dr. Hughes came up to him, all bluster and anger.

"Sorry. What is it?" He turned his attention back to his boss.

"Your little friend almost screwed up everything. I'm hoping her apology placated Dr. Wagner. If not, her actions could have severe consequences."

Would it come to that? Stuart's stomach churned as he imagined the university's reaction if the Turkish government revoked their permit again. All because he'd invited his best friend to join the dig.

He scrambled for an answer that might satisfy his boss. "I... suspect Dr. Wagner might keep quiet because of the humiliation. He might not want to admit he was fooled by three American girls who spoke perfect German."

"Let's hope so. If it were up to me, I'd send Dusty packing. It's what she deserves. But if we've truly found the cemetery, we're going to need her illustration skills. Clarissa has been helpful, but she's still too slow."

Thank God for that. "I'm so sorry. Believe me, I was in the dark about all of this."

Dr. Hughes snorted. "Obviously, your friendship with Dusty has clouded your judgment."

Stuart nodded. What else could he say? He could hardly defend her, not after her actions had nearly led to an all-out trench war. He went about the motions of setting up the food for their morning break, but he'd lost his appetite. As the crew sat down, buzzing about Dr. Wagner's visit, he walked away from the site, giving himself a little distance from the others.

Had he not been clear with Dusty before when he'd told her how much this job meant to him? Did she not understand how precarious his position was?

Back when he was applying for work, he'd been on edge constantly. He'd lost hours of sleep, envisioning a future where he ended up unemployed or toiling at a minimum-wage job in the service industry. Not that there was any shame in that kind of work, but he hadn't spent years in grad school with that goal in mind. Securing the post in Boston had been the lifeline he needed, and he couldn't do anything to put it at risk.

Even so, he felt bad about the way Dr. Hughes had exiled Dusty. Pulling out his phone, he considered texting her until Emilia stalked over and punched him in the shoulder.

"Hey, dipshit!" she spat out.

Rubbing his shoulder, he glared at her. "What the hell, Em? Is that any way to talk to me?"

"Fuck that. How could you let Hughes throw Dusty under the bus?"

"What are you talking about?"

"Do you honestly think that spy mission was her idea?"

"She did something like that once before in Egypt, and she's always been kind of fearless, so..." But even to his own ears, his rationale sounded weak. Dusty knew how much this dig meant to him. There was no reason she'd endanger it with a prank.

*Shit.* He'd misjudged her so badly.

"It was Hughes' idea, wasn't it?" he asked.

"Bingo. At first, he wanted Clarissa to do it solo, which is sleazy as hell. Dusty was so pissed she went after Hughes and yelled at him."

"She did *what?*" Hadn't she been listening when he'd begged her not to confront their boss?

"Not the wisest idea, but you know what her temper's like. Somehow, he got her on board with this scheme. Used some kind of leverage over her. I'll admit, it was a bonkers plan, but it wouldn't have failed if you'd warned us before inviting Wagner to visit."

Stuart's exasperation rose to the surface. "I wouldn't have invited him if you'd told me about it in the first place."

"Dusty was trying to protect you in case something went wrong. She knows you're incapable of lying. You should be grateful."

"You didn't even speak up for her," TJ said. "That's cold, man."

Stuart turned in surprise. Where the hell had TJ come from? Had he snuck up on them just to get a few words in? "You knew about this?"

"I ran into the girls when I went to find them at the café. After they told me the scoop, I agreed to keep it quiet, but only so you and Kerim wouldn't be implicated."

Stuart should have known. Even if he hadn't, he'd allowed Dr. Hughes to barrel over Dusty. And she'd taken it. Not only that, but she'd also claimed full responsibility, absolving Clarissa and Emilia of any blame.

"Who else was in on it?" he asked.

"Mort, of course," Emilia said. "He said it was like being in a

James Bond movie. If he were here, he would have stood up for Dusty."

Stuart took off his hat and scrubbed his hand through his hair, which was damp with sweat. "What should I do? I can't confront Hughes."

"Why not? This is all his fault."

As much as Stuart loathed his boss, the older man was still the one calling the shots. "I can't risk losing my job." When Emilia scowled at him, he stepped back and held up his hands. "But I'll apologize to Dusty and try to get her back on-site sooner."

It was a start, at least. Not good enough, but a start.

∽

THE REST OF THE MORNING PASSED WITH AGONIZING SLOWNESS. To Dr. Hughes' utter delight, his team found a second skeleton, which eased his fury over the confrontation with Dr. Wagner. If anything, he was in a better mood than he'd been all season, crowing about his inevitable victory over the Germans. Like this was an *actual* war rather than just two rival excavations.

When Kerim returned from dropping off Dusty, he went back to his trench in silence. With Emilia, TJ, and Kerim pissed at him, Stuart felt like a total pariah.

Once they were back at the field house, the others went to wash up for the afternoon meal. Stuart made a beeline for the lab. Dusty was hard at work, wearing earbuds as she sketched a gold bracelet they'd found in Kerim's trench last week.

"Dusty?" When she didn't answer, he raised his voice. "Dusty?"

She looked up at him but didn't remove the earbuds. She was pissed, all right.

"Can I talk to you?" he asked.

With a resentful sigh, she took out the earbuds and silenced her phone. But her stoic expression suggested she had no fucks to give. "Is it lunchtime yet?"

"Yes, but—"

She stood up. "Good. I'm starved." Setting her phone in her back pocket, she tried to push past him.

He grabbed her arm. "Wait. Dusty, please. I'm sorry."

She nailed him with a cool stare. "For what? For actually believing I'd do something that stupid on my own? Or for not offering to drive me back here so you could hear *my* side of the story?"

Now he felt even worse. "For all of it. Em told me what happened. She said you did it to help Clarissa."

"And because Hughes threatened to fire me. He told me I wasn't needed because he could use Clarissa to replace me."

"Wait. He said that? I didn't think he'd actually do it."

Dusty bristled. *"You knew?* You knew he was thinking of replacing me and you didn't tell me? What the fuck, Stuart? Why didn't you warn me?"

"I did warn you!" His voice had risen, but he didn't care. "I told you to play nice. I told you not to confront him. I begged you to keep quiet. But Em told me you went off on him, anyway. Why didn't you listen?"

"Because sometimes you can't just sit back and let terrible people do shitty things. Sometimes you have to take a fucking stand."

Didn't she get it? Even after their talk last night, she still didn't understand what he was up against. It wasn't like he condoned Dr. Hughes' behavior. But this was his boss. Not just his boss but a senior professor in the Classics Department at the University of Boston. If he didn't play by the guy's rules, he could lose everything.

"You make it sound so easy," he spat out. "But you can do whatever you damn well please. It's not like you have anything to lose."

She blinked quickly, as though his remark had wounded her. "How can you say that?"

"Because you don't have anything at stake! Not like me. If you get kicked out of Troy, what's the worst that could happen? You'll go work somewhere else. Knowing you, there's another job around the corner—in Cyprus or Tunisia or Egypt, or anywhere your mom's name carries a ton of weight. That's what you've always done. I don't have that luxury. I can't allow anything to jeopardize this job."

He knew his accusations weren't fair. Worse yet, they were hurtful and dismissive. But he wanted her to understand how much pressure he was under. A mistake like this could derail his teaching career before it even started.

"I know, and that's why I made sure you weren't implicated," she snapped. "So that I wouldn't put you at risk. But clearly, you think I can leave whenever I want. That it won't make a damn bit of difference because I'm so disposable. Maybe I *should* leave. Is that what you want? I'm sure it would make your boss happy."

*Fuck.* As upset as Stuart was, the thought of losing her made him physically ill.

His failure to respond only made Dusty angrier. "Your silence says everything. You want me to go? Say the word and I'll pack up my shit and take the next bus to Istanbul. Like you said, there's always another job."

"No." His voice broke in agony. "Please stay. Just…keep out of trouble. Okay?"

Taking a deep breath, she pulled herself from his grip. "You got it, Dr. Carlson. I'm going to lunch."

He said nothing, watching as she stormed away, his emotions a stew of anger, resentment, and guilt. Even if he had more to lose than she did, he'd just diminished her completely, acting like her contribution to the dig meant nothing. He'd never felt that way, not once. He'd just wanted her to realize why he couldn't speak his mind like she did and why he had to play things so carefully.

He glanced at the sketches she'd done. Perfect, as always. But under the drawings was a cartoon entitled "Operation Odysseus Fail" that showed three wide-eyed women in lederhosen, surrounded by Trojan warriors with spears. Of course she'd given the mission a code name. That was such a Dusty thing to do.

Setting down the drawings, he went to join the others. For now, he'd let her be. But once he got his turbulent feelings under control, he'd have to make things right with her.

# CHAPTER TWENTY

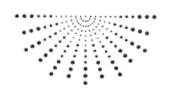

By her third day of banishment, Dusty had sunk into a grouchy funk. She couldn't remember a time when she'd felt this lonely on a dig. Her mood wouldn't have been as bleak if she'd been able to enjoy her time with the others when they returned from the site each afternoon. But the rift between her and Stuart was so painful that they could barely stand to be in the same room together.

Though she was still angry at him for keeping silent when she was exiled, what hurt the most was the way he'd lashed out afterward. Implying that she had nothing at stake. That she could pick up and leave Troy like a heartless bitch.

He was wrong. She had plenty at stake. Even if there was always another job, she wanted *this* one. Not just because of him but because she cared about the project and wanted to see it through to the end. Now she wondered if it was worth it.

After the crew left for the site at six thirty that morning, she resigned herself to another lengthy stretch of solitude. She'd been working at her illustration table for a few hours when the door opened suddenly. She jumped in fright, knocking over her coffee.

Grabbing a spare piece of paper, she blotted the spill, grateful it hadn't ruined any of her artwork.

Mort poked his head in. "Morning, Dusty. Sorry if I frightened you."

"It's fine. I'm just a little jumpy. How was your tour?"

He gestured to the chair opposite hers. "Mind if I sit? You'd think I'd be tired of sitting after all those hours on a bus, but we did a lot of walking."

"Please, have a seat. How did you like Ephesus?"

"Marvelous. The ruins were stunning. Aphrodisias was equally spectacular, so naturally, Clarissa took loads of photos. She told me she'd make me one of those digital scrapbooks when we get back. I'm not like your generation—having the photos on my phone isn't good enough."

"My dad's the same way. He still gets his photos printed from the drugstore." She stood up. "I'm going to get more coffee. Do you want a cup? I made the pot a half hour ago, so it's still fresh."

"Sure. Thank you. I take it black."

She went to the kitchen, refilled her cup, and poured one for Mort. When she brought it back, he took a sip. "Not bad. But I had real Turkish coffee on the tour, and it was much better."

"I couldn't agree more." She sipped hers slowly, glad to be sharing it with someone. "Where's Clarissa?"

"She insisted I drop her off at the site because she wanted to get right to work but then realized she didn't have her hiking boots. Can't exactly dig in sandals. I came back to get them and noticed the light was on in here. Why aren't you at the site?"

The last thing she wanted to do was relive the humiliating scene with Dr. Wagner, but Mort needed to know the truth. She gave him a quick recap, hoping he'd realize what a heartless bastard Dr. Hughes was. It was time he stopped idolizing the guy.

When she was done, Mort shook his head in dismay. "What a disaster. But I don't understand. Why'd you take the blame?"

She shrugged. "It was easier that way. Clarissa's here as a

volunteer, and Emilia's close to getting her doctorate. She can't take any risks."

"What about you? Aren't you working on your doctorate, too?"

Dusty released a ragged breath. "I should be, but the more I try to muddle through it, the more I realize it's not the path I want to follow. But try telling that to Dr. Louisa Danforth."

Given Mort's admiration for her mother, Dusty expected him to take her side. Instead, he nodded sagely. "I imagine it can't be easy living in her shadow."

"It's impossible. If I don't get my PhD, she'll be so disappointed."

"If I might offer a word of advice?"

She liked that he'd asked her first. Most guys his age would have just fired away. "Sure. Have at it."

"I spent my whole life trying to live up to my father's expectations. He was a successful businessman. Made millions. I did the same but neglected Clarissa in the process. You could say I gave her everything except my attention. But when I had a heart attack two years ago, I realized how foolish I'd been. Spending all this time trying to follow my father's dreams instead of my own. That's partly the reason I'm here, even if it's too late to pursue a career in archaeology."

His confession struck a chord with her. She loved that he hadn't given up on his dream. "At least you're trying. That's a huge step."

"Well, it helps if you have money. But when Clarissa told me she wanted to go into teaching instead of business, I supported her decision. I wanted her to do something she was passionate about, even if it wasn't that lucrative. Perhaps that's what you should do?"

She gave him a rueful smile. "Any chance you could call my mother and tell her that?"

He chuckled. "I don't think she'd appreciate it." As he set his cup down, his eyes fell upon her recent sketches. "Mind if I have a look?"

"Sure, but those aren't my illustrations for the site. They're just my own drawings, but...um...go ahead."

In between drawing artifacts, she'd slowly added to her collection of Trojan-themed pieces, including character sketches of all the Greek gods and goddesses who'd played a role in *The Iliad*. Creating those images had brought her more joy than any of the research she'd done for her dissertation.

As he took his time perusing them, her shoulders tightened. Since her style was more cartoonish than Clarissa's, he might consider her work inferior. When he set the pages down, she gnawed on her thumbnail, waiting for his verdict in nervous anticipation.

He gave her a broad smile. "Marvelous work. I didn't realize you were so talented."

Relief flooded through her. She didn't know why his opinion mattered so much, but given the week she'd had, she could use a boost. "Thanks. I used to specialize in Egyptian characters, but I'm having fun with *The Iliad*."

"I feel like I owe you an apology. On that first night, when Stuart told us you were an illustrator, I started bragging about Clarissa's accomplishments, completely undermining you."

She could smile about it now, especially since she and Clarissa had grown closer in the past few weeks. "It's fine. You have every right to be proud of her. She showed me the mockup for that picture book she illustrated—the one about the jungle. I wish I were half as good at drawing animals."

"You're still very gifted."

"Thanks. I have examples in color, too. On my tablet." She grabbed it and pulled up the file containing her artwork from *The Iliad*, detailed drawings where she'd taken the time to add shading, color, and elaborate backgrounds.

After he swiped through them, he stroked his chin. "These are splendid. I know you've got your hands full here, but would you be interested in illustrating children's books?"

Would she? Her heart started pounding. She set down her coffee cup with shaky hands. "What did you have in mind?"

"My friend—the one who runs the children's publishing firm in Boston—is looking for illustrators. Not for the picture books Clarissa is working on but for a different series. Are you familiar with the *Magic Tree House* books?"

The name brought back a delightful memory. The first time she'd met Stuart, he'd been seven. Anxious about living in Egypt for the first time, he'd brought a backpack filled with his favorite books, including five from the *Magic Tree House* series. Having never seen them before, she immediately fell in love with the concept of time travel via a tree house.

"Sure. Those books are great. I loved the one where they visited Pompeii."

"My friend's doing something like that, but for a younger age group. Picture books set in various time periods, like ancient Egypt, the Roman Empire, and the Middle Ages. Your drawings would be perfect. Do you have an agent?"

An agent? Hell, just creating her own Etsy site had been a big deal. She shook her head.

"That's fine. Clarissa could refer you to hers, or she could help you find one. But in the meantime, I'd like to photograph a few of these pages and send them to my friend."

"Thanks. If you give me your email address, I'll send you the digital files, too." Who could have imagined her morning would take such a turn? Suddenly, she didn't care that her dissertation was a giant failure. Though her illustrations had appeared in plenty of academic publications, the thought of seeing her artwork in a children's book was far more exciting.

After Mort photographed a few of her sketches, he glanced at his watch. "I should get back to Clarissa. She'll be wondering what's taking so long. When I get to the site, do you want me to talk to Hughes about allowing you back?"

"It's okay. I know you two are friends. You don't have to confront him on my behalf."

Mort let out a heavy sigh. "When we were on the tour, Clarissa told me how inappropriate he's been. She learned from Hayat that he's been making lewd comments about her. A few times, I've caught him saying things about other women, but I let it slip. Now I'm ashamed I kept quiet. There's no excuse for treating women with such disrespect."

"Or for any of his behavior," Dusty said. "I know you admire him, and he was once a big deal in the archaeological world, but he's not a nice guy."

"I'm realizing that. I'm sorry I got you tangled up in this. If I'd said no to the spy mission instead of being swayed by his promises, none of this would have happened. Let me help. I'll insist you come back next week. Unless you're happier here on your own?"

"Not really. Half the fun of working on a dig is the camaraderie. In the mornings, I'd rather be at the site with everyone else." Except for Dr. Hughes. But she could put up with him if it meant she wasn't stuck by herself in the lab.

Mort stood up. "If something like this happens again, know that I'm on your side. Clarissa told me how much you've taught her. This has been an incredible summer for her, and it's partly because of you and Stuart."

Hearing that brightened Dusty's mood. "Thanks. I've liked working with her."

As Mort left, she wondered if he'd be able to reduce her sentence. At least he was making an effort.

Which was more than she could say for *some* people.

# CHAPTER TWENTY-ONE

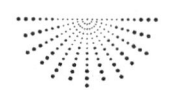

After spending five days alone in the lab, Dusty should have been eagerly awaiting her day off. Especially since most of the crew had planned for a lazy beach day. But going to the beach with everyone meant dealing with Stuart. She was growing weary of ignoring him, but how could she treat him like a friend when he'd done nothing to bridge the gap between them? The one time he'd tried talking to her, he'd gone into full mansplaining mode, and they'd ended up arguing again.

At the sound of wheels crunching on the gravel driveway, Dusty's stomach rumbled. Since all she'd had for breakfast were a few tea biscuits and a cup of coffee, she was desperate for the midday meal. When the door opened, she expected to see Emilia. Instead, Dr. Hughes came in and shut the door behind him.

As he approached her table, she flinched, then cursed herself for showing any weakness. "What is it?"

He stared down at her in contempt. "I came here to tell you that you can return to the site on Monday. It's a full week earlier than I planned, but Mort insisted on it. I wasn't about to piss off one of the university's biggest donors."

She hid her smile of victory. She'd have to thank Mort. Maybe even give him a hug.

Dr. Hughes continued. "He wasn't pleased I let you take the blame, but you're the one who messed up."

A white-hot fury surged through her. With trembling hands, she set down her pencil before she was tempted to jab it into his throat. "*I* messed up? It's not my fault Stuart invited Dr. Wagner to our site. And when he yelled at us, I took the fall. I didn't reveal anything that would get you kicked out of Troy again."

He picked up her pencil and twirled it between his fingers. "It's good that you kept quiet. If you'd told him the truth, the consequences would have been far more serious."

"Then where's the fucking gratitude?" She was careening dangerously close to losing her self-control again, but she couldn't help it. "Instead of thanking me, you've been treating me like shit. If anything, you owe me."

All at once, his calm demeanor vanished. He leaned in closer, his jaw twitching. "I owe you? After what your mother did to me on that wretched tour? That woman tried to tank my career. I'll never owe you *anything*. You're lucky you still have a job here."

Clenching her fists, she resisted the urge to lash out at him again. She didn't want to make the situation worse.

"Cat got your tongue?" he said. "What a surprise. I'm heading out to Çanakkale and won't be back until Monday morning. Make sure you've caught up on all the illustrations by then."

With that, he strode out, slamming the door behind him.

Dusty closed her eyes, willing the anger to fade. After a few calming breaths, she got her racing heartbeat under control. But as she replayed the conversation in her head, Dr. Hughes' words stuck with her. What had her mother done to him?

When her phone buzzed, she startled, her nerves still on high alert. Emilia had sent her a text. *We're back for lunch. Come join us.*

Ignoring the gnawing ache in her stomach, she stayed seated. With everyone at lunch, she'd have the lab to herself for a full hour. She fired off a quick reply. *Need to finish this task. Save a plate for me in the fridge?*

She texted her mother and asked if she was available to talk. Half the time, her mother didn't bother to answer her phone, especially if she was immersed in her research. But she called Dusty immediately.

"Dusty?" Her voice sounded breathless, as though she'd been running out the door. "I didn't expect to hear from you. Are you all right?"

Because it wasn't like either of them *ever* called to have a friendly chat. "I'm good. Sort of. This Troy gig has been harder than I thought."

"What's the problem? I'm heading out to a planning meeting at the Grand Egyptian Museum, so I don't have much time."

Typical Mom. At least she hadn't told Dusty to call her back later. "It's Dr. Hughes. I know you warned me about him, but he's worse than I imagined. Twice now, he's threatened to fire me because he's still carrying a grudge over that Ancient Excursions tour. What did you do to him?"

"Oh, dear." Her mother let out a lengthy sigh. "I should have told you the whole story, but I was hoping he'd moved on from that incident."

"What incident?" Dusty jolted up from her chair, too agitated to sit still.

"Calm down. It wasn't that bad."

"Mom, tell me. I need to know everything."

"It happened when we were halfway through the tour. We'd finished up in Egypt and were spending a week in Turkey. Until that point, I hadn't minded working with him. There's no denying he was the boastful sort—the type who always has to be the biggest person in the room. But he could also be a real charmer, especially with the older women on the tour."

Did this mean her mother had succumbed to his charms?

Dusty grimaced, not wanting to imagine it. "You didn't fall for it, did you?"

"Hardly. Only one man has ever won me over with flattery, and it's your father. Anyway, when we got to Istanbul, two of the women on the tour took me aside. Young women in their twenties. They told me Hughes had propositioned them privately. At first, I thought they'd misread his intentions, but the more they shared with me, the more I realized how inappropriately he'd behaved."

Dusty shuddered as she recalled everything that Clarissa, Hayat, and Mort had told her about Dr. Hughes' comments. How he'd often referred to women in a way that demeaned or objectified them.

Her mother continued. "I took up the issue with Hughes. Just a warning, nothing more. But he erupted in a rage. Said it was none of my business and that the women were overreacting to a few flirtatious remarks. So, I let it go. But he was so upset that I'd brought it up that he barely spoke to me the next day."

It sounded just like him. What an immature prick.

"That's it?" Dusty asked. "That's why he's so mad?"

Her mother gave a rueful laugh. "I wish that was all. Two nights later, one of the women came to me in tears, claiming he'd drunkenly groped her when they were at the bar. As you can imagine, I felt horrible I'd let it get that far."

"It's not your fault. It's his for being such an ass."

"Even so, I was the one who'd enabled him by not putting an immediate stop to his behavior. This time, when I talked to him, I was angry. But he blew me off again. So, I called the tour office to report him. I wasn't sure what the repercussions would be, but if he assaulted one of those women, I never would have forgiven myself."

When her voice broke, Dusty's throat clogged with sympathy. Her mother so rarely lost control of her emotions that this incident must have affected her powerfully. "What happened?"

"The company kicked Hughes off the tour, but it didn't end there. He was so furious that he tried to get back at me. After he flew home, he called your father and filled his head with lies."

"What kind of lies?" Dusty's heart constricted as she imagined her poor father picking up the phone only to be subjected to Dr. Hughes' vicious slander.

Her mother gave a dismissive snort. "That I'd slept with two of the men on the tour. Or was it three? Either way, I'd behaved like a complete slut—his words, not mine. I would never describe another woman that way."

"That piece of shit. What did Dad say?"

"He didn't believe a word of it. He's always stood by me, no matter what." Her mother paused. "Has Stuart been standing up for you on this dig?"

Dusty swallowed, suddenly uneasy. "Not exactly, but..."

"I'm sure he's acting out of self-preservation, but it's something to consider. When you finally decide to settle down —*if ever*—make sure you find someone who'll stand up for you." She gave a wry laugh. "Look at me, dispensing motherly advice."

"Um...thanks, Mom."

"You're welcome. Now, if that man ever lays a finger on you, tell me immediately. If I have to fly over to Turkey and take him on, I will."

Dusty could only imagine how well that would go over. "It's okay. I can fight my own battles."

"Just as I taught you. Now, I must rush. Don't want to keep those curators waiting."

She signed off, but her words resonated in Dusty's ears. *You need someone who'll stand up for you.*

Even if she loved Stuart, she wasn't sure he could fill that role.

Stuart was having a hell of a week. During the midday meal, he barely paid attention to the surrounding conversation as Emilia and Clarissa discussed their plans for the weekend. After shutting him out for days, they'd finally come around. He couldn't say the same for Dusty. He'd approached her yesterday, but instead of apologizing, he'd tried to make her see reason. To understand how much he had to lose. But his attempts had only infuriated her. Now things between them were so prickly he didn't know what to do.

Emilia nudged him. "Stuart? Are you listening to me?"

He pushed Dusty from his mind. "Sorry. What did you ask me?"

"Since tomorrow's our day off, we're going out tonight. A little drinking, a little karaoke, some late-night fun. You in?"

"I'll pass. I'm not up for it."

She rolled her eyes. "Enough moping. Go make up with Dusty so we can have our happy couple back."

He set his plate to the side. Normally he loved stuffed vine leaves, but he'd lost his appetite. "I tried, but she wouldn't listen."

Emilia waved her fork at him. "You mean she wouldn't listen when you tried to justify your actions? That's not a true apology."

"Just go in there and grovel," Clarissa said.

TJ walked over to their side of the table and grabbed a piece of pita bread. "Women love a good grovel. That's one of the first rules of rom-coms. Am I right?"

"Absolutely," Emilia said to him. "Teej, you coming on our bar crawl tonight?"

"Hell, yeah. We need to let off steam after this week. I got stuck in Hughes' trench three days running, and it's the worst. He's so focused on finding more skeletons that he wouldn't let us take our morning break."

Emilia shot Stuart a look. "See? Everyone's going. I'm sure Dusty will be up for it."

But she'd have more fun if he wasn't there. "I'll pass. Not because of her. I could use the time to catch up."

Maybe he was stretching the truth, but he had hours of work ahead of him, thanks to his boss. The director might behave like a petty tyrant while overseeing his trench, but he put minimal effort into writing up his field notes. Stuart had been cobbling together the daily site reports from the other students' notebooks.

Since Kerim and Dr. Hughes had already left for Çanakkale, Stuart was in charge of the afternoon's lab work. He didn't have the heart to play the role of taskmaster. Instead, he let everyone go early so they could get ready for their night out in Güzelyali.

For the next two hours, he holed up in the lab and concentrated on his report. At six, he heard a couple of vehicles pull onto the gravel driveway, followed by the sound of raised voices, a flurry of laughter, and the slamming of doors. He went to the open window, watching wistfully as the taxis pulled away. Rather than return to his work, he headed for the showers to wash off the day's dust and grime.

Though the water wavered between lukewarm and downright chilly, his mood improved once he was done. He ambled over to the kitchen to grab a beer from the fridge, only to recall they'd run out last night. As he was leaving a note to buy more, his phone buzzed.

TJ had sent him a text: *You there?*

He responded right away: *Yeah. Everything OK?*

TJ: *Go into the library.*

Had TJ left his wallet there? He'd just have to suck it up and borrow money from someone in the group because Stuart wasn't about to drive into Güzelyali to bring it to him. He walked over to the library and opened the door. Dusty sat at a far table, earbuds on, surrounded by a stack of excavation reports. He swallowed hard, rendered speechless at the sight of her. Over the past few days, he'd missed their closeness more than he thought possible.

She took out her earbuds and gave him a cursory glance. "What's up?"

"What are you doing here?"

"Working on my dissertation. Or attempting to. But these site reports are boring as fuck."

"I thought you were going out tonight."

"I am. We're leaving at six thirty." She peeked at her phone. "Shit, it's a quarter past six. I should get ready."

"I think you got the time wrong. They left fifteen minutes ago."

"Are you sure? Em told me six thirty." She grabbed her phone and typed quickly. When it buzzed with a response, she read it and let out an exasperated breath. "Seriously?"

"What is it?"

She snorted. "Here's her reply: *Sorry for the ruse, but you're too damn stubborn. Enjoy your time alone with Stuart. We won't be back until midnight.* Followed by a wink emoji. Really, Em? A wink emoji?"

Before he could ask to see the text, their phones buzzed. This time, Emilia had sent a message to both of them: *TJ and I cooked this up. We call it Operation Aphrodite.*

Stuart groaned. Aphrodite was the Greek goddess of sexual love. A week ago, he would have been thrilled at this opportunity. Now he was pissed. He hated being manipulated.

Dusty set down her phone. "Nice try, Em, but I've got work to do. This dissertation won't write itself."

"I'll let you get to it." If she wanted to work in the library, then he could take the lab. They could get a lot done without the others around to interrupt them.

But was that what he wanted? The thought of spending the next few weeks at odds with her made his stomach clench up. Despite their bitter argument, she was still his closest friend.

He plopped down in the chair across from her. "I'm so sorry. About all of it. I've been a complete idiot."

She shook her head, a regretful expression clouding her features. "I'm sorry, too. You warned me not to confront Hughes, but I didn't listen, and I almost got fired. I only did that stupid spy mission to keep my job. I didn't mean to make things worse for you." She gave a curt laugh. "If you can believe it, Hughes told me that if I helped him out, he'd also put in a good word for you with Dr. Fiorelli."

A painful ache tugged at his heart. "You never told me that."

"I didn't think it would make a difference, since it was probably just more of his bullshit. He obviously can't be trusted. Even though I covered his ass when Wagner showed up, it didn't change anything. He hates me because he'll never forgive my mother for what she did. When they were on that tour together, she reported him for predatory behavior, and he got sent home early. He retaliated by calling my father and telling him my mom had cheated on him."

"What?" Stuart stared at her in horror. "When did you find this out?"

"A few hours ago. Now I see why Mom warned me against working with him." She twisted her pencil between her fingers. "I'm trying to decide if I should stay or pack up and call it a day. Hughes is just too fucking toxic."

He reached over to take her hand. "Please stay."

"My being here isn't exactly helping you. Not like I hoped."

"I want you here. I'm sorry I was such a fucking coward. I need to stand up to Hughes."

"Don't do it on my behalf. Like you said, I'll be okay wherever I end up." There was no anger in her words, just a sad resignation. Like she'd already lost.

"It's not just you. This week, he's been so determined to uncover more skeletons that he's been pushing the students too hard and not letting them take their breaks. I need to remind him of the rules."

A ghost of a smile crossed her face. "You and your rules. That's the Stuart I know and love."

She'd said "love." That had to count for something. "Rules are important. They're one of the few things saving us from chaos. Well, that and spreadsheets." From the way her smile grew, he knew he was winning her over.

"You really want me to stay?" she asked.

"Please." He squeezed her hand. "You're my best friend. I don't want to do this without you."

"If you insist." She pushed the reports away. "I don't feel like working. You know what I'd love, though? A drink. Is there any beer left in the fridge?"

"Sadly, no. But Hughes has a ton of booze in his room. Want to snitch some?"

"Stuart Carlson? Are you suggesting we steal?" She stood and grinned at him. "I like this version of you. We've got until midnight, right? Let's have some fun."

# CHAPTER TWENTY-TWO

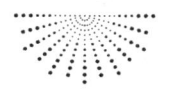

Dusty almost suggested they forget about drinks and head straight to bed. Thanks to Em and TJ, they'd been granted a golden opportunity. Six hours alone in the field house. They could go directly to Stuart's room, shuck off their clothes, and get down to it.

But they'd barely spoken in the past five days. During that time, Dusty had let her bitterness fester. She needed time to warm up to Stuart again. One drink, maybe two. Just enough to reignite the spark between them.

She followed him out of the lab and down the hall toward their boss's room. As he unlocked the door, she recoiled in disgust. The room reeked of stale booze, sweat, and unwashed socks. A mishmash of dirty laundry, crumpled wrappers, and books covered the floor.

"Why does his room smell like a teenage boy lives here?" She kicked a sweat-stained shirt out of her way. "There's no excuse for this shit, not when we have a washing machine right here in the field house."

"He refuses to do his own laundry. The housekeeper's been handling it when she comes to clean, but he might have forgotten to leave it out for her. He keeps his door locked because he doesn't want anyone coming in."

Dusty peered around, her curiosity piqued. "How'd you get in?"

"I found a spare set of keys inside one of the kitchen drawers." He gave her a sly grin. "But Hughes doesn't know that."

She grinned right back. "That's so devious. I love it."

He placed his hand over his heart and spoke in a lofty tone. "Normally I prefer to use my powers for good rather than evil, but in this case, I'll make an exception." He jangled the keys. "Though I should find a better place to hide these than the kitchen. Somewhere Hughes wouldn't ever think to look."

Dusty toed aside a pile of laundry and peeked under the bed. No booze. But she hit the jackpot when she opened the doors to his wardrobe. Along the bottom was a neatly arranged row of bottles: brandy, cognac, and raki, a Turkish liqueur with an aniseed flavor. Upon spotting three bottles of wine, she let out a cry of delight. "KK. This is good stuff."

"KK?"

"Kacelik Karasi. A local red, like pinot noir. Let's grab a bottle."

"You don't want something stronger?"

She considered stealing a bottle of raki, but it was powerful stuff. She couldn't risk them getting drunk. Whatever happened tonight, she wanted them to remember all of it. "Nope. This is perfect. We should eat something, too, since we're missing out on dinner. Let's scrounge through the leftovers and put together a meze platter."

In the kitchen, she set out a large ceramic platter and loaded it with odds and ends from the fridge and the pantry—beyaz peynir cheese, sour green olives, sliced tomatoes, spiced nuts, grapes, figs, and pita bread, along with hummus from yesterday's dinner. Stuart carried the platter outside to the picnic table while she brought the wine and the glasses.

She poured them each a glass of wine, then raised hers in a toast. "To Operation Aphrodite."

Stuart clinked his glass against hers. "I'll drink to that."

When his sea-blue eyes captured hers, his tender gaze made her heart soar. "I missed you."

"Same here. Not just on-site but at night, too. Getting to be alone with you, even for a few minutes. That's probably why this week has been rougher than usual."

His troubled expression brought her earlier guilt racing back. "Were things rough at the site? Sorry if I made it harder for you."

"Don't be. It wasn't just because of that incident with Wagner." Stuart popped an olive into his mouth. "Hughes' behavior has gotten more erratic. This morning, he yelled at his team, claiming they were working too slow because they haven't uncovered any more skeletons. He's worried the ones we've found are just isolated examples. Definitely worth studying, but hardly evidence of a burial ground strewn with fallen warriors."

She sipped her wine slowly, mulling over the information she'd gathered during Operation Odysseus. "When I talked to Dr. Wagner, he hadn't found anything noteworthy, either, though the potential is there. But he wasn't nearly as obsessed as Hughes."

"No one's as obsessed as he is. It's so frustrating. He still believes that if he finds something amazing, the scholarly community will magically forget the Turks banished him for ten years. He's so desperate to regain his former glory that he's coming across as pathetic."

Was that why he was so angry? Was it because it was looking more likely that this season wouldn't yield the success he wanted?

*Whatever.* At this point, she wasn't going to expend any more emotional energy speculating about him.

As she sat with Stuart in the cool evening air, all traces of the week's tension ebbed away. This dinner was exactly what she needed. By the time they'd finished eating—and knocked back all the wine—she'd loosened up considerably. Not quite tipsy but rocking a pleasant buzz. After they brought in the dishes and washed up, she knew exactly what she wanted next. Sex. And lots of it.

Stuart placed his hands on her shoulders and kissed the top of her head. One of those small gestures that made her feel cherished. "I don't want to pressure you," he said. "If you'd rather talk tonight, that's okay. We don't have to do anything else."

While she appreciated his thoughtfulness, she didn't want the platonic, best-friend version of Stuart. She wanted the guy who'd made her the star of his fantasies. "Are you serious? This is our one chance." She gnawed on her lower lip. "Unless you're having second thoughts?"

*Shit*. Was he? She turned to face him, worried he wasn't ready to take things any further.

The wicked gleam in his eye suggested otherwise. "Never. I was trying to be a gentleman."

"Well, knock it off. I want to see your wild side."

He laughed. "Glad to oblige. But let's go to my room in case the others come home early. I don't want to get caught in the act."

The thought made her wince with discomfort. "Em would never let me live that down."

As he took her hand and led her to his room, a naughty thrill surged through her. She felt like a teenager sneaking around with her boyfriend while his parents were out.

Compared to her cluttered dorm-style room, Stuart's was tiny, almost monk-like. As she expected, he kept it tidy. His double bed was neatly made, covered with a navy comforter. The nightstand beside it held a box of tissues and a worn paperback copy of *The Iliad*. And his suitcase, messenger bag, and hiking boots were lined up beside the tall wooden wardrobe that stood against the wall. If she opened it, she suspected she'd find his clothes hanging in a row, arranged by color.

Stuart shut the door behind them. "Let me close the blinds and switch on the fan. It's kind of stuffy in here."

He lowered the window blinds and angled the standing fan so it faced the bed. But when he turned to face her, all her blissful buzz vanished. She rubbed her bare arms, suddenly anxious. Though she'd never felt inadequate with any of her partners before, none of them had built her up the way Stuart had. What if she didn't live up to his fantasies?

Pushing aside her doubts, she closed the distance between them and locked eyes with him. The warmth she saw set her at ease. What was she so worried about? Even if tonight didn't match his erotic daydreams, they'd still have fun together.

With a flirtatious smile, she reached for the hem of his shirt and pulled it over his head. Over the years, she'd seen him shirtless plenty of times, but she'd never had the liberty of touching him freely, except when she'd lathered him up with sunscreen.

She ran her hands along his bare chest, relishing the feel of his firm muscles. Leaning in closer, she placed soft kisses on his shoulders and collarbone, his skin warm beneath her lips. She inhaled the familiar scent of his body wash, the same woodsy mix of cedar and cypress that he'd used for years. When she ran her tongue along the curve of his neck, he sucked in a breath and tangled his hand through her hair, sending spirals of heat racing through her.

She smoothed her fingers along a sturdy bicep. "You've been lifting, haven't you? The Stuart from last year wasn't this built."

"This is going to sound like a total cliché, but after Shelby and I broke up, I needed to get out of my head. I upped my gym workouts a lot."

"It shows. Not that I didn't appreciate your body before, but this is next-level."

Eager to explore further, she unzipped his shorts and tugged on them until they fell in a heap around his ankles. But as she reached for his boxers, he gently took hold of her hand. "Not until I get to see a little more of you. It's only fair."

"You know how much I love playing fair." She removed her tank top slowly, then unclasped her bra and tossed it aside.

The fan blew a gentle breeze across her nipples, making them perk up. He was looking at them with such undisguised longing that she trembled in anticipation. The heat from his gaze ignited a fire inside her, dousing her earlier inhibitions. She undid the button of her shorts and eased them off her hips; her panties followed seconds later. And then she was totally naked, facing her best friend, without a hint of shame or insecurity.

He regarded her in awe, like she was a precious treasure he'd just uncovered. "You're so beautiful. You have no idea how much I want you."

"Oh, I think I do." Taking a step closer, she looped her arms around his neck and ground her body against his. The feel of his hard length pressing into her made her ache with need.

When he kissed her, she tasted red wine on his tongue. They stood suspended in time as he devoured her mouth with kisses so deep and passionate that she could barely keep upright.

Still kissing her, he maneuvered her over to the bed. As she stumbled back against it, she pulled away. She hated to break their connection, even for a second, but she wanted to make sure they were prepared. "You have condoms?"

"Top drawer of the nightstand. But we won't need one yet." He leaned over to pull aside the bedding, then lowered her onto the thin cotton top sheet. Standing over her, he gave her a roguish smile. "There's a lot more I want to do to you first."

Her pulse raced at the thought of what he wanted. He straddled her body, pinning her down while his lips burned a trail along her neck and shoulders, lingering in the hollow of her throat. He took his sweet time arousing her. Tweaking her nipples, then sucking on them until she gasped with pleasure. Placing soft kisses on her stomach and hip bones. Brushing his beard along the inside of her thighs as his lips came tantalizingly close to the center of her desire.

By now, she was wet with longing, craving release, but she let him set the pace. She wanted him to be in control, acting out the fantasies he'd spun in his head.

When he placed his fingers between her legs and stroked her, she let out a cry. He stopped quickly. "Did I hurt you?"

"No. It feels good. Just touch me there. Right there." She guided his hand until he'd hit the perfect spot.

"Better?" He started stroking her again, slow circular movements that built up the friction inside her until she could hardly bear it.

"Yes. Like that." She tensed up, her breath suspended, her muscles tight. And just when she was almost there, so close she could feel herself cresting that delicious wave of pleasure, he lowered his head and used his tongue, licking and sucking and finding her sweet center. She moaned his name, begging him to continue. "*Please*, Stuart, please, please, please."

And then she was completely and utterly lost. She cried out again, long and loud, as the sensations surged through her, like the rush of a roller coaster on a downward plummet. He kept going, letting her ride that high again until she climaxed a second time in a wail that stole her breath away.

She tugged on his hair, forcing him to stop until she'd drawn in a lungful of air. She'd never felt like this, so breathless, so out of control, her whole body thrumming with sensation.

"Wait. Stop," she said. "I need a minute to recover."

He released her gently. "I can wait. But we're not close to being done yet."

# CHAPTER TWENTY-THREE

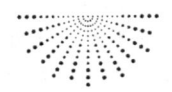

Stuart loved that he'd made Dusty beg. For once, she'd relinquished all control and let him take the reins. And he'd loved every minute of it, especially the way he'd made her cry out in passion. No shame, no filter, just a breathy wail of joy. Like she'd been waiting years for that orgasm. Having her naked beneath him was sexy as hell. But hearing her moan his name? Even more of a turn-on. By now, he was aching to enter her, but he wanted to wait until she was ready.

He drew himself up until he was facing her in bed. Pushing a strand of hair from her forehead, he regarded her tenderly. "You okay?"

"I'm...good. So good. I can't believe I lost control. I never do that." She let out a shy laugh. "Sorry I was so loud."

"Don't apologize. I loved hearing you moan."

Her laughter rolled out freely. "That's what you said the first time we—"

She stopped and drew in a sharp breath. But now his curiosity was aroused. "The first time? You mean in your fantasies?"

"I..." Her eyes widened in fear. "I'm sorry, I should have told you."

"Told me what?"

She didn't answer. Instead, she closed her eyes, as though too ashamed to face him.

He shivered, suddenly chilled by the breeze coming from the fan. What could have made her retreat like this? "What is it? I promise I won't be mad."

"I'm so sorry."

"Just tell me. Please." Had he done something wrong? Hurt her?

"Do you remember when you came to that conference in Boston two years ago?" Her voice was so soft he could barely hear her. "It was right after the first time Shelby broke up with you. When you arrived on Thursday night, we went on a bar crawl and got really wasted."

"Sure, but I was so drunk I barely remember any of it."

"Do…do you remember kissing me?"

"Vaguely? I think I passed out after that. I woke up with the world's worst hangover."

He remembered goofing around with her on the couch, doing another round of shots, and kissing her. Drunken, sloppy kisses fueled by his secret desires. He couldn't remember much else except that his dreams that night had been vivid and erotic. The next morning, he'd apologized for kissing her, but she'd brushed it off like it was no big deal. He'd felt a profound sense of relief, knowing he hadn't taken advantage of her.

"You told me it was nothing," he said. "A few kisses. Just some drunken shenanigans."

Dusty's breath caught. She grabbed the sheet and pulled it over her naked body, shielding herself from his gaze. "I lied. You did more than just kiss me. We…um…"

"What did we do?" He tried to keep his voice calm, even as his heart was racing.

"Almost everything that…we did just now. When I came, I was so loud that you teased me about it. We…um…we wanted to have sex, but I said we should stop. I didn't want our first time to be a big, drunken mistake. I got up to get us some water, but by the time I got back to the couch, you'd passed out. And then, when you woke up on Friday morning and didn't remember most of it...I let you believe nothing happened."

He stared at her, too stunned to speak. At the time, he'd felt guilty about kissing her. But he'd done so much more. All along, she'd kept it to herself, never saying a word, even when he went back to Shelby three days later.

Her eyes welled up with tears. "I'm sorry. I know I promised I'd be honest, but I thought you'd be angry that I never told you. And tonight, it just slipped out. But that's not the hardest part. It's what you said to me."

He was almost afraid to ask. "What did I say?"

"You said, 'It's you, Dusty. It's always been you.' I'd waited so long to hear those words, only to have you forget you'd ever said them."

Now he felt worse than ever. Deep down, he'd meant them. But if he hadn't been drunk, he never would have had the courage to say them out loud.

She sat up, holding the sheet around her chest. "I should go."

"No." He placed his hand on her arm. "Please stay. I'm the one who should apologize. I'm so sorry. You were drunk, and I took advantage. That's not the way I treat women."

"I wasn't *that* drunk. If anything, I'm the one that took advantage. I should have told you to stop after a few kisses, but it felt so good."

The anguish in her voice shredded his heart to ribbons. He pulled her down beside him and drew her close. Stroking her hair, he held her as she trembled in his arms. "It must have killed you to keep this hidden for so long."

"I was going to tell you that morning, but we both had such miserable hangovers. Then we were so busy at the conference that we never got the chance to be alone. The night before you left, I couldn't keep it to myself any longer, so I decided to tell you everything. I wanted to see if we had a shot at being together. But then Shelby called, and..."

"And I went back to her." Remorse washed over him. "I still wish you'd told me."

"I couldn't because you were in so deep with her. If I kept quiet, I figured we could still be friends. I didn't want to ruin our friendship."

The fact that she'd kept such a big secret, all because she didn't want to lose him, made him love her even more. "Thank you for never giving up on us."

"You're not mad?"

"No. But let's not keep any more secrets. Is there anything else you need to tell me?"

She gave him a coy smile. "Nothing else, except I'd like to finish what we started. If you're up for it. Otherwise, we can wait. I know I dropped a big bombshell, but..."

But they were together now, and Boston was in the past. If they didn't act on this chance, they wouldn't get another one until the dig ended. And he *really* wanted her. "We shouldn't waste this night. Not when Em and TJ went to the trouble of setting up Operation Aphrodite."

"I couldn't agree more. Let's keep going." She trailed her hands down his stomach and tugged on the waistband of his boxers. "But these need to go."

He pulled them off and tossed them aside, then reached over to his nightstand to retrieve a condom. Before putting it on, he met her eyes. "You sure about this?"

She smiled up at him, her expression radiant. "Yes. But I want you on top. In total control."

"There you go, ceding control to me again. I like this side of you."

"Don't get too used to it, Dr. Carlson. Except maybe in bed."

Her sassy tone made her even more irresistible. After putting on the condom, he rolled her onto her back, parted her legs, and pushed himself deep inside her. The sensation of being enveloped by her was so much better than he could have imagined. "How's this?"

"It's good. So good." Her hazel eyes brimmed with warmth as she tightened her grip on his shoulders. "Don't hold anything back. You can take it as hard and fast as you want."

"If I've waited this long, I'm not about to rush."

At first, he took his time, pausing between thrusts to suck on her nipples, eliciting cries of pleasure from her. But when she dug her nails into his back and urged him on with more of those breathless pleas, he couldn't hold out any longer. He picked up the pace until the bed was creaking beneath them. Sweat beaded on his forehead, but the fan cooled them with its gentle breeze.

He didn't want to forget any of it. The feel of Dusty beneath him, the scent of her skin, her delightful little moans, and the connection he felt when he looked into her eyes. As her cries grew louder, he held back until she'd climaxed again before finally letting go, coming in a rush of ecstasy. He let out a loud groan, relieved that no one but Dusty could hear him.

When he finally stilled, his breathing was ragged, his heart pounding. At first, he didn't speak, not wanting to break the moment. When she murmured his name, ever so gently, he placed a tender kiss on her forehead. "Dusty...that was incredible."

She gave a contented sigh. "The best. And you know what's even better? We still have three hours left. And we're going to remember *all* of it tomorrow."

~

When Stuart woke, the room was dim, the morning light filtering through the blinds. Dusty was curled up beside him, her head nestled against his chest. His heart swelled with affection, remembering everything she'd shared with him. He still found it hard to believe that she'd kept such a painful secret for two years and that she'd waited for him, even when he'd been foolish enough to reconcile with Shelby.

From now on, he wasn't going to let anyone ruin things between them.

Dusty blinked slowly and opened her eyes. "Is it morning already?"

"Barely." He reached over to the nightstand and grabbed his watch. "Not quite six, but we can sleep in. It's our day off."

She placed a soft kiss on his bare shoulder, then sat up beside him. "If it's six, there's still time for me to sneak back into my bed."

He laughed. "I'm pretty sure Em and Clarissa noticed it was empty when they came in last night." He wasn't sure what time they'd returned from their bar crawl since he and Dusty had drifted off after making love a second time.

"I know, but I don't want to do the walk of shame back into my room." She stretched, then regarded him with an affectionate smile. "Thanks for last night. It was amazing."

"My pleasure." He wanted her to stay and cuddle, but he needed to respect her boundaries. Overnight, things between them had changed. Now that they'd crossed the line from friends to lovers, there was no going back.

She hopped out of bed, scooped up her clothes, and put them on quickly. Blowing him a kiss, she tiptoed across the room, eased the door open, and shut it quietly behind her.

Then he was left alone with just his thoughts. While he was grateful they'd gotten to spend the night together, instead of feeling satisfied, he wanted more. Not just a summer romance but an actual relationship once they returned to Boston.

But was that what she wanted? Most of her flings had lasted the length of a dig season. Whereas he'd spent far too long tied up in a lengthy relationship that had shattered his self-confidence.

Maybe he needed to start slowly. Instead of worrying about the future, he could take a small first step.

If he recalled correctly, Dusty was spending a week in Istanbul after the dig ended. She loved exploring the older parts of the city, checking out the flea markets, and indulging in her passion for street food.

While he couldn't commit to a full week there, he could spend three or four days with her. Knowing her, she was probably saving money by staying in one of the student rooms at the American Research Institute. But what if he rented a place for them instead? Somewhere small and cozy where they could make love every night with no one else around.

While mulling over the idea, he remembered a conversation with his friend Olivia. Over the past few weeks, he'd been texting her off and on. As a fellow archaeologist, she'd been eager to hear about his experiences at Troy. At one point, she'd asked if he'd be staying in Istanbul after the dig ended since she'd visited the city last fall.

He grabbed his phone and sent her a text. *When you were in Istanbul with Rick, where did you stay?*

When no text bubbles appeared, he tried to recall what time it was in California. Eight p.m.? Nine? If it was later than that, he didn't want to disturb her. A minute later, his phone buzzed with an incoming call from her. He answered it in a hushed voice. "Olivia?"

"Hey, Stu. I'm driving right now, but Rick saw your text. He said you were asking about Istanbul?"

"Yeah. What's the name of the place you stayed after you guys finished working in Bodrum?"

"Let me think a minute." He heard her talking to Rick, and then she came back on the line. "I booked it through Airbnb but can't remember what it was called. Rick can send you the link. It wasn't super cheap, but it was totally worth it. In the heart of the Old City, near the monuments in Sultanahmet Square. Lots of light, a big kitchen, a rooftop patio overlooking the Sea of Marmara."

Rick's voice chimed in. "Don't forget the king bed."

Olivia snorted. "Right, because that's just what Stuart needs. He's not planning a romantic getaway." She paused, then addressed Stuart. "Wait. *Is* this a romantic getaway?"

No sense in hiding the truth from Olivia. If he didn't tell her, then Dusty would. Heat crept into his cheeks. "Uh…yeah. I thought I'd book it and surprise Dusty."

"You two are together? Yes! About time!"

"You knew?"

"Of course, you goofball. Last year, when we were in Cyprus and I was pining for Rick, she told me in solidarity. She wanted you to stop treating her like a sister."

He chuckled. "Definitely not treating her that way now."

"I'm gonna need more details than that," Olivia said. "How long has this been going on? Is this a summer thing or a legit relationship?"

"It's only been a few weeks, but I'm hoping we can stay together once we're back in Boston. Right now, I'm taking it one step at a time."

"Good plan. Spending a few days in Istanbul would be perfect. Dusty'll love that place, too. The light is fantastic. Just right for drawing." Olivia gave a dramatic sigh. "I'm so happy for you. Dig romances are the best."

No doubt she was remembering her own experience last summer when she and Rick had fallen in love while working at a field school in Cyprus. By now, they'd been together for almost a year. If Stuart was lucky, maybe he and Dusty could follow in their footsteps. "Thanks. I'm trying not to blow it."

"You won't. I have total faith in you. I've got to go, but Rick will text you that link."

A few minutes after she ended the call, Stuart's phone buzzed with a link to the Airbnb listing. To his immense luck, it was free on the dates he wanted.

For once in his life, he didn't overthink his decision or make a mental list of pros and cons.

Instead, he booked it immediately.

## CHAPTER TWENTY-FOUR

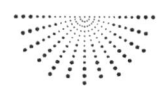

After sneaking back to her bed without waking her roommates, Dusty closed her eyes and curled up under the sheets. Given her blissful state of contentment, she expected to drift back to sleep immediately. But her mind insisted on replaying every detail of her night with Stuart. When she'd told him about their drunken hookup in Boston, she had feared it would drive a wedge between them. Instead, it had brought them closer than ever. So much that when they'd had sex, it had been more than just a fun romp in bed. They'd shared a real connection. But allowing herself to feel this way had left her strangely vulnerable.

Easing out of bed quietly, she grabbed her towel and headed off to the shower. As usual, the water turned from comfortably warm to arctic within minutes, making her teeth chatter. She finished up quickly, then changed into a tank top and shorts.

With everyone sleeping off last night's bar crawl, the field house was silent, save for the ticking of the ceramic-tile clock on the kitchen wall. After starting a pot of coffee, she retrieved her sketch pad and pencils from the library. Last night's antics had left her with an irresistible urge to doodle.

Once the coffee was done, she poured some into a mug and took it over to the table in the common room. Outside the window to the east, the sun was rising, bathing the sky in a pinkish glow. She took a sip of coffee, then turned to a fresh page in her sketch pad.

Her first drawing was a playful cartoon of her and Stuart holding hands, with little hearts swirling above them. In the corner, Emilia looked on, dressed as the goddess Aphrodite, while TJ played the part of Cupid, shooting them with one of his arrows. She followed it up with another drawing, where she and Stuart were floating in a hot-air balloon over the rock formations in Cappadocia, once again surrounded by swirly hearts.

She shook her head in disgust. When had she become so sappy?

This wasn't just the delicious buzz she got after a great night in bed. These were full-blown romantic *feelings*. The type that led to a relationship with a capital *R*.

*What's wrong with that? Why can't you and Stuart stay together once you're in Boston?*

In the past, she'd avoided getting in deep with any of her partners. She took pride in her independence, not wanting to be tied down to anyone. But Stuart was different. She could easily envision sharing her life with him. Not that she wanted to spook him by moving too quickly, but at some point, she should tell him she wanted more than a summer romance.

As she drew, her mind kept circling around Boston. Of all the cities she'd lived in, it was the one that felt the most like home. Back when she was three, her parents had purchased a large condo in a gorgeous old building in the Back Bay neighborhood. Filled with overstuffed bookshelves, memorabilia from their trips, and antique furniture, it had a cozy, lived-in quality. Unlike their modern apartment in Cairo, the Boston condo suited her dad perfectly, which was why he lived there for most of the year, puttering over his research.

Dusty was looking forward to spending time with him once she got back.

But she'd still have to deal with her dissertation. The thought of all that writing made her shudder.

Unless she charted a new course.

Could she be that bold? The more she considered it, the more excited she got. What if Mort's offer panned out? What if she could make a career as an illustrator—not just of archaeological publications but children's books as well?

"Morning, Dusty." Emilia strolled into the common room, with Clarissa following on her heels. "I'm surprised you're awake. Last night's shenanigans should have left you exhausted."

Dusty groaned. "Can we not, Em?"

"We certainly can. After all, Operation Aphrodite was my idea. Well, mine and TJ's. The guy is surprisingly well-rounded in his knowledge of rom-coms."

Dusty cast a knowing smirk at her friend. "Is he looking more appealing now?"

"No." Emilia scowled. "Besides, we're not talking about him. You're the one who's under interrogation. We want to know if our mission succeeded." She turned to Clarissa. "Right? Don't you want to know what happened?"

Clarissa peeked at Dusty's drawing. "From that sketch, I'm guessing it went well."

Dusty turned the page over. "It worked perfectly, thanks. But that's all the details I'll share."

"I'm glad you're back together," Clarissa said. "Stuart was miserable on-site without you."

"Yeah, he was a real grump." Emilia wandered over to the kitchen counter and poured herself a mug of coffee. "You want one, Clarissa?"

"Yes, please. With two lumps of sugar." Clarissa sat down across from Dusty. "Speaking of the site, did Dr. Hughes talk to you yesterday about coming back on Monday?"

"He did. I owe your dad a giant thank-you. I can't believe he stood up for me like that." Dusty still wished Stuart had been the one to speak up for her, but he had more to lose than a wealthy donor like Mort.

"Dad and I were shocked at Dr. Hughes' behavior. I'm sorry I wasn't around to take my share of the blame." Clarissa shivered. "Though I'm glad Dr. Wagner didn't yell at me. I cry really easily."

"It was rough, but it's over now." Dusty flipped her pencil between her fingers as she pondered her next move. "Or maybe not. I had an idea…"

"What?" Emilia returned, setting the two mugs of coffee on the table, along with a package of Ülker tea biscuits. "Please say you're not planning another spy mission. We just got you and Stuart back together."

"No spying." Dusty grabbed a biscuit. "I was thinking about Dr. Wagner. I still feel guilty that I lied to him. I'd like to make amends."

Emilia gaped at her. "Are you serious? He was a total jerk when he confronted you."

"He had every right to be. He spent a long time showing us around the site only to find out we were bullshitting him. I'm going to apologize on Monday, but I'll clear it with Stuart first."

"You think Wagner will listen to you?" Emilia said.

Dusty shrugged. "It's worth a try, except I won't be approaching him as Hilde. I'll be Dusty Danforth, the daughter of renowned Egyptologist Dr. Louisa Danforth." Though she rarely used her mom's name to gain favors, this time, she'd make an exception. "Stuart said Dr. Wagner met my mom in Berlin. Maybe he's a fan."

"Are you going to tell him the spy mission was Hughes' idea?" Emilia asked.

Dusty shook her head. "Nope. I'm just going to apologize for what we did. Hopefully, that should be enough."

"I think it's a fabulous idea," Clarissa said. "I could go with you and bring a peace offering. If I could find the right ingredients, I'd be glad to bake him an apple strudel. I love baking. Cookies, pies, pastry, you name it. It's one of my hobbies."

*Of course it is.* But now that Dusty wasn't competing with her, she didn't care if Clarissa outshone her in every way. "Sounds perfect. We'll call it Operation Strudel. After our beach day, we can stop by the grocery store in Güzelyali, and you can pick up the ingredients you need."

"I'll pass," Emilia said. "I need to stay out of trouble."

"No problem," Dusty said. "It shouldn't be a big deal. I just want to make things right."

~

STUART WAS IN A RARE STATE OF BLISS. IT WAS HIS DAY OFF, HE WAS sitting on a towel facing the Aegean Sea, and Dusty was smoothing sunscreen over his back. She took her time with it, massaging the lotion onto his shoulders and rubbing it along the nape of his neck. Her every touch reminded him of their night together. The feel of her bare skin, the taste of her lips. What he wouldn't give to lower her onto the blanket and continue where they'd left off.

*Enough.* Since they were on a public beach, he couldn't exactly give in to his fantasies.

"I'm done." Dusty handed him the bottle of sunscreen. "Do you want to do me now?"

He turned to face her. "Do I want to *do* you? Is that a trick question? Besides, I already got your back."

She thrust her chest out at him, the swell of her breasts barely covered by the tiny bikini. "How about you do my chest and shoulders?"

"Not until I get things under control here." He adjusted himself as discreetly as possible.

"Sorry about that." Laughing, she stretched out on her towel, tilting her face up to the sun. "Isn't it gorgeous out? I love the beach."

Right now, he wasn't focusing on the beach. Instead, he could barely draw his eyes away from her. He wanted to lean over and brush his lips against her bare stomach. Stroke her beneath that bikini until she made more of those delightful noises. But he forced himself to look away.

Shading his eyes, he gazed out at the water. The Aegean was a perfect shade of turquoise, glimmering in the sunlight. Though the tourists were out in full force, their group had gotten to the beach early enough to stake out a large swath of sand. Ever thoughtful, Clarissa had purchased a giant beach umbrella in Güzelyali in case anyone needed a break from the sun.

He lay down beside Dusty. Lulled by the steady crashing of the waves, he'd almost fallen asleep when her voice roused him. "Stuart? Can I talk to you about something? Before I do, promise you won't get mad?"

His serenity vanished, but he refused to let his anxiety get the best of him. Opening his eyes, he turned on his side so that he was looking at her. "What's up?"

She rolled over to face him, propping herself up on one elbow. Giving him a mischievous grin, she traced her fingers along the curve of his shoulder. "I came up with a new plan this morning. I'm calling it Operation Strudel."

As enticing as her touch was, he couldn't let it sway him. "No more covert ops. Please. Even if I'm grateful Operation Aphrodite worked out, I'd like to keep things above board."

"Above board? Who says that? You sound like my dad." A little furrow appeared between her brows. "Anyway, it's not about spying. It's about making peace with the Germans. And bringing them strudel."

Rather than dismiss her idea outright, he forced himself to listen. To his surprise, she and Clarissa had dreamed up a thoughtful way to repair the damage done by their first spy mission. He waited until she finished speaking before he weighed in. "It's a good plan, but you don't need my permission to run with it. You're not doing anything wrong."

"I didn't want you to be blindsided. You hate that. So, if you're okay with it, Clarissa and I are going to stop by the Germans' site on Monday morning."

He liked that she'd asked. That she'd told him everything and hadn't tried to sneak it past him. "I'm definitely okay with it. Anything else you want to share with me?"

"Well, actually…"

"Just tell me." Brushing his hand across her cheek, he softened his tone. "Whatever it is, I won't get angry."

"It's not that bad. But remember yesterday evening when you came into the library? Before we went off to snitch Hughes' wine?" When he nodded, she continued. "I couldn't focus. Not just because of our fight but because I was having such a hard time with the opening chapters of my dissertation. I couldn't figure out what to say or how to approach my topic in a way that didn't sound trite or boring."

At the risk of coming across as too eager, he spoke up quickly. "Do you want my help? I could read what you've written and give you some feedback."

"Hold it, Professor. I'm not done. What I'm trying to say is that it's still not going well, despite all the help you and Kerim have given me. And this morning, when I was drawing, I had an epiphany. It's amazing the clarity really great sex can bring."

He grinned. "Really great sex, huh? Glad I could be of service."

"You were *extremely* helpful. Anyway, I started thinking about this fall. If I want to stay on my mom's good side, I need to go back to Boston. Which wouldn't be so bad if I wasn't facing another year of grad school. It doesn't matter what my topic is, I'll never want to write that dissertation. So it's time I faced the facts. Getting a doctorate isn't the right path for me." She gave a short laugh. "I know you already told me that, but I had to figure it out by myself. I'd be much happier if I was doing something I loved. Like my artwork."

Hearing her speak with such honesty made his heart soar. Not that he *ever* wanted to discourage her from finishing her degree, but she'd spent far too long struggling over a task that made her miserable. "That's a great idea. You're such a talented artist. I'll bet you could find illustration work if you wanted it."

She gave him a bright smile. "I never told you about Mort's offer, did I? He liked my cartoons so much that he put me in touch with his publisher friend. If it works out, I could end up illustrating children's books, like Clarissa does. It's an incredible opportunity."

He listened as she described the project—a time-travel series for the picture book set. This was exactly what she needed. "That sounds awesome. I'll bet even your mom would be impressed."

"I doubt it." Dusty blew out a breath. "Nothing less than a PhD will win her over. But I have to stand up to her, even if she cuts me off."

"What does that mean, anyway? It's not like you get an allowance."

"Yeah, but I've been using my parents' frequent-flier miles for years. And I've never had to chip in for rent when I've stayed at their apartments in Cairo or Boston."

"If you got a bunch of illustration work, you could probably afford your own place. But from what you've told me, your mom's hardly ever in Boston. Most of the time, your dad's the only one there, and he likes having you around. He also doesn't care if you get your doctorate."

Stuart respected Dusty's father immensely. Even though the man was a world-class archaeologist and a scholar of ancient languages who had published ten books, he was also easygoing and compassionate. Unlike Dusty's mother, he'd never insisted their daughter follow them into academia.

Dusty traced a circle in the sand with her finger. "He'll

definitely take my side. The question is whether he'd assert himself if my mom loses her shit."

"Would you still stay in Boston? If you're not tied down to grad school, then you could keep traveling since you could do your illustrations anywhere." As soon as the words were out of his mouth, Stuart longed to take them back. What was he doing? He wanted her to stay in the city with him, not jet off to another project.

"I didn't think of it that way." She chewed on her lip. "Right now, I don't have anything else lined up. Besides, I was looking forward to showing you around."

While her answer relieved his immediate fears, it wasn't as romantic as he'd hoped. Playing the role of tour guide was something she would have done for him, regardless of whether they were friends or lovers. By making the offer, she wasn't implying that they'd still be together romantically. Was it too much to hope for?

He was about to prod her into making a bigger commitment but stopped himself in time. This conversation wasn't about him. It was about Dusty and her decision to alter the course of her life. He needed to stop worrying about the future and support her as best he could.

He kept his voice light. "Don't forget, once I'm settled, you promised me dumplings and Italian pastries."

She grinned. "Like I'd ever forget? We're going to eat our way into a food coma."

He reached across the blanket and took her hand. "No matter what happens with your mom, I'm here for you. I promise."

"Thanks. I'm going to email my graduate adviser on Monday and let her know what I decided. I can formally withdraw once I get back to the States in September."

"Will you still keep working in the field?"

"Hell, yes. It's not like I'm giving up archaeology. I'm just going to do it without a PhD." Giving him an adorable smile, she lay back on her towel and closed her eyes. "But now I can do *anything*. The world is wide-open."

As much as he loved this free-spirited version of Dusty, he didn't want to lose her. If he had any hope of keeping her in Boston, he'd have to be brave enough to tell her exactly how he felt.

## CHAPTER TWENTY-FIVE

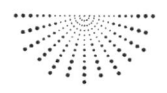

On Monday morning, Dusty got ready with the others, eager to return to the site. When she went out to the Land Rover to load up her supplies, Clarissa was already waiting, occupying the front passenger seat. On her lap was a basket, with the strudel wrapped in a dish towel.

Dusty inhaled the delicious scent of cinnamon and apples. "Is that the strudel? When did you make it?"

"I prepped everything last night, then got up at five to bake it." Clarissa yawned. "I'll probably need an extra dose of caffeine today, but strudel is better when it's warm."

"Seems a shame to give it all to the Germans. Do you think—"

"I made two. One for us and one for them. We can have ours during the morning break."

Because *of course* Clarissa would bake two strudels. She was just that thoughtful.

Once they got to the site, Dusty and Clarissa let the others go on ahead. While Dusty wasn't trying to keep their mission a secret, she didn't want to deal with a bunch of questions. The rest of the group headed west along the boardwalk while she and Clarissa followed the path leading to the eastern part of the site.

She took a deep breath, enjoying the brisk morning air. She loved the site at this hour, before the sun beat down without mercy and the tour groups arrived.

Clarissa tugged on her arm. "I'm nervous. What if they yell at us?"

"Worst case, we apologize and promise never to bother them again. But there's no harm in trying." Even if Dr. Wagner shooed them away, Dusty's conscience would be clear, knowing she'd made an effort.

When they reached the Germans' trenches near the Temple of Athena, she stopped short at the sight of a guard standing in front of the barrier. She recognized him as Mehmet, one of the friendliest workers at the café. The few times she'd gone there to get coffee, he'd always made time to chat with her.

"Mehmet?" she asked. "Are you working as a guard now?"

"Yes. The German archaeologists needed someone to guard the site, so I offered to take the job."

"Isn't it kind of dull standing around here all day?"

He shrugged. "The pay is better, and my family can use the money. There are enough tourists coming by with questions that I don't get bored."

Dusty had little patience for nosy tourists, but Mehmet's people skills were probably better than hers. "We were hoping to talk to Dr. Wagner. Any chance you could get him for us?"

"Sorry, he's not allowing visitors on the site. Especially not your group."

While Dusty could understand Mehmet's need to play by the rules, she hadn't expected an additional hurdle. But Clarissa seemed undaunted. Looking past Mehmet, she spotted one of the German students and waved at him. "Yoo-hoo! We're back."

Naturally, it was Leo, the blond hottie they'd met during Operation Odysseus. *Great.* He'd probably send them packing.

Frowning, Leo approached them and spoke in English. "Liesel? And Hilde? What do you want?"

Even if his voice was gruff, Dusty didn't miss the way his eyes lingered on Clarissa's figure or the way his Adam's apple bobbed when she met his gaze head-on. Before Dusty could speak up, Clarissa beat her to it. "I'm sorry we tricked you. We brought you a peace offering." She held up the basket, then lifted the dish towel, giving Leo a peek. "I made strudel."

No human could resist the delicious smell emanating from that basket. Leo stared at it with undisguised longing. "I...don't think that's a good idea. Dr. Wagner was furious with you."

Clarissa batted her eyes. "Were *you* furious with us?"

Leo's lips twitched up in a smile. "Tell no one, but we thought it was kind of funny. We were also surprised you spoke German so well. Most Americans can't be bothered to learn another language."

"I'm half-German on my mother's side. When I was younger, I used to spend my summers in Berlin visiting my relatives." Clarissa gave him a sweet smile. "Even now, I'm always looking for opportunities to practice my German."

Was she flirting with him? Or putting on an act to win him over? Either way, she was crushing it. Still, Dusty didn't want to lose focus. "I see you have a guard now. That's new."

"It's because of you," Leo said. "Well, not you, personally, but your whole group. We can't risk having any of you poking around. Mehmet is here from six in the morning until four."

Mehmet nodded. "Then my brothers come to take over. One of them does the evening shift, and the other works from midnight until six. That way, the site is guarded around the clock."

"Can't say I blame you," Dusty said. "But since we're here, is there any chance we could talk to Dr. Wagner? I'd like to apologize in person."

Leo gave a good-natured shrug. "I guess it couldn't hurt."

As he ambled off, Dusty nudged Clarissa. "Nice job buttering him up."

"I wasn't faking. He's kind of a cutie." She flushed scarlet, then turned away, as if hesitant to meet Dusty's eyes. "I...um...I wouldn't mind knowing him better."

But her shy smile morphed into a look of sheer terror when Dr. Wagner strode up to the barrier and nailed them with a withering glare.

He directed his wrath at Dusty. "*You*. I can't believe you have the gall to show your face at my site. Thanks to you, we've had to hire guards for the rest of the season."

Dusty bowed her head and kept her voice humble. "Sorry about that. We came to apologize properly. To make up for our thoughtless behavior, we brought an apple strudel for your team's morning break."

Clarissa brandished the basket. "It's not poisoned. It's my grandmother's recipe."

Dr. Wagner let out a weary sigh. "Why are you doing this? What goal does it serve?"

"No goal except to make amends," Dusty said. "I'm sorry we lied about everything, including our names. This is Clarissa Jones, and I'm Dusty Danforth." She tensed up, hoping her name would prompt recognition.

Dr. Wagner nodded, as though a light had gone on. "You're Dr. Louisa Danforth's daughter, aren't you? I've heard of you before."

"You have?" At most, she'd expected him to remember her mother.

"Dr. Danforth mentioned you during her talk. Somewhat of a troublemaker, if I remember correctly."

"Yep. That's me. Living up to my reputation, once again. But I'm genuinely sorry I wasted your time."

He eyed her sharply. "Did you think it was a waste of time? You seemed so interested."

"I *was* interested. I've spent my whole life around ruins, and they fascinate me." She glanced down at the trenches where the

German students were digging. Or rather, pretending to dig while they attempted to listen in. "If anything, I wish our two groups could combine forces. When my mom worked in Egypt, she was part of an international team—British, American, Egyptian, German. Everyone contributed."

Dr. Wagner gestured for them to come closer. "Have a look. And bring that strudel."

Clarissa gave a cheeky salute. "Yes, sir."

Giving Mehmet a quick smile, Dusty pushed past the rope, with Clarissa following her. In the twelve days that had passed since they last visited, the Germans had dug up an even bigger swath of territory, occupying four separate trenches.

"Leopold, take Clarissa over to the break area so she can leave her strudel there," Dr. Wagner said. "Dusty, you come with me."

Clarissa went with Leo, talking to him softly as they walked together. Dusty followed the dig director to the area he'd been excavating. "Any evidence of that archive?" she asked. "Not asking for Dr. Hughes, just curious."

As soon as she said it, she cursed herself inwardly, realizing she'd put her boss in the line of fire and jeopardized her job again. But Dr. Wagner only responded with a sardonic laugh. "So that ridiculous plan was his idea? I suspected as much."

She cringed. "You won't report him, will you?"

"No. Despite what you might think of me, I'm not that petty. But I'm angry that he coerced you and your friends into carrying out that scheme for him."

The tension eased from her shoulders. "Thanks. I'm not proud of what I did, but I needed to stay on his good side. Not that it helped. He's one of the most toxic people I've ever met."

"He wasn't always like this. Yes, he was a boastful man who insisted on being the center of attention. But he wasn't so mean-spirited. Did you know he and I once worked together here at Troy? Years ago, our two teams were part of a joint excavation project."

"What? I thought you were rivals."

"No. We were collaborating until Dr. Hughes..." He trailed off. "You know what happened?"

She shook her head. "Just that there was a dispute, and the Turkish government ruled in your favor. Stuart said everyone involved with the dig had to sign an NDA."

He looked away briefly, as though the memory pained him. "Maybe so, but I think you deserve to hear the truth. Our last season together, we made some valuable finds. Gold jewelry, like the kind found by Heinrich Schliemann back in the 1870s. You've heard the stories?"

"Sure. Schliemann claimed it was the treasure of King Priam of Troy, then took photos of his wife wearing it. He smuggled it into Greece, but when the Turks found out, they revoked his excavation permit for three years."

"Dr. Hughes was doing the same thing. Stealing artifacts, then passing them along to a contact to sell. But when I accused him, he said I was lying. That I'd set him up so I could sabotage him and take full control of the dig."

This went beyond mere jealousy. This was criminal shit. "Now I get why they kicked him out. Why'd they agree to let the University of Boston come back here?"

"There were artifacts from the Turkish sites of Ephesus and Hierapolis in the university's archaeological museum—valuable pieces the Turkish government wanted repatriated. So they made an arrangement."

No wonder the university had tried so hard to keep the incident a secret. Hiding it from everyone, even Stuart. She was astonished Dr. Hughes hadn't gone to jail, but it was truly mind-boggling what an entitled male authority figure could get away with. "That's terrible. We'll have to keep an eye on him."

"I doubt he'd make the same mistake twice. He's more intent on restoring his good name. That's why he wants to find something notable—so he can brag about it at that symposium in Amsterdam."

Dusty was tempted to reveal that her boss had only found two skeletons, but she held her tongue. Eventually, Dr. Wagner would find out. For now, she'd keep quiet, but she'd watch Dr. Hughes more closely. As far as she could tell, no one in their crew had excavated anything worth smuggling. The few pieces of jewelry she'd drawn were small and poorly preserved. But that didn't mean he wouldn't try something. And if he pulled any criminal shit, it wouldn't just affect him but Stuart as well.

By the time she left, she'd established a strong rapport with Dr. Wagner. Not only had he forgiven her, but he also sympathized with her for working under Dr. Hughes. As she and Clarissa were leaving, he invited them to drop by again. "Or come lend a hand," he added with a hint of a smile. "There's always room for more German-speaking archaeologists on *our* team."

～

THE FIRST HALF HOUR AT THE SITE HAD LULLED STUART INTO A STATE of complacency. Since Kerim and Dr. Hughes hadn't returned from Çanakkale yet, he was in charge. The prospect no longer intimidated him. Having spent hours working on the site report, he had a better overview of the project than Dr. Hughes, who only cared about his own trench. When Stuart reviewed the day's objectives with the team, they all listened. No one bickered or grumbled as they took their places and began another day of excavation.

If only the rest of the dig could be like this.

Stuart was helping Emilia outline a wall in the far corner of his trench when Kerim arrived, bringing Dr. Hughes with him. Emilia let out a pained groan. "Please don't make me work with him. I can't deal with his attitude this morning."

"Same here," said Hayat, who was working nearby.

"I'll do my best." Stuart stood and went over to greet the two men.

"Good morning," Kerim said. "Looks like you've got everything under control."

Dr. Hughes pointed to his empty trench off in the distance. "Hardly. Why isn't anyone working there?"

*Because they can't stand you.* Stuart forced a bright smile. "I figured we'd wait until you arrived since you're the one with the vision for that part of the site."

"True." Dr. Hughes scanned the area as if seeking someone. "I don't see the Danforth girl. I thought she was coming back today. Did she decide to stay in the lab? If so, all the better."

"She's here, just…" He paused, trying to think of an answer that wouldn't lead to an explosive rant.

"And where's Clarissa? What are they up to?"

Before Stuart could answer, Dusty and Clarissa strolled up to the site, smiling triumphantly. Dusty gave them a hearty wave. "We're back."

Clarissa walked over to her father, who lounged on his camp chair next to Stuart's trench. She leaned down and pecked him on the cheek. "Dad, the Germans were so excited about my strudel. I used Grandmother's recipe."

"That's my girl. No one can resist that strudel."

Setting down her trowel, Hayat turned toward Clarissa. "Did you save any for us?"

"Of course. I baked an extra one."

By now, all the students were advancing closer, no doubt curious as to what was happening. Dr. Hughes' booming voice stopped them in their tracks. "What's going on? Did you just say you brought strudel to the Germans?"

"As a peace offering," Dusty said. "And we apologized for lying to them earlier."

Dr. Hughes turned to Stuart in fury. "Did you authorize this?"

Stuart's spine stiffened, but he kept his voice firm. "I did. Like I said before, I wanted to make peace with the German archaeologists. When my earlier efforts failed, I was pleased Dusty took the initiative."

"It worked out just fine," Dusty said. "Dr. Wagner accepted our apology. He's not angry about any of it. Though he now has a guard posted at the site."

Clarissa laughed. "Not a full-on security guard. The Germans recruited Mehmet—you know, the one who works at the café?"

"A shame," Mort said. "I always enjoyed chatting with him during my visits there. Such a friendly chap."

Though Stuart wouldn't have admitted it in front of his boss, he was grateful the Germans had someone watching their site. Now he wouldn't have to worry about Dr. Hughes sneaking over there and causing problems. He smiled at Dusty. "Thanks for making the effort. You, too, Clarissa. Maybe we can have Dr. Wagner's group come visit our site during one of our morning breaks. In the meantime, let's get back to work."

"Sounds good," Dusty said. "Where do you want me?"

Talk about a loaded question. But Stuart wouldn't let his mind wander down that path. "You can go back to Kerim's trench. Clarissa, you can work with me."

She flashed him a dazzling smile. "Wonderful. I'll just set this strudel down."

"Not so fast." Dr. Hughes blocked her path. "What else did the Germans tell you? If they felt the need to hire a guard, they must have found something of note."

"I don't know. I was too busy talking to Leo." Maneuvering around him, Clarissa walked over to the picnic blankets and set her basket by the coolers.

"We weren't there to spy," Dusty said. "So, there's nothing to report."

"Don't take that tone with me," Dr. Hughes said. "If you can't show me the proper respect, I'll send you back to the lab again."

Taking a deep breath, Stuart addressed his boss, hoping to redirect him. "Sir? Why don't you pick out a couple of students to help in your trench today? Maybe someone who hasn't had the chance yet? I'd also like to remind you of our schedule. *Everyone* gets a break at ten, regardless of where they're working. It's to our benefit to keep them hydrated and well-fed."

"Are you telling me what to do?" Dr. Hughes said.

"This is the schedule we agreed on. It's in one of the spreadsheets I gave you."

"You and those damn spreadsheets." But the fire had gone out of Dr. Hughes' eyes. He turned and stormed off toward his trench.

Still maintaining a calm facade, Stuart didn't let on that his heart was pounding, his mouth dry. He'd never spoken to a supervisor that way before—not a dig director, not a professor, not *anyone* above him. He had the utmost respect for authority. But for once, it had felt remarkably good not to roll over and show his belly.

# CHAPTER TWENTY-SIX

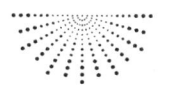

In the four days that had passed since Operation Strudel, Dusty had seen a noticeable improvement in everyone's morale. Now that the Germans were no longer their enemies, she and the others could freely walk past their site and chat with them. Mort and Dr. Wagner had shared tea at the café. And Leo and Clarissa had become an item. Not only had she been bubblier than usual, but Dusty had also caught her singing in the bathroom like a lovestruck Disney princess.

The only one who hadn't benefited from the détente? Dr. Hughes. With each passing day, the lack of a cemetery—or any other spectacular find—soured his mood even further. By now, his behavior had gotten so toxic that no one wanted to work with him. To ensure fairness, Stuart had drawn up a new schedule. Though everyone had to take a turn in the dig director's trench, they only had to endure it for two days in a row.

Unfortunately, Dusty was on the first day of her rotation, which meant putting up with Dr. Hughes' nasty barbs. But even though he clearly resented her, he hadn't made any more threats to kick her off the dig. She figured if she kept her temper under control and did her job, he wouldn't have any reason to get rid of her. Even without a cemetery, they'd found enough artifacts that both she and Clarissa had plenty to draw.

She could hardly believe they only had two weeks left at Troy. While she wasn't in a hurry to leave Turkey, she was looking forward to returning to Boston. Then she and Stuart could stop pretending they were just colleagues. If they wanted, they could spend every night in each other's arms. Not that they'd gotten far in discussing the future. But Dusty suspected Stuart wanted to stay together as much as she did.

At the sight of Leo strolling over to their trench, she waved at him. "Hey, Leo. What's up?"

"I came to fetch Clarissa. She's coming back to the field house for our midday meal."

Clarissa straightened and brushed the dirt off her knees. Unlike the rest of them, she always looked good, even after seven hours of digging in the scorching sun. She flashed Leo a radiant smile. "Thanks for coming to get me."

Dr. Hughes strode over to the edge of their trench. "You can't leave yet. You've got fifteen minutes left before it's time to go."

Clarissa shrugged. "Sorry. I'll make up for it tomorrow."

Dusty bit back a grin, secretly pleased Clarissa didn't sound sorry at all.

Leo squatted at the side of their trench and peered into it. "Find anything good today?"

"Nothing special," Dusty said. "More horse bones than usual. Not sure what that means yet. What about you?"

He broke into a wide smile, revealing adorable dimples. "We made a significant find, or rather, I did, by the Temple of Athena. I dug up a small clay fragment that might have come from a larger tablet. It's hard to tell, but it looks like it has writing on it. Cuneiform, if I'm not mistaken."

"That's so exciting," Clarissa said. "Do you have a picture?"

Leo jumped into the trench and brought up a photo on his

phone, displaying it for them to see. The piece wasn't much bigger than Dusty's thumb, but she could make out faint scratch marks. She could only imagine how excited Dr. Wagner must have been when Leo made the discovery.

"That's a sweet find," she said. "What if it turns out to be the oldest example of writing at Troy?"

"Didn't someone find a bronze seal with writing on it from this time period?" Clarissa asked.

Dusty nodded. "The Luwian seal. It's from the Late Bronze Age, but it's tiny. Like the size of a button. And it only has a couple of words on it. This piece could be part of something much bigger. Like an engraved tablet." The thought filled her with a burst of joy. Now that she and Dr. Wagner had become friends, she'd be thrilled if his team scored a major find.

Dr. Hughes lumbered down to join them, then demanded Leo show him the photo. After squinting at it, he gave a dismissive snort. "Looks like garbage to me. I doubt it's anything valuable."

Dusty refrained from rolling her eyes at his blatant rudeness. Instead, she smiled at Leo. "Tell Dr. Wagner congrats from us. I hope it leads to an entire tablet."

"That's what he's hoping for, too. He wanted to keep digging, but one of his colleagues—an archaeology professor from Berlin—is stopping by our field house for lunch. That's why I invited Clarissa to join us."

"He's from the same neighborhood as my cousins," Clarissa said.

"Have fun," Dusty said. "Don't get into any trouble."

She laughed. "That's your department." After climbing out of the trench with Leo, she grabbed her daypack and left with him.

Dr. Hughes' lip curled in disgust as he watched them go. Was he annoyed because Clarissa had left early? Or jealous of Leo's discovery?

Either way, Dusty didn't need him taking out his anger on

her. She crouched back in her corner and continued digging until her grumpy boss announced it was time to go.

∼

Once they were back at the field house, Dusty washed up for lunch. Before heading outside with the others, she stopped by her room, plopped down on her bed, and booted up her laptop.

Emilia popped her head in. "Coming to eat?"

"In a minute. I need to check my Harvard email account. I still haven't heard from my adviser." Last week, Dusty had emailed her to announce that she was dropping out of grad school, only to get an out-of-office auto-reply. Frustrating, to be sure. Now that she'd made her decision, she wanted to file the paperwork as soon as possible.

"Didn't you say she was in Greece?"

"Yeah, but I was hoping she'd check her email while she's there. If she's going to be mad at me, I want to get it over with."

Emilia sat on her bed and unlaced her hiking boots. "She won't be mad. If anything, she'll be relieved she doesn't have to deal with you."

"I'm not *that* bad."

"No, but you weren't exactly a model doctoral student, what with cycling through six different dissertation topics."

"It was only five. But you're right. That's why I want her to reassure me she's not angry." As she was scrolling through her inbox, she paused at a new message.

Emilia tossed her boots on the floor and grabbed a worn pair of flip-flops. "Let's go. I think we're having kofte today, and you know how much I love those yummy little meatballs."

"Hang on." Dusty scanned the message, her excitement growing as she read it. "I got a job offer. From Professor Biancuzzo at the University of Parma."

"Sweet. Have you worked for her before?"

"Three years ago. In Italy. She's leading a dig in Sardinia this fall and needs an illustrator. I'm touched she remembered me." Dusty took pride in getting offers based on her own merit rather than on her parents' connections. To her, it was proof that she'd made a solid name for herself and that she didn't need a PhD to succeed.

"You probably did a kick-ass job. Have you ever been to Sardinia?"

"No, but I've always wanted to visit. You've dug there, right?"

"Yep. Two years ago. The island's famous for these mysterious stone towers called nuraghi, which are from the Bronze Age. That's what I was working on." Emilia leaned back on her hands and let out a wistful sigh. "I'd give anything to go back. When does the job start?"

"September fifth. I'd have a week to get there after Istanbul. But..."

"But what? Now that you're not tied to grad school, you don't have to go back to Boston. You could go anywhere."

She could. A gig in Sardinia would mean breathtaking beaches, delicious food, and new experiences. She'd get paid, brush up on her Italian, and eat her weight in pasta. If she accepted the offer, she could also delay finding a real job until after Thanksgiving. Saying yes should have been a no-brainer.

But it wasn't what she wanted.

"What's the issue?" Emilia asked.

Dusty looked down, unable to meet her friend's eyes. Why was it so hard for her to admit that she wanted a little stability in her life? "I...kind of want to go back to Boston."

"Because of Stuart?"

She nodded, her heart torn. In the past, she hadn't allowed anyone to tie her down. But Stuart wasn't just anyone. He was the guy she'd loved for years. "I want us to stay together. Like, be a couple and everything."

"Nothing wrong with that. If I met the right person, I could see doing the same thing."

"It's not just Stuart. Thanks to Mort, I have a shot at illustrating children's books. I'd also like to spend more time with my dad. Does that sound too boring?"

"Honestly? It sounds great. I'm sure Stuart would love it if you stayed in Boston."

Though he hadn't said as much, Dusty knew how his mind worked. Just last week, he'd mentioned Boston three times, suggesting things they could do together and restaurants he wanted to try. Sardinia might be an amazing adventure, but she'd been on amazing digs all over the world. For once, the thought of being with the man she loved, in a city that felt like home, was the most exciting option of all.

~

AT LUNCH, STUART LISTENED WITH THE OTHERS AS DUSTY SHARED the news of Leo's discovery. He didn't want to jump to conclusions, but he suspected the fragment was part of an incised tablet. The implications were so exciting that he wasn't even jealous the piece had come from the Germans' site.

For the rest of the meal, the crew discussed the topic at length until Dr. Hughes declared it to be "a worthless piece of junk" and left in a huff. But the conversation continued without him, even during the afternoon lab session, to the point where Stuart desperately hoped the Germans *would* unearth something substantial. Otherwise, everyone would feel let down.

After dinner, the crew hung out in the common room, playing poker. Ever since TJ had emerged victorious from their last tournament, Emilia had been determined to beat him. So, she'd suggested a rematch but with higher stakes. Rather than join them, Stuart sought out Dusty, who had retreated to the library. She sat at one of the tables, humming while she sketched. Beside her was a thick tome entitled *The Illustrated History of the Medieval World*.

Curious as to why she'd be researching that era, he pointed to the book. "What are you working on?"

She took out her earbuds and gave him her full attention. With a luminous smile, she held up a picture of two knights jousting on horseback. "Mort's friend loved my illustrations so much he asked to see a few more. This time, he wants examples for the medieval time-travel book, so I've been drawing knights and princesses."

As always, her talent blew him away. "That's great. Can I peek at the rest?"

"Sure. They're kind of rough. I've been so obsessed with the ancient world that I haven't quite captured the feel of the medieval era. But it's fun."

He leafed through sketches of knights, castles, kings, and princesses. The last drawing was a cartoon depicting the two of them sharing a bottle of wine over dinner, no doubt inspired by Operation Aphrodite. "You weren't going to send him this one, were you?"

"Nope. That's just for me."

"Considering how the evening turned out, it's very G-rated."

"I wasn't about to draw us having sex." She clasped her hands under her chin and flashed him a naughty smile. "Even though I've dreamed about it. A lot."

When she looked at him like that, he was helpless to resist her. "Want a break? Why don't you come outside with me?"

"I'd love to." She stood and cocked her hip. "Tell me, Professor Carlson, what will it take to free me from Hughes' trench? A few kisses? Or something more?"

He laughed. "You can offer all you want, but I'm not budging. I have to be fair."

"Fine. Be that way. But he's gotten even more unbearable. Today, he yelled at me for taking too long during one of my bathroom breaks, and he snapped at Clarissa for leaving early. He also treated Leo with total disrespect. I think it's awesome the Germans found that fragment, but all he said was that it looked like garbage."

"He was probably jealous. Only two weeks left, and we have yet to find his cemetery. He's running out of chances to reclaim his glory."

"I guess." Dusty followed him out of the library, shutting off the lights as she left. "Did I tell you I caught him harassing Mehmet?"

"When did this happen?" For once, Stuart wanted to experience a day when his boss behaved like a mature adult.

"Yesterday morning when we first arrived at the site. Em and I were walking past Wagner's trenches. The Germans weren't there yet, but Hughes was standing next to Mehmet, totally laying into him. I felt sorry for the poor guy."

"He was probably demanding access. What an asshole. Do you think I should say something to him about it?" After the success of Operation Strudel, Stuart had gained more confidence in asserting himself around Dr. Hughes.

"Probably not since he'll know I'm the one that told you. I don't need him hating me more than he already does. It's gotta be killing him that Clarissa and I can hang with Wagner's crew anytime we want, but he's not welcome." She grinned. "The power of strudel."

"Well, it was damn good strudel." Taking her hand, he led her outside to the picnic table under the olive trees.

Since they were alone, he had no qualms about pulling her onto his lap. After a full day of working together as colleagues, he relished the chance to drop the professional facade. She turned so she was straddling him and ran her fingers through his hair. Cradling his face in her hands, she pulled him closer and kissed him. Softly at first, then with more urgency, nipping at his bottom lip.

All the day's tension ebbed away as he gloried in the taste of her lips, the delicate flicker of her tongue against his. He could sit for hours like this, enjoying her delicious kisses. But when she ground into him and his body reacted accordingly, he pulled away with a reluctant groan.

"Dusty, no. I won't be able to walk back into the field house."

Laughing, she eased off his lap but kept her hand resting on his thigh. "Only two weeks left. Then once we leave Troy, I'm all yours. You're spending a few days in Istanbul, right?"

This was the perfect opportunity to share his surprise. "Yeah. I wanted to talk to you about that. I planned something for us there."

"What is it? Does it involve a huge bed? Because we need to make up for lost time."

"There might be a king bed involved..." He took out his phone, eager to show her pictures of the apartment he'd booked, but a gruff voice stopped him cold.

"Enjoying the evening?" Dr. Hughes strode past them on his way to the field house. Phone in hand, sweat dripping from his brow, he looked like he'd been out power walking while engaging in a late-night conversation.

Stuart flinched under the professor's scrutiny, feeling like a kid caught with his hand in the cookie jar. "Um...yeah. It's a pleasant night."

"Were you out for a walk?" Dusty asked.

Dr. Hughes stared at them for a beat before responding. "Yes. Out for some air. I wouldn't suggest staying up too late. We have a busy day tomorrow." With that, he turned and went into the field house.

An uneasy sensation skittered along Stuart's spine. Even if his boss hadn't reprimanded him, he was still aware he'd been caught behaving unprofessionally.

Dusty stood and smoothed down her clothing. "We should get

back inside. I feel kind of creepy thinking he might have been watching us."

Stuart agreed with her. He wanted to tell her more about Istanbul, but this wasn't the right time. Tomorrow night, he could share his secret, but he'd make sure Dr. Hughes wasn't around to spoil it.

# CHAPTER TWENTY-SEVEN

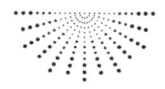

Dusty yawned, fighting off a wave of tiredness as she filled the coffeepot with water. For whatever reason, she'd woken up an hour early and couldn't drift back to sleep. If she didn't get some caffeine into her veins soon, she'd be a grumpy bitch all morning.

As she was retrieving a box of sugar cubes from the pantry, the door to the field house opened. She froze, watching in shock as Dr. Hughes dashed inside. He looked a mess—red-faced and sweaty, his shirt untucked and strands of gray hair plastered to his head. Over his shoulder was a faded green knapsack. The sight of him was so jarring she couldn't pull her eyes away.

"What's wrong?" he snapped. "Do you have a problem?"

"No. I just didn't expect to see you out this early. Are you all right?"

"I'm fine. Out for a walk, not that it's any of your business." Pushing past her, he marched down the hall toward his room and slammed the door shut.

Another walk? If last night wasn't odd enough, today was even more out of character. He never walked anywhere. The last time he'd taken a "morning constitutional" was when he'd gone with Mort to spy on the Germans.

What the hell had he been up to?

She set down the sugar cubes and crept over to the door. Opening it quietly, she slipped outside and ran to the garage. When she approached the nearest Land Rover and placed her hand on the hood, it was warm, the engine still ticking.

Her curiosity turned to irritation. If that asshole had tried to bully his way onto the Germans' dig site, then someone needed to rein him in. Not her, since she couldn't risk antagonizing him again, but she could mention it to Stuart or Kerim.

When she went back inside the field house, TJ was in the kitchen, hovering over the coffeepot. Pushing Dr. Hughes out of her mind, she laughed at her friend's eagerness. "Give it a minute. You know how slowly it brews."

"I know, but I need my morning go juice. I'm pumped to see what's going to happen today." He rubbed his hands together. "What if the Germans find an engraved tablet? It could be the oldest evidence of writing at Troy. What an incredible score."

"I know, right? It'd blow that Luwian seal right out of the water." Seeing that the coffeepot had filled up, she poured TJ a mug. "Here. I tried to make it a little less strong."

He took a sip, then grimaced. "Still extra bold, but I'm getting used to it."

She took a container of evaporated milk out of the pantry, opened it, and set it on the counter. "We have to be realistic, though. A tablet might not provide evidence that the Trojan War took place. It could be a set of administrative records or a list of items in storage."

"But what if the Trojans were stocking up their supplies for a lengthy siege?" TJ's voice rose. "That could indicate *some* kind of war took place. Or what if the tablet contains a treaty between the Trojan rulers and the Mycenaean Greeks? Or—hear me out—imagine if it's part of a royal archive?

Like a bunch of tablets? That would be a total game-changer."

A flare of excitement shot through her. Even if the Germans were the ones to make the discovery, their find would be a win for the entire site of Troy. Like TJ said, it could change history.

Still, she couldn't resist teasing him. "If the Germans find a tablet, there's no way any of us can top that. Which means neither you nor Em can claim victory in your challenge."

"Whatever. We've already let it go."

"Does that mean you're becoming friends?"

He scoffed. "Hardly. But I had fun teaming up with her to pull off Operation Aphrodite. She's gotten a little more bearable, but that's it."

~

ONCE ON THE SITE, DUSTY RESIGNED HERSELF TO ANOTHER DAY IN Dr. Hughes' trench. Though she was meant to be working with Clarissa, she'd been on her own for the past hour. Clarissa had left at nine, claiming she was desperate to snag a cappuccino at the café, but she still hadn't returned. No doubt she'd stopped by the Germans' site to flirt with Leo.

"Hey, there!" Clarissa hopped back into the trench. Her face was flushed, her blond hair coming loose from her ponytail.

"Hey, yourself. How's Leo?"

Clarissa's mouth turned down in a pout. "Not good. When they started digging this morning, Dr. Wagner thought looters might have tampered with the trench. Like they dug up something and tried to put the dirt back into place."

Looters or Dr. Hughes? From the odd way the professor had been acting, Dusty suspected he'd been the one to disturb the site. But how could he if it was guarded around the clock? "Did Mehmet and his brothers see anyone there last night?"

"No. According to them, no one came through the site after

hours. And the Germans got here at 5:00 a.m. because they wanted to start digging as early as possible."

A nasty chuckle made Dusty shiver. Dr. Hughes had made his way over to the edge of the trench, where he stood looking down at them. "If you ask me, Wagner's trying to cover his ass. I doubt anyone messed with his site. He's just ashamed he made a fuss about a piece of garbage."

Dusty's skin prickled, but she wouldn't give her boss the satisfaction of knowing how much his words annoyed her. "They could still find something. They've only been digging for a few hours."

"It's nothing but a fool's errand." He checked his watch. "Time for break. Not that you've earned it, working as slowly as you have. Especially you, Clarissa, gallivanting with the Germans as though you're on vacation."

Ignoring him, Dusty and Clarissa clambered out of the trench. But as Dusty waited in line to wash her hands, the prickling sensation continued. Where had Dr. Hughes been earlier this morning? Why had he been carrying a knapsack?

Deep in her bones, she knew he'd been up to something. She was tempted to pull Stuart aside and share her suspicions with him. But if she was wrong, she'd be putting him in an uncomfortable position. He wouldn't risk accusing Dr. Hughes unless he had definite proof.

But she couldn't let it go, either.

If she went back to the field house now, she could poke around while everyone else was still at the site. This way, she could make sure Dr. Hughes wasn't hiding anything. In a flash of inspiration, she clutched her stomach and let out a loud groan.

Clarissa turned toward her. "You okay?"

She shook her head. "I just got the worst pain. Like my insides are twisting in knots."

"Need some Midol? I have a bottle in my daypack."

"I...I don't think it's that." She let out another cry. "It could be something I ate. I don't know. I need to sit down."

She stumbled over to the shaded area and sat on one of the blankets. Closing her eyes, she put her head between her knees. In less than a minute, Stuart was by her side.

He crouched beside her. "Are you all right?"

She looked up at him with a pained grimace. "I don't know. I started feeling awful. Horrible stomach pains. But I can't think of what's causing them. I ate the same dinner last night as everyone else." She wiped her forehead. "I'm kind of light-headed, too."

"You should go back to the field house. Do you want me to drive you?"

His concern made her squirm with guilt, but she kept up the act. "You should stay here and supervise. Maybe Mort could drive me back."

"I'll check with him." He placed a gentle hand on her shoulder. "But if you go back, get some rest. I don't want to find you've spent the entire time working."

"I just want to lie down," she said. "Maybe sleep a little."

When Mort approached her, she pasted on a humble expression. "I'm so sorry, but do you mind driving me back?"

"It's fine." He held out his hand and pulled her up. "Being able to help makes me feel useful."

She passed by the rest of the group, who were setting out the food for the morning break. "Sorry, but I'm leaving early. I don't feel well."

Dr. Hughes frowned. "Female troubles, is it? I thought you were stronger than that."

His dismissive tone was clearly intended to bait her, but she replied calmly. "It's more like a stomach bug. I'm going back to the field house. I'll see all of you later."

She waited for him to challenge her. He said nothing, though his contemptuous expression spoke volumes. *Good.* If he regarded her as a weak, pathetic female, he wouldn't suspect her of trying to carry out another spy mission.

As she and Mort walked back to his car, she slowed her pace, occasionally clutching her stomach for good measure. Once they were driving back to the field house, she rested her head against the window, enjoying the powerful blast of cool air. After weeks of driving the Land Rover, a vehicle with air-conditioning was a true luxury.

Mort turned to her, his face etched with concern. "You can be honest with me, you know."

Had he guessed her true intentions? If so, her acting ability was worse than she thought. "What do you mean?"

"I mean, if it's menstrual cramps, you don't have to pretend it's a stomach bug. There's no shame in having your period. It's part of your natural cycle."

*Whoa.* That was not where she expected the conversation to go.

He continued. "I've been a single father since Clarissa was a baby. Even with nannies and housekeepers to help out, I still got a crash course in puberty when she turned twelve. She used to have such bad cramps that she'd miss school. A few times, I stayed home from work to keep her company." He gave a wistful sigh. "I wish I'd done it more often. I loved our time together. For what it's worth, she found chamomile tea to be helpful."

"Um...thanks. I'll see if we have any in the pantry." Dusty was tempted to tell Mort the truth since he'd probably jump at the chance to assist her on another covert operation. But she couldn't risk involving anyone else until she found more evidence.

"Do you want me to stay at the field house with you?" Mort asked.

"Thanks, but I'll be okay."

Though his concern was touching, she was relieved when he dropped her off and drove away. As soon as his car was out of sight, she bolted inside, ran to Dr. Hughes' room, and tried the door. Locked. Giving a huff of exasperation, she went to the kitchen to find the spare set of keys. Hadn't Stuart told her he kept them in one of the drawers?

But after opening every drawer, looking through the pantry, and poking around the cupboards, she came up short. Maybe Stuart had tucked them away in his room. She went into it, smiling at the neatly made bed and the orderly way he'd arranged his belongings. Seeing the bed filled her with a pang of longing. She wanted to spend the night with him again. To feel his arms around her, hold nothing back, and nestle in his embrace until they drifted off to sleep.

*Stop it. You need to focus.*

Shaking off her daydreams, she searched every inch of his tiny room. She checked the drawers in his nightstand, the inside of his wardrobe, the pockets of his suitcase. Nothing. Would he have taken the keys to the site? Doubtful, since he'd be at risk of losing them. They had to be somewhere in the field house.

*But where?*

She blew out a frustrated breath. Faking illness had been a bold move, but she'd done it for nothing. Since she was stranded at the field house until the others came back, she could work in the lab. But first, she had to change into something resembling pajamas. In case anyone else returned early, she needed to keep up the appearance of being sick. She went into her room and rooted through her pack, only to realize how few clean clothes she had left. A peek inside her stinky, overstuffed laundry bag made her reel in disgust.

She'd planned to do a load last weekend, but the washing machine had been in high demand. With the field house to herself, she could catch up on her laundry. After shucking off her hiking boots and changing into a comfy pair of shorts, she hauled her laundry bag over to the washing machine, which was set in an alcove by the back door.

She dumped her clothes into the machine, but as she was

scooping a cup of powdered detergent onto them, she recalled what Stuart had told her about the spare keys. Hadn't he said he wanted to put them somewhere Hughes wouldn't think to look?

Since he refused to do his own laundry, this was the last place he'd be snooping around.

Beside the washer was a wooden cabinet used for holding detergent and bleach. She opened one of the top drawers, only to find it filled with junk: screws, rubber bands, nails, paper clips, and random pens. But in the drawer beside it?

A full set of keys.

∼

DURING THE MORNING BREAK, STUART'S THOUGHTS KEPT TURNING to Dusty. In all the years he'd known her, she'd rarely been hampered by illness or cramps. Even when she was sick, she often powered through her discomfort and kept working.

Still, if she wasn't feeling well, at least she'd been sensible enough to take a break. Maybe she'd actually rest once she was back at the field house.

Setting his water bottle down, he turned to Clarissa, who sat beside him on the blanket. "Did Dusty seem off this morning? It's not like her to get sick."

She held up her hand, waiting to speak until she'd finished eating. Like Dusty, her favorite morning snack was peasant bread loaded with cheese and tomatoes. "Sorry about that. I didn't want to talk with my mouth full. She seemed fine, but I wasn't in the trench that much. I stopped by the Germans' site to visit Leo and spent longer there than I intended. Sorry."

"Don't apologize. You're here as a volunteer. Thanks to your strudel, our two teams aren't fighting anymore. How are things with Leo?" If nothing else, Stuart was glad Operation Strudel had brought her and Leo together. The two of them made an adorable couple.

She gave him a shy smile. "They're good. It's nothing serious, just a fun summer fling."

"That's the best kind."

"But you and Dusty want more than that, don't you?"

Her question caught him off guard, but he allowed himself to speak honestly. "I hope so. Since we'll both be in Boston this fall, I'd like us to stay together." He still hadn't talked to Dusty about it. Later today, when he went to check on her, he could bring it up or at least mention the place he'd rented for them in Istanbul.

A hand clapped him on the shoulder, startling him so much he choked on a tea biscuit. "Stuart. I need to talk to you." Dr. Hughes stood over him, his face contorted in agony.

Stuart coughed and cleared his throat, hoping the older man hadn't heard him talking about Dusty. "Are you all right?"

"No. My stomach's in knots, and my head's pounding. Normally, I'd keep working, but I don't want to risk getting worse. Given that Dusty had the same symptoms earlier, I suspect there's a bug going around."

*Shit.* Since everyone lived and worked together, an illness like this could knock out the whole crew. "Do you want a ride back to the field house? Kerim or I could drive you if you're not up for it."

"I can drive myself. I'll take the truck. That way, you'll have the two Land Rovers, plus Mort's car."

"Okay. I think Em can handle the other Land Rover."

"Good. I'll see you back at the field house this afternoon. Text me if anyone else gets sick. I'm hoping this bug won't spread."

"Will do. Hope you feel better soon."

As Stuart watched him walk away, he pressed his hand over his stomach. So far, he didn't feel ill. No pain, no dizziness, no other symptoms. Whatever had sidelined Dusty and Dr. Hughes, he hoped it wasn't too contagious.

# CHAPTER TWENTY-EIGHT

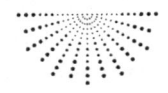

Leaving her clothes in the washing machine, Dusty ran to Dr. Hughes' room and unlocked his door. The room smelled as bad as she remembered, with dirty socks and balled-up underwear on the floor. After stuffing the spare keys in her pocket, she opened the doors to his wardrobe. There, behind the bottles of wine, brandy, and raki, was the faded green knapsack Dr. Hughes had been carrying that morning.

She grabbed a strap and hauled it up, surprised at the weight of it. Pushing aside the pile of rumpled bedclothes, she set the pack on the bed. She unzipped it and pulled out a heavy rectangular object wrapped in a towel. As she unfolded the towel, she fumbled and dropped the object on the bed.

With a small bounce, it landed faceup, revealing an inscribed tablet.

Her breath hitched, her heart galloping like a runaway horse. She couldn't imagine anything worse than dropping a three-thousand-year-old tablet and watching it shatter into pieces.

Placing a hand over her chest, she inhaled slowly, willing herself to calm down.

But it was hard to keep composed while staring at a piece of history.

The tablet was dark grayish brown, baked out of clay, about the size of a hardcover book. The top edge was jagged, as though a few pieces had broken off, but the rest was in perfect shape, other than a slight weathering around the edges.

Every inch of the tablet was covered in cuneiform script—a system of writing used during the Bronze Age. It consisted of small, wedge-shaped indentations created by a stylus, an ancient version of a pen usually made from reeds.

Over the years, Dusty had encountered plenty of awe-inspiring finds. She'd seen her parents uncover intact tombs, ancient mummies, and golden jewelry worth thousands. But this worn tablet filled her with a sense of awe she hadn't experienced in a long time.

She recalled one of her favorite lines from *Raiders of the Lost Ark*, a movie her parents loathed but which she secretly loved. When Indiana Jones had tried to blow up the Ark of the Covenant, his rival Belloq had dissuaded him by saying: "We are simply passing through history. But this, this *is* history."

This tablet *was* history.

If the inscriptions had been written in Greek or Latin, she might have been able to decipher them. But she'd never studied cuneiform. For all she knew, the writing on the tablet could be one of a dozen ancient languages, including Sumerian, Akkadian, Hittite, or Linear B. She didn't have the first clue where to start.

But she knew someone who did.

Not only was her father an expert in ancient languages, but he also loved a challenge.

She pushed aside the blankets until she'd cleared a space for the tablet on the bed. Using her phone, she took a series of photos, zooming in on the details. Not for the first time, she wished her father owned a smart phone so she could text him the pictures immediately. Instead, she'd have to send him an email.

Sitting on the edge of the bed, she pulled up the email app on her phone. After attaching all the photos, she fired off a quick message: *Any chance you can read this writing? I promise I'll explain later.*

She hit Send but knew better than to wait for an immediate response. Since it was only 3:00 a.m. in Boston, chances were good he wouldn't check his email for another four or five hours. Then she'd have time to tell him the whole story. For now, she needed to contact Stuart. She was just about to text him when a gruff voice shattered the silence.

"What do you think you're doing?" Dr. Hughes demanded.

She gasped and dropped the phone, sending it clattering across the floor.

Before she could grab it, he swooped in and snatched it up. He pressed his fingers on the screen, no doubt to stop it from locking up. "Were you texting Stuart? Showing him what you'd found?"

"N...no. I...didn't..." Though her heart was pounding furiously, she refused to let him intimidate her. "Give me my phone."

He scowled at it. "Not until I get rid of all these photos."

As he took his time deleting them, her jaw tightened, her fear giving way to irritation. Once he was done, he stuck her phone in his pocket and regarded her with a smirk. "There. That's better."

She could barely contain her rage. "Give it back. Now."

"You're not in any position to be giving orders. Not after that stunt you pulled at the site. I knew you weren't sick. Turns out my instincts were right. You're a sneaky little thief, breaking into my room like this."

Her furor grew, filling her with a rush of adrenaline. "Are you kidding me? You're the one who robbed an archaeological site. Planning to smuggle this out of the country? Because that worked out *so well* for you last time."

He scowled. "Wagner told you about my illustrious past, did he? I'm not surprised."

"So, you admit you did it?" She'd expected him to claim Dr. Wagner had been lying.

"An antiquities dealer in Istanbul talked me into it. Turned out to be the worst mistake of my life." For once, his voice wasn't boastful or authoritative but heavy with sorrow. "Wagner caught me. Then the Turks exiled me from Troy for ten years. Even though the university kept it quiet, they couldn't quell all the rumors. My academic reputation took an enormous hit."

Did he expect her to feel sorry for him? Not a chance. Her mother had been approached by dealers before. People who promised her a small fortune if she'd smuggle artifacts out of Egypt. But her professionalism and her moral compass were too important to her.

Still, Dusty was curious why he would have succumbed to the lure. "Why'd you do it? You're a tenured professor at a prestigious university. It's not like you needed the money."

He barked out a coarse laugh. "You'd think so, wouldn't you? But I'd just gone through a nasty divorce. My ex ran up enormous credit card bills, then had the gall to fleece me dry in the divorce settlement. I'd also made some terrible investments, thanks to a chum who had no business calling himself a broker."

Now he sounded more like the Dr. Hughes she knew—blaming everyone but himself.

She looked at the tablet again, trying to piece together his endgame. If he wasn't going to smuggle it out of Turkey, then why had he risked stealing it from the Germans? And how had he done it? "How'd you get it from Leo's trench?"

To her surprise, he pulled up the desk chair and sat across from her, like he was engaging in a friendly chat. He spoke with a touch of pride. "It's simple, really. I paid Mehmet and his brothers a hefty sum. Did you know their father has been out of work for months? It wasn't hard to bribe them into helping me. If anything, they were grateful for my benevolence."

The hell? "Did it ever occur to you that they could end up in jail?"

"That's not my problem. Anyway, when Leo mentioned the fragment yesterday, I suspected it might lead to something. Last night, after Troy closed to visitors, the boys started digging. They found two more fragments before they uncovered this tablet. Mehmet called me early this morning with the news. We couldn't do the handoff at the site because he'd heard the Germans were planning on getting there early. So he met me in Güzelyali. Tonight, after dinner, I'll go back there and set it in my trench. As long as no one else is around, it shouldn't be difficult to stage it properly. Then I can dig it up tomorrow morning, first thing."

Dusty couldn't speak, too stunned at the audacity of his scheme to form a coherent sentence.

He gave her another of those condescending smirks. "You have to admit it's a brilliant plan."

"It's not brilliant—it's criminal. You stole a valuable artifact so you could plant it in your own trench. Is this so you can have bragging rights at that symposium in Amsterdam?"

"It's more than that. For years, I was one of the foremost experts on the site of Troy. Now I'm all but forgotten, other than the ugly gossip that destroyed my reputation. A find like this could restore my good name."

Talk about a monstrous ego. "Don't you think Dr. Wagner will know you stole it? Leo's the one who found that fragment."

He snorted. "It's a *very* small fragment. Even if the Germans suspect foul play, they won't be able to prove anything."

Dusty got to her feet, too aggravated to sit still. "You can't take an artifact out of context. It'll mess up the provenance. That's one of the most basic rules of archaeology."

"Does it really matter? Even if our excavations are from two different parts of the site, they're from the same era. In the end, no one's going to care. They're just going to be astonished that *I* uncovered a tablet bearing the earliest example of writing ever discovered at Troy."

"But..." Did he not see how wrong this was?

He raised his eyebrows at her. "Let's be honest—you're only here as an illustrator. Do you actually care that much about Troy?"

"Stuart does. He's one of the most ethical guys I know. It doesn't matter what your justification is, he won't buy it." She could only imagine his horrified reaction.

Dr. Hughes shrugged. "Then I suggest you keep your mouth shut. This is my one shot at glory, and I'm not about to lose it."

She swallowed, her mouth dry as dust, as she imagined keeping a secret like this from Stuart.

*No.* It was wrong on so many levels.

If Dr. Hughes wouldn't be swayed by ethics, she had to convince him of the risks involved. "You're making a huge mistake. If you're caught, you could be banned from Troy. Not just for a few years but for life. Imagine what your colleagues would think of you then."

"I won't get caught." He stood to face her. "All you have to do is forget we had this conversation."

Her gut tightened. If she let him carry out his scheme, he'd probably get away with it. Even if the Germans suspected his find, even if they insisted on comparing his tablet to the fragment they'd found, they'd still have no proof that he'd taken the tablet from their site.

If she kept quiet, no one else would know what he'd done.

But she'd know. And if Stuart ever discovered the truth, he'd be appalled.

"No. I have to tell Stuart."

Dr. Hughes advanced toward her. "I didn't want to threaten you, but you haven't left me much choice."

She clenched her fists, hoping to hide the rush of fear surging through her. Even with her rudimentary knowledge of self-defense, he was easily a foot taller and a hundred pounds heavier than her. "Don't touch me, you bastard."

"I wouldn't dream of it. I know better than to touch a graduate student. But apparently, Stuart didn't get the memo."

A chill ran through her. "What are you talking about?"

He leaned in closer, giving off the rank aroma of stale sweat. "Were you aware the university's code of conduct forbids professors from engaging in sexual relations with their students?"

She backed away, only to bump up against the side of the bed. "I'm not one of Stuart's grad students."

"That's right, you're at Harvard. A legacy, if I'm not mistaken. Over the years, I'm sure your parents have been generous donors. How else could you have gotten in?" He gave a barbed laugh. "As much as I loathe your mother, I can't help but pity her. Having a daughter who's not cut out for academia must be a grave disappointment."

Two weeks ago, his words would have wounded her, tapping into her deepest insecurities. Not anymore. "For your information, I'm dropping out of grad school."

"That's even more pathetic. But you're a student *now*, and that's what matters. I'm assuming that Stuart, for all his spreadsheets and rules, didn't bother to read the updated code of conduct. The university amended it last year after a professor made the mistake of screwing a grad student who was working on his dig."

"You?" She wouldn't put anything past him.

"No. A colleague of mine had an affair with a student from Yale when they were excavating in Belize. Big mistake. After he broke things off, she accused him of sexual harassment. Since then, the rules were changed to prevent it from happening again. *All* students are off-limits, regardless of where they're from."

*Fuck.* Had Stuart known about this? When he'd first talked to her about the dig, he'd mentioned dealing with a mountain of paperwork. Since he'd been so busy packing up to move to Boston, she'd told him not to worry about it. For once in his life, he'd failed to read the small print, and his lapse had come back to bite him in the ass.

She tried to mask her anguish, but her voice came out wobbly. "Wh...what happened between me and Stuart was entirely consensual."

"Was it? I know the two of you stole a bottle of wine from my room. Who's to say he didn't get you drunk and take advantage?" He crossed his arms. "In six hours, Dr. Valeria Fiorelli, the chair of the Classics Department, will be in her office. She doesn't look kindly on issues of sexual harassment. I could call her then and report Stuart's infraction. Or…"

"Or what?"

"Or I could let it go."

Dusty clutched her stomach, fighting off a wave of nausea. It didn't matter that she'd been a willing partner. That she loved Stuart. This could destroy him.

*Shit.* Why hadn't they waited until Istanbul to have sex?

*Because you both wanted it. And you didn't know any better.*

Ignorance was no excuse. They'd still broken the rules and, in doing so, endangered Stuart's career.

"Are we done here?" Dr. Hughes said. "Because I'd like you to leave my room."

Without saying a word, she followed him out. He shut the door firmly behind them.

"For the time being, why not make yourself useful?" he said. "Get a little work done. Then, when the others come back, you can tell them you've recovered from your upset stomach."

She was about to retreat to the lab and take refuge in her drawings, but she stopped herself.

What was she doing? She couldn't let him get away with this.

And she couldn't lie to Stuart. The secret would eat away at her forever.

She took a deep breath, bracing herself for his wrath. "No. Do your worst, but I can't keep this quiet."

He stared her down, his face blotched with outrage, but she met his gaze and held firm. As he took a step toward her, her flight response kicked into gear. She dodged around him and sprinted for the front door. Wrenching it open, she raced to the truck, which he'd left parked on the gravel driveway. If she drove back to the site now, she could tell everyone what he'd done.

Her heart hammered as she tugged on the driver's-side door. Locked. Same with the front passenger door.

Letting out a groan of frustration, she glanced back at the field house. Since Dr. Hughes hadn't dashed out to stop her, he clearly held the upper hand. When she went back inside, he was leaning against the kitchen counter, bearing a smug expression.

He held up her passport. "While you were attempting your little getaway, I found this in your room on the nightstand. It would be a shame if you lost it, wouldn't it?"

"Give that back, you fucking criminal. And give me my phone."

"Not until I've put you on a bus to Istanbul."

"What?"

"You're fired, Miss Danforth. I'll give you half an hour to pack up your things, and then I'm driving you to the bus depot in Çanakkale."

"If you force me onto that bus, then I'll call Stuart the first chance I get. Kerim, too. Once they hear about that tablet, they'll come racing back here."

He let out a mean laugh. "You won't do that. You know why? Because if you report me, then Kerim and Stuart will have no choice but to tell Dr. Wagner. Then he'll report it to the Turkish authorities. Imagine the fallout. It could be the last time that anyone from the University of Boston ever sets foot at Troy again."

She swallowed. This wasn't just about Stuart. It was about all of them. Despite the weeks of work they'd put in, a scandal like this would taint their dig forever.

"While I'd rather avoid another hit on my reputation, I'm due for retirement," Dr. Hughes said. "I didn't want to go out like this, but at least I've had my day in the sun. That's not the case with Stuart. He's just starting his career. Do you think he wants this on his record? Can you imagine—a charge of sexual misconduct *and* a dig where artifact tampering took place? He'll be lucky if the university doesn't fire him outright."

Dusty let out a whimper, knowing he'd spoken the truth. If she revealed what Dr. Hughes had done, she'd bring everything crashing down.

"Now, stop wasting time," he said. "Get packing. While you're at it, leave a note for Stuart. Tell him I'm the reason you left because you couldn't deal with my toxic masculinity or some other bullshit. Make sure he understands you're not coming back."

She stood there, hands clenched, awash in frustration.

*You can't give in. You just can't.*

There had to be a solution. Some way to stop him without causing a tremendous scandal.

But she couldn't think of what it was.

For now, it was easier to let him believe he'd won. In a matter of minutes, she'd packed up her clothes, toiletries, drawing supplies, and laptop. Under Dr. Hughes' watchful eye, she dashed off a parting note to Stuart and left it in his room.

When she stopped by the library to gather up her notebook and sketch pad, she looked through the drawings she'd done yesterday. Mixed in with the knights and princesses was the cartoon of her and Stuart. The one he'd noticed last night, with the two of them drinking wine.

After checking over her shoulder to make sure she was alone, she drew a heart around the two characters and added the words "I love you" at the bottom. She left it under the pile of drawings, hoping Stuart would find it. Maybe it would ease the blow of the note she'd written. She'd just turned to leave when Dr. Hughes came in and ushered her out.

"Let's go," he said. "There's a bus leaving in an hour. I want to make sure you're on it."

# CHAPTER TWENTY-NINE

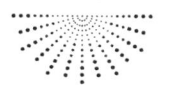

During the drive to the bus station, Dusty's mind worked frantically as she tried to figure out her next move. Right now, she was helpless. But as soon as she got on that bus, she'd have her phone. She still didn't know who to call or what to tell them, but at least she wouldn't be cut off. There had to be *someone* who could help her sort through this mess.

Once they arrived, Dr. Hughes bought her a ticket, asked the driver's assistant to load her giant backpack onto the bus, and escorted her to a seat in the back. Only then did he hand over her passport. She snatched it from him and held it tight.

"Now I want my phone," she said.

He smirked. "You can buy a new one in Istanbul. I'm sure your parents will foot the bill. But after that farewell note you wrote for Stuart, I can't have you backsliding and sending him a bunch of frantic texts."

"You asshole," she muttered. "You're a terrible excuse for an archaeologist. And for a human being."

Her words didn't appear to make a dent. He gave her a small wave as he exited the bus. "Goodbye, Dusty."

She wanted to go after him and raise a loud, angry ruckus, but all the fight had drained out of her. Whether due to sheer frustration or lack of food, her stomachache had grown worse. She hadn't thought to pack any snacks other than a bag of candied ginger. She took out a few pieces and popped them into her mouth.

As the bus pulled out of the station, she placed her head on the seat back in front of her.

She'd failed. Miserably.

Once again, she'd confronted Dr. Hughes only to have it end in disaster. Even if her intentions had been good—not just good but *ethical*, damn it—she'd fucked up everything. Now she was stuck on a bus, with no way to contact anyone. Their next stop was at least an hour away, and their route took them through farms and small villages in the middle of nowhere.

Maybe arguing with Dr. Hughes hadn't been the best move. If she'd played along with his scheme—acted like she was in on it—she wouldn't be trapped on this damn bus.

But even if she'd stayed at the field house, the bigger issue would still remain. The minute she told Stuart about the tablet, he'd insist on reporting the theft to Dr. Wagner. This time, the German dig director might not go easy on them. If he got the Turkish authorities involved, they might revoke the University of Boston's excavation permit again. Not just for ten years but forever.

Even if this entire debacle was Dr. Hughes' fault, Dusty would never forgive herself if Stuart and the others got kicked out of Troy.

She closed her eyes, trying to clear out the clutter in her mind.

*There has to be a solution.*

But right now, she had nothing.

～

Over the course of the day, Stuart had sent Dusty so many texts that his attempts to reach her had gone from thoughtful to pathetic. But she still hadn't responded. Maybe her illness was worse than he thought. At least no one else in the crew had complained of stomach pains.

Kerim approached him and placed a hand on his arm. "We're almost done here. Why don't you go on ahead and let me pack up the site? I know you're concerned about Dusty."

*Damn.* Was it that obvious?

Of course it was. "Sorry, but she usually doesn't ignore her phone. Thanks for letting me take off early."

He walked back to the Land Rover with Clarissa and Emilia, who were speculating about why the Germans still hadn't found a tablet. Just before the workday had ended, Leo had stopped by to visit. His team had found three more fragments but nothing else. In all, a disappointing day for everyone.

Upon pulling up to the field house, Stuart caught sight of the two local women setting out lunch. The delicious aroma of chicken kebabs made his mouth water. The women always served them with pearled couscous and a medley of roasted tomatoes, peppers, and eggplant. It was one of his favorite meals, but he was more concerned about Dusty than his growling stomach.

He poked his head into her room but didn't see her. Typical Dusty. Even if he'd asked her to take it easy, she'd probably grown restless. But she wasn't in the lab or the research library. A chill iced his spine as he circled back to her room. This time, when he opened the door, Emilia stood beside Dusty's bed.

"She's gone."

"What do you mean?" His voice came out as a strangled gasp.

"Her giant backpack's gone, and I don't see any of her clothes. Did she leave her drawing supplies behind?"

"I'll go look." Trying to tame his steadily growing apprehension, he raced back to the lab. Her illustration table was empty, her art supplies, measuring tools, and laptop all gone. In the library, she'd left nothing behind except a pile of sketches.

What the hell? She wouldn't have run off without telling him. Would she?

He bolted over to his room to see if she'd left a note. Propped up on his pillow was the baseball cap he'd given her on the first day. The navy blue one with the Trojan horse on it. Beside it was a note, written on a page torn from her sketch pad.

> Stu,
> I'm sorry to leave you like this. I planned to see this dig through to the end, but I couldn't do it. Like I said before, Hughes is too fucking toxic. When I was alone with him this morning, he insulted my mother, and we got into a huge argument. I don't apologize for what I said, but my actions were totally unprofessional. So, he fired me. Given how much trouble I've put you through, I thought it was time I left. I also think it's better if we put some distance between us. Hughes hates me so much that I've become a liability, and the last thing I want to do is mess up your teaching position at the University of Boston. I'm headed for Sardinia, where I got a job offer starting in a few weeks. Sorry for letting you down.
> Much love,
> Dusty.

He read it twice before the words sunk in. She'd left without warning, without the courtesy of a simple farewell text. Though her actions weren't out of character, he thought he'd meant more to her.

Had he been fooling himself this entire time?

He sat on his bed and put his head in his hands. Why hadn't she talked to him? If she couldn't bear to work with Dr. Hughes, she should have insisted on being removed from his trench.

*She asked you to do it last night. Remember?*

At the time, he'd assumed she was kidding around. He didn't think her animosity toward Dr. Hughes was powerful enough to merit this kind of reaction. But it must have been. Otherwise, she wouldn't have left so abruptly.

"Stuart?" Emilia stood over him. "Any news?"

He held out the note, then looked away, unable to watch Emilia's reaction as she read it. When she was done, she placed it on the bed beside him. He took a deep breath and forced himself to meet her eyes. "Did you know about Sardinia?"

"Yeah, but she learned about it *yesterday*. She also told me she wasn't going to take it. She wanted to go back to Boston so she could be with you."

"She did?" He allowed himself a small measure of hope.

Emilia nodded. "I think there's something she's not saying. Like what if..." She rubbed her bare arms, as though a chill had come over her. "What if this disagreement with Hughes wasn't about her mother? What if he did something to Dusty?"

Stuart's stomach twisted in knots. "He wouldn't. He can't stand her."

"But sexual violence is about hate, not physical attraction."

A white-hot rage blurred Stuart's vision. His heart pounded furiously. "If he did...I..."

"Hold on. We don't know anything yet. Go talk to him but do it calmly."

"Right. Okay." For all he knew, Dusty's argument with the director had been nothing more than a heated exchange of words. Maybe her fiery temper had finally pushed him over the edge.

He walked over to the professor's room, but when he tried the door, it wouldn't open. He knocked on it. "Dr. Hughes? I need to talk to you."

When no one answered, he pounded harder. He was thankful the others were already at lunch so that he didn't have an audience.

The door opened and Dr. Hughes faced him, cranky and rumpled, sporting dark bags under his eyes. "Do you mind? I'm quite ill, and I'm trying to sleep."

"What did you do to Dusty?"

"Nothing except making the unfortunate mistake of mentioning her mother. She yelled at me and called me a sexual predator. I've put up with a lot of nonsense from her, but that was the last straw. I had to let her go."

Stuart rubbed his hands over his face. "Why didn't you talk to me and Kerim first?"

"Because I'm the one in charge here. I gave Dusty plenty of chances, but this time, she went too far. Now it's done. I drove her to the station in Çanakkale and put her on a bus to Istanbul."

Stuart couldn't believe what he was hearing. "Sounds to me like you forced her to leave."

"It was a mutual agreement. She said she couldn't stand working around me. That I was a toxic male or some other millennial bullshit." Dr. Hughes backed away. "It's clear your emotions have affected your professionalism. I'll let it go this time. Don't let it happen again."

With that, he slammed the door. Stuart stood there, frustrated and heartbroken, craving answers but coming up empty. Bringing out his phone, he texted Dusty again. *I don't know what happened with Hughes, but please tell me you're okay. I'm worried about you.*

He stared at his phone, waiting for a reply, but none materialized. Rather than join the others at lunch, he returned to the library, where Dusty had left her sketches. He shuffled through the medieval ones until he came to the drawing at the bottom of the pile—the one that depicted them drinking wine together. He picked it up, intending to keep it. No matter how much Dusty had hurt him by leaving, he wanted a tangible reminder of their night together.

But the drawing had changed. She'd added a heart around the two characters and the words "I love you."

This was new. It had to be. If he'd seen these three words last night—words that were clearly meant for him—he wouldn't have forgotten them. And he would have told her he felt the same way.

As he folded up the drawing and put it in his pocket, his mind traveled back to his last conversation with her. When he'd lured her outside to share a few kisses, she'd been as passionate as ever. She was the one who'd brought up Istanbul, saying they needed to make up for lost time.

Those weren't the actions of a woman intent on ghosting him.

Heart pounding, he worked his way through the day's events. The Germans claiming someone had tampered with their site. Dusty leaving abruptly with an illness. Dr. Hughes following her shortly thereafter, then kicking her off the dig.

Had she discovered something about him? Something so awful that he had to get rid of her?

Stuart needed answers. But this time, he wasn't going to knock. All he needed was the key to Dr. Hughes' room.

He walked over to the alcove that housed the washing machine. Beside it was the cabinet where he'd stashed the spare keys. The top drawer was open, but the keys weren't in it. Someone must have grabbed them. Dr. Hughes? Dusty?

Either way, he was too late.

He glanced around the alcove, still hoping to spot the keys. To his surprise, the washing machine was open, loaded with a mound of clothes covered in a layer of powdered detergent. Looking down at his feet, he caught sight of Dusty's familiar laundry bag, the one she'd embellished with a drawing of a cartoon skunk. He reached into the washing machine and pulled out one of her favorite shirts—a faded blue tee bearing a picture of the Muppets.

Why had she left her clothes in the washing machine? Even if she'd been furious at Dr. Hughes, she wouldn't have dashed off without taking all her stuff.

Stuart marched over to his boss's room and banged on the door. "Open up!"

When Dr. Hughes opened it, his face was red, his voice thick with rage. "I already fired one member of the team today. Don't make me do it again."

"I know you're not telling me the whole story. What are you hiding in there?" He tried to push past Dr. Hughes, but the older man shoved him away.

"My room is off-limits. Understand? I'm not hiding anything. I realize you're hurt because your girlfriend left, but for God's sake, be a man about it."

Stuart wanted to shake some sense into him, but he controlled the impulse. Violence solved nothing and could get him fired. He forced himself to speak humbly. "Please tell me what happened. I'm worried about her."

"There's nothing to tell. She's gone."

"Then I'm going after her." Saying it infused Stuart with a powerful surge of energy. Why was he wasting time seeking answers from this asshole? The only person who knew the truth was Dusty. He had to find her.

"Good luck with that," Dr. Hughes said. "She's probably halfway to Istanbul."

As if that would stop him? "It's only five hours away. If I leave now, I can be there by eight."

"Are you mad? It's a city of fifteen million people. And you don't know where she is, do you? I'm guessing she's not answering your texts." His boss gave a smug smile, as if to assert his superiority.

Stuart didn't bother to answer. Instead, he was trying to figure out what Dusty would do once she arrived in Istanbul. Thanks to her parents' connections, she knew people who worked at the American Research Institute in Turkey. She'd probably see if they had a spare room available.

"I'm leaving. If all goes well, I should be back by tomorrow morning." He kept his voice firm, as though his decision wasn't up for debate.

Dr. Hughes frowned. "I'd think twice about that. If you leave, I'm going to report you to Dr. Fiorelli. I'll tell her you abandoned your post—and your responsibilities—to go after your wayward girlfriend. The same girl who insulted me and threatened me with violence. Your actions are hardly becoming of an assistant dig director. Or a professor."

Stuart's shoulders tightened. Every time he thought his boss couldn't stoop any lower, the man proved him wrong. "Are you threatening me?"

"Consider it a warning. I can't condone such unprofessional behavior."

Stuart swallowed, not wanting to imagine Dr. Fiorelli's response. She'd asked him to keep the dig on track, but he was allowing his feelings for Dusty to derail everything. But for the first time in his life, he couldn't do the prudent thing. Not if it meant losing the woman he loved. He'd have to take the risk and live with the consequences.

Without responding, he turned and left. Dr. Hughes shouted something after him, but he ignored it.

Grabbing his messenger bag from his room, he went to the kitchen and loaded it with supplies for the drive: a water bottle, a can of Coke, an apple, and a package of Ülker sesame stick crackers. On his way to the Land Rover, he stopped by the picnic table, where the others were in the midst of their midday meal.

He stood for a moment, hesitating over how much to reveal. Should he tell them Dusty had gone missing? Insinuate that Dr. Hughes was involved—not just in Dusty's departure, but in something more nefarious? Though he was loath to make any accusations, he wanted them to understand the serious nature of the situation.

Clapping his hands together, he called them to attention. "Sorry to leave you in the lurch, but Dusty's gone, and I'm going to bring her back."

"Is she okay?" Clarissa asked.

Mort banged his fist on the table. "It's foul play, isn't it? Is that wretched Dr. Hughes involved?"

"I think so," Stuart said. "I'm still not sure, but I'll know more once I talk to Dusty. In the meantime, don't let Dr. Hughes leave the field house."

"Stuart." Kerim's expression was grim. "What's going on?"

"I don't know yet. But I need to find Dusty. I'm worried about her."

"Are you sure you want to do this?"

"I'm sure. And I'm also sure Hughes needs to be watched. Trust me on this, okay?" His spine stiffened as he waited for Kerim's response.

To his relief, Kerim nodded. "All right, my friend. Go after her."

# CHAPTER THIRTY

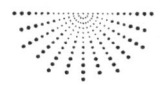

After an hour and a half on the road, Dusty's bus made its first stop at the station in Teskidag. She stood and stretched, grateful for a chance to grab something to eat. She'd spent the entire time battling a painful stomachache. Between her hunger pangs and her guilty conscience, she'd wallowed in misery, unable to do anything but agonize over her next move.

It killed her that Dr. Hughes still had her phone. By now, Stuart must have tried reaching out to her. She could only imagine his frustration when she didn't respond.

But now that she was at the bus station, she could take action. Even without a phone, she could use the station's Wi-Fi to contact someone. But who? And how could she report Dr. Hughes' crime without putting the whole dig in jeopardy?

Slinging her messenger bag over her shoulder, she hustled into the brightly lit bus station. It contained the usual amenities—restrooms, a mini-mart selling snacks, a cafeteria-style restaurant, and a large seating area with tables and benches. Rather than wait in line at the sketchy-looking cafeteria, she dashed into the mini-mart and bought a soda, a package of hazelnut cream cookies, and a bag of cashews.

Settling herself at an empty table, she scarfed down two cookies and drank half the soda. As the sugar rushed through her system, she perked up a little. Any minute now, a solution would come to her.

Next to her table, a faded sign on the wall displayed the station's Wi-Fi password. She turned on her laptop and logged in, racking her brain over whom to contact. But the first thing that popped up on her screen was a notification that she'd missed a Skype call from her dad. Not one call but three of them.

What was going on?

Being the old-school academic that he was, her father had never installed Zoom on his computer. Instead, he used Skype to communicate with everyone overseas—his friends, his colleagues, and his family. If he'd tried contacting her three times, something dire must have happened. Dusty popped in her earbuds and clicked on the Skype icon, waiting as the familiar tone rang out.

Her father's face appeared right away. He looked slightly flustered, his hair sleep-mussed, his glasses askew. "Dusty? Is that you?"

"It's me, Dad." She could barely control the hitch in her voice at seeing him. "Are you okay? I didn't wake you, did I?"

"No, no. Of course not. I was up when you sent your first message. Working through a tricky bit of translation on an inscription your mother found last year in Luxor. And then—when I saw those photos in your email—I couldn't sleep. I tried contacting you, but you didn't respond. I was getting worried."

"I'm here. Sorry to keep you up all night."

He gave her an indulgent smile. "You never have to apologize for that. You know how much I love a good mystery. But where did this come from?"

She sighed. "It's a long story. And I don't have much time." She still hadn't figured out what to do. Then again, if anyone could help her sort out this mess, it might be her dad. "But maybe you can help."

"I'll do my best. Because if this tablet is from Troy, it's a very significant find. Groundbreaking, in fact." His brow furrowed. "You aren't in possession of it illegally, are you?"

"No, but..." She glanced across the cafeteria. Over at a far table, the bus driver and his assistant were enjoying a hearty meal. If her experiences served her correctly, they'd take fifteen or twenty minutes to eat before returning to the bus. "I'm going to give you the abridged version, okay?"

She raced through her explanation but emphasized Dr. Hughes' threats, so that her dad wouldn't feel like she'd left without putting up a fight. Even so, she sensed his disappointment when she was done.

"Dusty, I know he put you in a terrible position, but you can't leave."

"What about the dig? And Stuart?"

"Stuart will be fine. If it's an issue of his character, your mother and I can testify on his behalf. Our names still carry some weight in the field."

At Harvard, sure. Or in Egypt? Definitely. But at the University of Boston, not so much. "I don't think that will be enough."

"Think of how many important people Stuart has worked with. His reputation is impeccable. Or rather, it was until he fell in love with you." He favored her with a wry smile. "I'm not surprised the two of you ended up together. I always hoped it would happen."

A flush of heat flooded her cheeks. As awkward as it was to talk to her dad about her love life, she was glad he approved. "Me, too. I really love him."

"That's why you can't leave him this way. You need to go back and make things right."

"But there's so much at stake. We could all get kicked out of Troy."

"You might. But if I know Stuart, he'd want you to tell the truth. Maybe if you're lucky, the blame will fall solely on Dr. Hughes, and the rest of you will be spared. Either way, you'll be able to sleep at night knowing you made the right call. That's what your mother would do."

His words resonated with her. Over the years, her mom had dealt with a few sticky situations in the field, but she'd never backed down or compromised her ethics.

*And I won't, either.*

Dusty caught sight of the bus driver and his assistant leaving their table. They were heading outside, which meant she had a decision to make. Keep going, keep her head down, and keep Stuart out of trouble. Or go back, make trouble, and live with the consequences.

The decision was obvious. She hadn't gotten a reputation as a troublemaker for nothing. "All right. I'm going back. Thanks, Dad."

"My pleasure."

"Before I go, can you call Stuart for me? He must be worried sick. I know you don't have a cell phone, but—"

"My landline works just fine. I'll tell him he can find you at the station in Çanakkale."

"Thank you." Relief flooded through her. "Maybe don't mention this to Mom, either. She already hates Hughes enough as it is."

"I think that's the right call. Otherwise, she might fly over there and drop-kick that bastard into the nearest trench."

As she envisioned the scene, Dusty couldn't help but laugh. "I'd like to avoid that, if possible. I should go, but I have to ask—have you had any luck translating the tablet?"

He chuckled. "This isn't a minor task by any means. It's a

version of cuneiform I'm not familiar with. But trust me, I'll figure it out. I'll email you as soon as I know more."

"Thanks. Love you, Dad."

"Love you, too, kiddo."

She shut down her laptop and raced toward the bus. In rapid, halting Turkish, she told the driver that she had a family emergency and needed to get her luggage. Though the assistant grumbled at the inconvenience, he helped unload her backpack. Then the bus rumbled back to life and pulled out of the station, leaving her behind.

She was tempted to go back inside and email Stuart and Kerim. By now, they'd be at the field house and might check their messages. But as she was turning to leave, a gleaming coach bus pulled into the closest bay.

Among the list of stops posted on the window was Çanakkale.

∼

Stuart had been on the road for twenty minutes when his phone buzzed. He jolted, his pulse racing in anticipation, as he reached for it. *Please let it be Dusty.*

No luck. Instead, the caller ID displayed a number he didn't recognize. He answered the phone and set it on the console of the Land Rover. "Yes? Hello?"

"Stuart? This is Roger Danforth."

A rush of fear gripped Stuart's heart, making it beat in double time. If Dusty's father was calling him, something horrible must have happened to her. He tightened his grip on the wheel. "Is Dusty okay?"

"I just talked to her. She's fine. It's a long story, so I'll let her explain when she sees you. Are you at the field house?"

"No, I'm driving to Istanbul. I should be there in about four or five hours, depending on traffic. Did Dusty tell you where she'll be staying tonight?"

"No need to drive all that way. She's heading back to Çanakkale on the next bus. I'm not sure when she'll arrive, but you need to go to the station and wait for her there."

Stuart's shoulders loosened in relief. He no longer cared she had run off without warning. Her safety and well-being were the only things that mattered. "Thank you so much."

"You're welcome. Best of luck."

Stuart signed off and watched for the exit leading to the bus station. After parking the Land Rover in the lot, he checked his messages. Still nothing from Dusty, which seemed odd, considering she'd just spoken to her father.

No one else had texted him except Dr. Hughes, who'd sent five messages, each more threatening than the last. Stuart read them with a sense of foreboding, fully aware he might have sabotaged everything—his position at Troy, his teaching job, and his reputation—just to go after the woman he loved. But in his heart, he knew he was doing the right thing.

He hustled over to the station, checking out the coach buses in their bays. Buses headed to Bursa, Diyarbakir, and Kuşadaci. Families carrying oversized bags, drivers taking a smoke break, a vendor hawking tea and coffee. Chances were good he'd have to wait a while, but in the meantime, he could text Kerim and the others to let them know Dusty was all right.

When a new coach bus pulled in a while later, he stood up, his breath tightening. The bus door opened, and the passengers filed out. Among them was Dusty.

He let out a yelp and ran toward her. She collided into his arms, hugging him so tightly he almost fell over. He buried his face in her hair, inhaling the faint scent of her rosemary shampoo.

When she looked up at him, her eyes were damp. "You came after me."

"You came back."

"I couldn't leave. I just couldn't." She wiped her eyes. "I'm so sorry."

"It's okay. But this rescue mission would have been easier if you'd answered your phone."

She gave a sad shake of her head. "Hughes took it from me."

"What? What the hell was he thinking?"

"Let's get my bag. Then I'll tell you everything."

Letting out a growl of frustration, Stuart grabbed her backpack from the bus, carried it over to the Land Rover, and stashed it in the back. She got in beside him and placed her hand over his. "Don't be upset. I'm just glad you're here."

"Sorry, but I'm so pissed at Hughes. I can't believe he did this to you."

"I'll be okay." She retrieved her laptop from her messenger bag. "Before we head back, I have to show you something. Do you have your phone? I need to use it as a hotspot."

"Sure." He brought it out and waited for her to make the connection.

She angled the laptop so that the screen was facing him. "This is the email I sent my father. Look at the attachments."

At first, he could barely comprehend what he was seeing. Ten photos of a worn clay tablet, inscribed with cuneiform markings, resting on a white bedsheet. "Where did this tablet come from? I don't understand."

"You will once I explain. But you have to let me tell the whole story."

He listened, his emotions wavering between shock and fury, as Dusty filled him in on the morning's events. When she recounted her confrontation with Dr. Hughes, he clenched his fists, barely able to keep his rage in check.

She tugged on his arm. "Please don't be mad at me."

"I'm not mad at you. Not in the slightest. I can't believe Hughes had the balls to steal that tablet and think he could place it in his own trench."

"I wanted to tell you about it. Even after he threatened me, I insisted on it. But he took my passport and strong-armed me onto that bus."

"Did...did he hurt you? Physically, I mean?" Stuart's breath caught as he waited for her to answer, afraid of what Dr. Hughes might have done to her. But when she shook her head, a little of the tension ebbed from his body. "I'm so sorry he forced you to leave. But...were you going to tell me once you had a way to call me? When you were in Istanbul?"

She bowed her head. "I don't know. I was worried if I said anything that I'd put the whole dig in jeopardy. Not only that, but if you confronted Hughes, he'd report you for sexual misconduct. I didn't want to ruin your career."

"Oh, Dusty." He pulled her closer until her head was resting on his shoulder. "I'm sorry I didn't know about the new code of conduct when we spent the night together. But I still don't regret anything we did. I love you, and I want you in my life, no matter what it costs me."

She sniffed and rubbed her eyes. "I've waited for years to hear you say that. I love you, too. It was so hard to leave you."

Her declaration filled him with a rush of happiness that eclipsed his earlier doubts. He took her sketch out of his pocket and unfolded it. "Thanks for the drawing. Once I saw it, I knew you didn't leave by choice."

"Trust me, I didn't want to."

"What about Sardinia? Were you actually going to take a job there?" Maybe he was pushing her a little too hard, but he didn't want any more secrets between them.

"No, but Hughes wanted me to hurt you. He insisted I act like I was making a clean break. But I hadn't planned on going to Sardinia. I wanted to come back to Boston with you so that we could be together. Like, together-together. You know?"

Now that he knew her feelings matched his, he had no qualms

about speaking honestly. "I do. That's what I wanted, too. I even booked a romantic getaway for us in Istanbul."

"You did?" She placed her hand over her heart. "That's so sweet. When were you going to tell me about it?"

"I almost told you last night until Hughes ruined the moment. I booked the place where Olivia and Rick stayed when they were in Istanbul last fall."

"I love that idea. Olivia said it was so romantic." She tugged him toward her until their lips met.

He kissed her passionately, tangling his hands through her hair and tasting ginger on her tongue. More than ever, he was glad he'd gone after her. A love like this was worth fighting for.

But he had to keep them both on task. With great reluctance, he pulled away. "We need to head back to the field house and deal with Hughes. It's gonna get ugly."

"I know. And I'm worried the Turks will exile all of us from Troy. But when I Skyped with my dad at the bus station, he told me to go back and fight."

"That's the Dusty I know and love." Whatever happened, he could deal with it now that she was at his side. "I couldn't do this without you."

She flashed him a cheeky grin. "Damn right. Now, let's go kick some ass."

# CHAPTER THIRTY-ONE

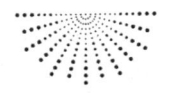

During the drive, Dusty wavered between giddy happiness at being back with Stuart and sick dread at the thought of him losing his job. Or, worse yet, of the Turkish Ministry of Culture ordering all of them to leave Troy in disgrace. But she was glad she hadn't let Dr. Hughes drive her away. If Stuart wanted her at his side, then that was where she'd stay, regardless of the consequences.

When they pulled onto the gravel driveway, Stuart killed the engine and took a deep breath. "No matter what happens to me, I love you. Okay? I can handle it."

She gave his hand a quick squeeze. "I love you, too."

Upon entering the field house, they stopped short. The entire team, including Mort and Kerim, had gathered in the common room. A few sat on the couch while the others sprawled on the floor. They were still grubby from the day's work at the site, as though they hadn't wanted to waste time showering. Instead, they'd banded together to watch over Dr. Hughes, who occupied an armchair with a peevish expression on his face.

Emilia leaped up to greet them. "Stuart! You found her!"

"Thank God," Clarissa said. "We were so worried."

"Not me," Mort added. "I knew you wouldn't fail. That's the power of love."

TJ stood and placed his hands on the back of Dr. Hughes' chair. "Our esteemed professor tried to leave, but we wouldn't let him. I told him we'd tie him up if need be, but it didn't come to that."

Dusty cringed. "That's probably for the best."

"You realize you're all sabotaging your academic futures?" Dr. Hughes blustered. "This isn't going to end well for any of you."

Kerim approached Stuart and Dusty, his brow furrowed with concern. "Could you please explain what's going on?"

Dr. Hughes glared at Dusty. "Before you open your mouth, I want to remind you what will happen if you keep going. Not only will you jeopardize our entire season at Troy, but you'll tank your boyfriend's career. Stuart's already in deep trouble for leaving his post to go after you. Don't make me report him for sexual misconduct."

She shot a nervous glance at Stuart, but he crossed his arms and scowled at Dr. Hughes. "Do your worst."

"I don't think you realize how much damage I can do to your reputation," Dr. Hughes said. "You're a new hire with everything to lose. I could make your life hell. There are few things more powerful than a tenured professor."

Dusty wanted to smack the smug look right off his face. She wished he didn't have the clout to ruin Stuart's career. But she'd spent her life around academics. She knew how ruthless and competitive the system was and how tenure could give unfavorable types like Dr. Hughes too much power. Right now, he held the cards to Stuart's future and had no qualms about exploiting that imbalance.

Stuart placed his hand on her shoulder. "Go on, Dusty. Don't let him intimidate you."

Before she could speak, Mort stood and cleared his throat. "If I might interject?" He turned to Dr. Hughes. "Do you know the only thing more powerful in academia than a tenured professor? An exceptionally wealthy alumnus."

"Sit down, you useless idiot," Dr. Hughes sputtered. "No one wants you here, taking up space and boring us with your endless stories."

Mort's face fell, but Dusty was quick to respond. "That's not true! We all like Mort."

"Of course," Emilia said. "He's been wonderful."

"Yeah, he's the best," TJ added. "His stories rock."

Mort chuckled. "While I'll admit I've spent more time sitting outside at the café than in the trenches, I've enjoyed being a part of your dig. I'm grateful you've let an old man live out one of his dreams. But this recent turn of events has made me question my next donation to the University of Boston. At the end of the year, I usually dole out a hefty sum to various causes. Clarissa was trying to convince me to give it all to the animal shelter where she volunteers rather than donate anything to the university's archaeology museum."

"I didn't say *all* of it," Clarissa added. "But the shelter could use more money."

"Right. So…" Mort drew out the words. "Imagine if I were to call the dean of Humanities—whom I golf with regularly—and tell him I'm considering leaving the museum off my list because of the unprofessional behavior I witnessed. To be clear, I'm referring to Dr. Hughes' behavior, not Stuart's."

Dusty stared at him in awe. "You'd do that?"

"Without question. Stuart doesn't deserve to have his reputation tarnished. If anyone should be called out, it's Dr. Hughes." Mort pulled a small notebook out of his shirt pocket. Dusty had seen him writing in it on numerous occasions. "When it comes to sexual misconduct, he's the worst offender here."

"What are you talking about?" Dr. Hughes demanded. "I haven't laid a finger on any of the female students."

"True," Mort replied. "But I've noted every indecent,

lascivious comment you've made about them, including lewd remarks about my daughter. In English *and* in Turkish."

"You don't speak Turkish," Dr. Hughes said.

"Hayat does." Mort graced her with an approving smile. "She made sure I didn't miss anything." He turned his attention back to Dr. Hughes. "At best, your remarks were crude and insulting. At worst, they're evidence of your predatory nature."

Dusty couldn't hold back her grin. She wanted so badly to give Mort a hug.

Clarissa scowled at Dr. Hughes. "You're despicable. You mess with Stuart or Dusty, and my dad will *bury* you."

Seeing sweet, lovable Clarissa go into attack dog mode stunned all of them into silence.

Clearly, her words affected Dr. Hughes just as powerfully because he gave a full-body shudder. "Enough. You win."

Stuart held out his hand. "We'll need the keys to your room. Otherwise, I'll have Dusty pick the lock."

TJ perked up. "We're allowed to pick the lock? Can I try?"

"Hang on. I can open it." With a laugh, Dusty pulled the spare set of keys from her pocket. She gave Stuart a sheepish grin. "Sorry. I used them to open Hughes' room earlier but forgot I still had them with me."

Before Stuart could chastise her for taking off with the keys, she dashed over to the professor's room and unlocked his door. The tablet wasn't on his bed, but she found the familiar green knapsack in the wardrobe. She brought it out, laid it on the coffee table next to the couch, and opened it. Inside was the tablet, wrapped in a towel. She slid it out and unwrapped it carefully. Once she revealed the tablet, the entire crew stared at it in silence.

"Holy fuck," Emilia said. "Is that...cuneiform?"

"Linear B?" TJ asked. "Akkadian? Elamite? Hittite?"

"That's not the issue," Dusty said. "The point is, it came from Leo's trench. After the Germans left the site yesterday, Dr.

Hughes paid Mehmet and his brothers to keep digging there. Once they found the tablet, they brought it to Hughes. He was going to sneak it into his own trench later tonight and miraculously 'uncover' it tomorrow morning."

"Bro, are you serious?" TJ said to him. "Ever heard of provenance?"

"Oh, shut up," Dr. Hughes muttered.

Kerim cursed under his breath. "This is terrible. If the Germans press charges, the University of Boston could lose their excavation permit again. Not just for this season but for the foreseeable future."

"That's what I was afraid of," Dusty said. "Dr. Hughes told me if I reported him, then we'd all suffer. I didn't know what to do."

Kerim placed his hand on her shoulder. "You made the right call."

"No, she didn't," Dr. Hughes said. When the others stared at him in horror, his bluster vanished, replaced by a pitiful expression. "Why can't we keep this quiet? What harm will it do if you let me uncover it tomorrow? This way, we'll all get to avoid a huge scandal and share in the glory."

The pathetic look on his face was painful to witness. If he hadn't just put Dusty through hell and threatened the man she loved, she might feel sorry for him.

"Absolutely not," Kerim said. "Dr. Wagner needs to be alerted. Then we'll deal with the consequences."

TJ punched his fist into his palm. "This sucks. We've worked so hard this season."

Dusty fought back a fresh wave of guilt. "I'm sorry. I didn't want it to end this way."

"Trust me, no one's blaming you," TJ said.

"The only one we blame is that asshole over there," Emilia pointed to Dr. Hughes, "who put himself above the law."

The others nodded, and TJ muttered, "Fucking treasure hunter."

As the group sunk into despair, the only one who appeared undaunted was Clarissa. "Maybe Dr. Wagner will go easy on us. Let me call Leo and see if we can work something out. That way, no one has to get kicked out of Troy."

"You think Leo has that much pull with Dr. Wagner?" Stuart asked.

"Of course he does. He's Wagner's oldest son." Clarissa grinned. "He just keeps it quiet so that no one will accuse his dad of nepotism. I'll call him and see what I can do."

While Clarissa went to make the call, Dusty relayed the entire turn of events to the crew. By the end of her story, she was glad she'd had the courage to come back. And even more glad that Mort had stepped up to help them. If Clarissa could work her magic with Dr. Wagner and his son, then the Jones family would have single-handedly saved their asses.

She cast Mort a warm smile. "I owe you, big-time."

"Think nothing of it," he said. "I was happy to help."

"Is there anything I can do for you?" When he shook his head, she pressed on. "Don't forget, I've got serious pull with Dr. Louisa Danforth."

Mort brightened. "Well, now that you mention it, there is something I might want…"

~

AN HOUR LATER, DR. WAGNER, LEO, AND THREE MEMBERS OF THE German team showed up at the field house. At the sight of the tablet, Dr. Wagner exploded in anger and accused them of betraying his trust. After Leo and Clarissa begged him to listen, Dusty walked him through the entire story. By the end, he was still seething over Dr. Hughes' treachery, but he'd calmed down enough to realize the rest of them weren't at fault.

He gazed at the tablet. "We'll never have the exact context. It's a shame."

"I know," Dusty said. "But if you talk to Mehmet and his brothers, they can show you where they found it, more or less. Now you can record it as coming from the mound near the Temple of Athena rather than from a trench in the lower city. You'll also know where to keep looking in case there are more tablets in the same area."

"True. We found three more fragments this afternoon. Maybe we'll get lucky."

"With that in mind, is there any way you can keep this quiet?" Stuart asked. "If you feel the need to report the incident to the Turkish government, I'll understand. Rules are rules. But we'd like to keep working here. And come back next year, preferably as part of a joint excavation with your university."

Dusty tensed as she waited for Dr. Wagner's response. After everything they'd been through, she didn't want Stuart or anyone else punished on account of Dr. Hughes' greed.

Dr. Wagner gave a slow nod. "I see no reason to get the government involved. I'd also like it if our two teams could collaborate, as we once did. But I have a few conditions."

"Name them," Kerim said. "We'll do our best to accommodate you."

"First, Dr. Hughes must be removed from the dig. He's not to set foot at Troy ever again. Second, he should not speak on behalf of your university at the Amsterdam symposium."

Dr. Hughes bristled with anger. "That's completely unreasonable."

"If word gets out about what you did, people aren't going to forget it," Kerim said. "Is that what you want? To be known as a trench robber? You'll be the laughingstock of academia."

He lowered his head. "Fine. I'll concede."

"We'll need to send someone to Amsterdam," Stuart said. "The university wants a presence there."

"Then I suggest you go," Dr. Wagner said. "Take Miss Danforth with you."

Dusty grinned. Amsterdam? With Stuart? *Hell, yes.* Maybe by then, her dad would have translated the tablet, and they could share its contents with the scholarly community.

"All this fuss because I moved a tablet," Dr. Hughes said. "It's ridiculous."

"It's not just because you moved the tablet," Kerim said. "You bribed three young men into looting a site and risking arrest, you stole Dusty's phone and her passport, kicked her off the dig, and threatened Stuart's job. Not to mention the lewd comments you've made about the women on the crew. These are not the actions of a professional."

Dr. Hughes stood and straightened to his full height. "If we're quite finished with the inquisition, I'd like to retire to my room."

"Can I have my phone first?" Dusty asked.

Grumbling, he pulled it out of his pocket and gave it to her, then strode off to his room, slamming the door behind him.

Dusty peeked at the notifications on her phone, only to stare in shock. So. Many. Missed. Texts.

"Ah…there might be a lot of messages from me," Stuart said. "And a few calls. I was a little frantic."

She pressed the phone against her chest. "I think it's sweet, but I'll read them later." She placed it in her back pocket. "How much beer do we have in the fridge?"

"I just restocked two days ago. Why?"

"Because we need to show our German visitors some hospitality." She smiled at Dr. Wagner. "How about a drink? All we have is Turkish beer, which isn't up to the standards of a good German lager, but…"

"A cold bottle of Efes still tastes good on a hot day," Dr. Wagner said. "We'll join you."

As Dusty went to get the beer out of the fridge, Clarissa spoke up. "What about Mehmet? Will he be punished? I don't think he wanted to help Hughes. It sounds like he just needed the money."

"He can't work for us anymore," Dr. Wagner said. "I'll have to see about hiring someone else. But I won't report him, either."

Dusty was glad to hear it. She liked Mehmet and pitied him for getting roped into Dr. Hughes' scheme.

She took out the beer and set the bottles on the counter. She couldn't think of anything she wanted more than to share a celebratory drink with their new allies now that they'd all emerged victorious in the (second) Trojan War.

# CHAPTER THIRTY-TWO

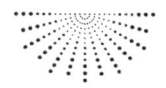

Stuart looked out the window, gazing at the skyline of Istanbul in the distance. Given the dense traffic and the vast sprawl of the city, their bus wouldn't reach the station for another hour. But the longest part of the journey was over. By seven, he and Dusty would be comfortably settled at their rental place in the Old City, near the historic monuments in Sultanahmet Square.

Beside him, Dusty slept peacefully, her head resting on his shoulder. The last few days at the site had been so busy that the whole crew had put in extra hours, staying up late to get their finds cleaned, sorted, and documented before the season ended. Even if they hadn't found a cemetery, they'd made considerable progress in expanding the lower city and revealing more about life at Troy during the Late Bronze Age.

The season's biggest win had been the Germans' discoveries. The day after Mehmet had shown Dr. Wagner where he found the first tablet, Leo had uncovered two more—both engraved with the same cuneiform markings. Though they had yet to be translated, their discovery marked a significant turning point in the history of Bronze Age Troy.

In November, Dr. Wagner would present his finds at the Troy symposium in Amsterdam. Stuart would be there as well, representing the University of Boston, and Dusty planned to join him. For all their travels, neither he nor Dusty had ever spent time in Amsterdam, so the trip would be a new adventure.

Dusty blinked and rubbed her eyes. She graced Stuart with a sleepy smile. "That was such a good nap. Please tell me we're almost there."

"Not quite. Another hour or so. Glad you got to rest."

"Thanks for letting me sleep on your shoulder. Apologies if I drooled on you." She pulled out her phone and scrolled through it. "Clarissa says hi. She and her dad are flying to Cappadocia tomorrow for a three-day tour, including a hot-air balloon ride over the rock formations. Oh, and Mort's friend loved my medieval sketches. Now he wants some of Regency England, which means I'll get to draw dukes and duchesses and horse-drawn carriages."

"That's fantastic." Stuart was so proud of her for taking this leap into the world of children's book illustration. She was happier about this project than she'd ever been about her dissertation. "Any more news?"

"Dr. Wagner also sent me a message. His crew found two more tablets." She handed Stuart her phone. "Take a look."

He regarded the photos with awe. Both tablets were engraved with dense lines of cuneiform. It was looking more and more like the Germans had discovered the royal archive of Troy. "That makes five so far."

"I know, right?" Dusty took her phone back. "I can't wait to find out what they say. Dad's been conferring with Dr. Wagner on the translation. They think the script might be a variant of Linear A or B."

"Whatever's on them, the news is going to rock the archaeological community. Kerim said the Troy Museum is already working out where they're going to display them once they've been translated."

"What a coup for Turkish history." She grinned. "I love that I was in the middle of all this discovery. I'm so glad we didn't let Hughes win."

Stuart chuckled. "He went to all this trouble, got himself barred from Troy, and for nothing. Finding one tablet might have seemed like a big deal when he came up with his plan, but that's a minor win compared to digging up a whole archive."

"Yeah, he wasn't thinking about the big picture at all." She checked her phone again. "Speaking of Wagner, he invited me to join their dig next summer if I'm looking for work."

From her saucy tone, he sensed she was hoping to get a rise out of him. "Are you considering it?"

"I would, but I already promised this superhot, sexy-as-hell American professor that I'd spend the summer with him."

He laughed at her blatant attempt to flatter his ego. "With any luck, you can work with both of us since I'll probably be back at Troy next July, collaborating with Wagner."

During his last week on-site, Stuart had discussed the idea of a joint excavation with Kerim and Dr. Wagner. Kerim had not only been in favor of a collaboration, but he'd also agreed to propose the concept to the Turkish Ministry of Culture. Stuart didn't know if he'd be asked to lead the American team or just serve as the assistant director again, but he was eager to go back. He'd enjoy it even more if Dusty could join him.

"I'd be totally on board with another season at Troy," Dusty said. "As long as I don't have to work with Dr. Hughes again. Ever."

"Not an issue. His days in the field are over."

After Dusty had revealed the professor's subterfuge, he left the field house the next day. A week later, Stuart had been pleasantly surprised when Dr. Fiorelli called him with the best possible news. Dr. Hughes had informed the department chair of his retirement, claiming his health had taken a turn during his time at Troy. While it meant he wouldn't be punished for what he'd done, he'd spared the university from further scandal.

Dusty set her phone back in her pocket. "Can I ask you something? It's kind of personal."

Her serious tone alarmed him. "Is everything okay?"

"It's fine, but I wanted to know—that night in Boston two years ago, when you said, 'It's always been you.' Did you mean it? What about Shelby?"

He sighed, wishing he hadn't botched things so badly. "I did mean it, but it was complicated. When I was with Shelby, I thought she was the right person for me. Even when it was painfully obvious to everyone else that she didn't respect me, I kept trying to make our relationship work. That's why I stuck with her for longer than I should have.

"But as for you and me—there's always been something special about us." He stroked her hand. "Do you remember when we first met? I was this scared seven-year-old who dreaded the thought of living in Egypt for three months, but you convinced me it could be an adventure. Even at age six, you were a total badass."

Dusty gave him a wistful smile. "We had a lot of fun, didn't we? You were my favorite dig buddy. Every year, when my parents started packing up to go to Egypt for another season, I'd ask them, 'Is Stuart's family coming, too?' I was fourteen when I started crushing on you."

"I've got you beat. I was thirteen. Remember when we stole your dad's brandy and got drunk for the first time? I was so wasted I almost told you how I felt."

She laughed. "Good thing you didn't because that night went horribly sideways. We both ended up huddled over the toilet, puking our guts out."

He shuddered at the memory. "That was the worst. After that, I let my feelings simmer. We were such good friends that I didn't want to mess things up. But the older we got, the more I wanted you. Except we didn't want the same things out of life. Right before you left for college, you told me you couldn't imagine *ever* getting married because you didn't want anyone to tie you down or stop you from having adventures. I wasn't like that. All the traveling my family did made me crave stability. That's why I never had any luck with flings or one-night stands. It's also why I stayed with Shelby for as long as I did."

"I get it. For the record, seventeen-year-old me didn't have a clue. There's nothing wrong with settling down with the right person. Not that I'm in any hurry. I still want to have adventures, but I also want more than that. I want to be with you. For as long as you'll have me."

"I feel the same way. I'm so glad we'll get to be together in Boston. But to answer your question, I meant it then, and I mean it now. It's always been you, Dusty. You captured my heart a long time ago, and now you have it for real."

"Aww, Stuart." She blinked quickly. "You've turned me into such a sap."

He loved that he'd softened her up. Still the same adventurous Dusty but with no qualms about showing her vulnerable side around him.

She peeked out the window. "We're getting closer, I can feel it. I'm so glad you booked us our own private love nest. Did I tell you what my dad said when I told him about it?"

"I don't think so."

"He wanted to know where it was, so I sent him the Airbnb link. This is wild, but the last time he and my mom were in Istanbul, they stayed at a hotel on the same block. Apparently, the shop next door sells the best baklava in the city. He asked me to bring him a box."

"Good to know. I was planning to buy some for my mom. And for us as well." He grinned at her. "I never got any of that baklava from our romantic dinner in Güzelyali."

"Sorry about that, but now we can share an entire box and eat it *naked*." She squeezed his arm. "I can't wait to dive into bed with you. A king bed, if I'm not mistaken. Are you excited?"

"Of course." Four nights alone with her, where they could indulge their secret desires and wake up together each morning. It was better than any of his fantasies.

But he was even more excited about what lay ahead. While the past two months at Troy had challenged his resolve, he'd finished the dig with a newfound sense of confidence. Instead of brimming with anxiety over the future, he was eager to start teaching at the university. Not only was he embarking upon a new life in Boston, but he'd also be sharing it with the woman he loved.

∼

Just before sunrise, Dusty woke to the distinctive sound of the call to prayer. She peeked out the window. Still dark outside, but she could spot the lights of the nearby minaret where the muezzin was reciting the call. Even if it was only 5:00 a.m., she wasn't tired.

After arriving in Istanbul last night, she and Stuart had tried to stay awake. They'd rambled through the Old City like a couple of tourists, grabbing doner kebab from a nearby restaurant and sharing a few beers. By the time they returned to their apartment, they were running on fumes. No sooner had they changed for bed than they crashed out immediately, too tired to attempt more than a good-night kiss.

But with the entire day ahead of them, plus three more nights, they still had plenty of chances for steamy shenanigans.

Dusty slipped out of bed and went into the bathroom to relieve herself. She looked ridiculous, clad in one of Stuart's old T-shirts, which dwarfed her small frame. But last night, she'd been so wiped that she hadn't unpacked anything except her toiletries case.

When she returned to the bedroom, Stuart was awake, lying on his side. "Good morning," he said. "You doing okay?"

"I'm doing great. It's astonishing what a full eight hours of sleep will do for you."

"Sorry I conked out so early. I was exhausted."

"Same here." She bit back a grin, unable to resist teasing him. "But now that you're up, we can get ready to explore Istanbul. Right?"

"Now? It's not even six."

"That's the best time. We can go to Eminönü before the tourists get there and buy fresh cheese and olives." She rubbed her hands together. "Make our own Turkish breakfast."

To his credit, he managed an enthusiastic smile. "Sounds great. Can I take a shower first?"

Laughing, she slipped back into bed with him. "Just kidding. There's only one thing I want to explore this morning, and it's *not* the city of Istanbul."

"Naughty girl. You could tell I was disappointed, couldn't you?"

"You have a terrible poker face, but you get an 'A' for effort." She reached for his shirt and pulled it over his head, then peppered his bare chest with kisses, loving how warm and solid he felt.

As he pulled her closer, his hands wandered beneath the hem of her shirt. He cupped her bare ass and gave it a squeeze. "What are you wearing? Or, rather, not wearing?"

"Just your shirt. Nothing else. I was too lazy to unpack last night." She stripped off the shirt, then flung it to the side. Naked, she pressed her bare skin against his. "It's so nice to wake up with you. Though at some point, I *would* like to go out and buy fresh cheese and olives."

Now that they had complete privacy, she wanted to take her

time with him. To do all the things she'd dreamed of during their weeks together at Troy. After pushing the covers aside, she scooted down on the bed, running her lips across his chest and stomach. She reached for his boxers and tugged on them. He eased them off his hips and kicked them away.

She stroked his rigid length and swirled her tongue around the tip—just a little tease to let him know what she intended. When his breath hitched, she looked up at him in concern. She hadn't gotten the chance to give him a blowjob yet. Maybe it wasn't something he was into.

"Is this okay?" she asked.

"Yes, but you don't have to. It's not my birthday or anything."

*Oh, Stuart.* She had so much to make up for. "Can I do it, anyway? *Please?*"

His warm laugh heated her from the inside out. "Like I'd say no? I wanted to make sure you were on board."

"I'm on board. Very much so." She stroked him with her tongue before taking him into her mouth.

When he groaned and tangled his fingers in her hair, her body flooded with a rush of longing. An ache built up between her thighs, making her yearn for release, but she could wait. Right now, she wanted to give him as much pleasure as humanly possible.

She continued sucking, tightening her grip on his butt, her desire increasing each time he gasped or begged her to keep going. But when he tugged on her hair with a little more force and called out her name, she pulled away. "Do you want me to stop?"

"I want to come inside of you. If that's okay."

"Of course it's okay." But she loved that he'd asked.

He pointed to the nightstand. "The condoms are in my toiletries bag."

She crawled across the bed and reached for them. "Good thing they're not buried in your suitcase." Pulling out a long strip, she let out a low whistle. "Ambitious, much? Kidding. We're going to use all of them."

After unwrapping one, she placed it on him. Then she straddled him and lowered herself onto him, adjusting her body until he was deep inside her. The sensation was so incredible that she paused and gazed down at him, awed by the love in his eyes. After everything they'd been through this summer, sharing this bed felt like a hard-won victory.

"I'm so glad we're here." She'd never felt this connected to anyone before.

"Me too. Thanks for never giving up on me." He pulled her closer, capturing her mouth in a tender kiss.

Sliding his hands down her back, he clasped her butt. He squeezed it, urging her on as she moved against him with slow, steady thrusts. She angled her body until he was hitting the right spot and drew in a ragged breath. As good as it felt, she wasn't sure she could reach orgasm in this position.

When she stopped, he locked eyes with her. "Tell me what you need."

"Flip me over. I want you in control again." A throaty laugh tumbled out of her. "But don't get too used to it."

"That's what you said last time. Deep down inside, you enjoy relinquishing control to me, don't you?" With a wicked grin, he maneuvered her until she was beneath him. "Is that better?"

"It's perfect." She wrapped her legs around him and pulled him even deeper. He brushed his tongue over her nipples, licking each taut bud until she whimpered with pleasure. "Yes, Stuart. More of that. Please."

He quickened his pace, thrusting into her with more force. She closed her eyes, overwhelmed by the sensations coursing through her: the feel of his body pressed against hers, his scent, his lips on her skin. All of it so much better than she'd ever imagined. She clutched his shoulders as the orgasm rolled over her, the rapture so intense that she cried out his name in abandon. No sooner had she reached her peak than he let out a loud, utterly shameless groan. Hearing him lose control filled her with a sense of pride. *She'd* done this. Taken straightlaced Stuart and brought him to the heights of ecstasy.

As his movements stilled, she held him tight, wanting to prolong the moment. She never wanted to forget how it felt to be loved so thoroughly.

He eased off her gently, as though reluctant to break their connection. After grabbing a tissue from the nightstand, he disposed of the condom and then took her in his arms. She nuzzled her face into his neck, feeling warm and cozy and blissfully happy.

"Stuart?" she asked.

"Mmm?" His voice was thick with sleepy contentment.

"The olives can wait. Right now, I just want to stay in bed with you."

# CHAPTER THIRTY-THREE

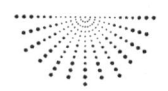

Dusty sat with Stuart on the rooftop patio of their rental apartment, taking in the view. Below them, the Sea of Marmara glistened under a clear blue sky. Seagulls swooped overhead, catching air currents as they glided on the breeze. Huge cargo ships plied the waters, slowly headed for the port at Istanbul.

She sipped her coffee and let out a satisfied sigh. Clad in Stuart's T-shirt and a pair of worn sleep shorts, she was grateful for the privacy of their apartment. Since she'd been too lazy to opt for real clothes after her shower, Stuart had volunteered to get dressed and fetch them breakfast at a local café. He'd come back with cappuccinos, chocolate croissants, and simit—a Turkish version of a sesame seed bagel.

Truly, he was the perfect boyfriend.

All day yesterday, the two of them had barely left the apartment, other than a few forays into the neighborhood to grab food. Dusty couldn't remember spending this much time in bed with anyone. Though she'd known Stuart for years, she was discovering a whole new side of him. A wicked, sexy side that delighted in physical pleasure as much as she did.

When he grinned at her, she flushed under his scrutiny. "We should probably leave the apartment today. Like, for real."

"Come on, Dusty. How many times have you been to Istanbul?"

"Three times. Maybe four?"

"I've been here twice. So we've both seen all the highlights—the Hagia Sophia, the Topkapi, the Blue Mosque, the ferry to the Princes' Islands. We can skip all that touristy stuff."

"True. But we could still explore the city." She laughed. "Stop looking at me like you want to sweep me off to bed again."

He grinned. "Well, now that you mention it…"

She loved how insatiable he was. No one had ever wanted her this much, had ever craved her body and worshiped it the way he did. But their connection wasn't just about sex. They'd also spent hours lying in bed and talking—sharing memories, dreams, and plans for the future. She'd opened up to him in a way she never had with anyone else.

As eager as she was to go back to bed with him, she loved teasing him too much to concede right away. "Let's go to the Grand Bazaar and do some shopping."

He groaned. "That's the biggest tourist trap of them all. If you're not careful, some crafty salesman will whisk you off to his shop. He'll compliment you and offer you apple tea, and then his associates will swoop in and give you the full-on kilim hard sell."

"The full-on kilim hard sell? Are you speaking from experience?" She bounced in her seat, brimming with giddy enthusiasm. "Come on, let's do it."

"You want to bring home a rug?"

"We can play off each other. You can be the nerdy tourist who wants a souvenir, and I'll be your grumpy girlfriend who's trying to talk you out of it."

"For you, I'll go to the Grand Bazaar, but I'm not buying anything that doesn't fit in my suitcase." He waggled a finger at her. "Don't even think about it."

She finished her coffee and set the cup down. Giving a lengthy stretch, she tried to decide whether she wanted to lure Stuart back into bed or get ready for an expedition to the bazaar. At the sound of the doorbell, she turned to him. "You didn't order any food, did you?"

"Nope. I'll go check it out." He stood and raked a hand through his sandy-blond hair, still mussed from where she'd tangled her fingers in it.

A panicked thought came to her as he went inside the apartment to answer the door. She'd been extra loud when they'd made love this morning. Like, multidecibel loud, moaning in ecstasy, calling out his name, begging for him to give it to her harder. Was it possible the next-door neighbors had heard her? Were they coming to complain about her lack of decency?

*Sorry. I couldn't help myself.*

At the sound of a raised female voice, the hairs on the back of her neck stood up. Their visitor wasn't an angry neighbor. It was her mother.

Dr. Louisa Danforth strode onto the balcony, impeccably dressed in a navy linen pantsuit and matching heels. Trailing behind her, Stuart shot Dusty a desperate look as if to say, "I have no idea what the hell is going on."

She didn't, either, but she forced a quick smile onto her face. "*Mom.* What are you doing here?"

Her mother pulled up one of the patio chairs and settled herself in it. She glowered at Dusty. "I called you three times yesterday. Why weren't you answering your phone?"

"Sorry." She'd put it on "do not disturb" after they reached Istanbul, not wanting any distractions from her steamy escapades with Stuart. "Is everything okay? Is Dad okay?"

"He's fine. I'm glad he told me where to find you, otherwise, I wouldn't have had a clue. He said he's looking forward to seeing you in Boston next week and that you're working together on a little translation project."

*Thanks, Dad.* While she wasn't thrilled that he'd disclosed her location, at least he'd kept quiet about the tablet. "Yep. Just a father-daughter side project." She twisted her hands together. "When I talked to him last week, he didn't mention you were coming to Istanbul."

"I asked him not to. I'm here on business, but I thought I'd surprise you."

*Yep. Definitely surprised.* At least her mother hadn't shown up earlier, when she'd been in the throes of passion with Stuart. "It's nice to see you. But is there something urgent you wanted to talk to me about?"

"Yes. I got a call from a brash fellow by the name of Mortimer Jones. Apparently, he signed up for the VIP tour of Egypt that I'm leading in November with Ancient Excursions. He's under the impression that he'll get special treatment, with exclusive access to the recent excavations at Luxor. When I asked him who authorized this, he said *you* gave him my number."

"I'm sorry. I forgot to tell you. He did me a huge favor, and I wanted to repay him. But he's a sweet guy. If it wasn't for his help, Stuart might have lost his job."

"*Dulcinea.* What on earth are you talking about?"

Dusty caught Stuart's eye. When he nodded, she took a deep breath and launched into the tablet saga. By now, she'd recounted the story four times and was growing weary of it. But she wanted her mother to know the truth, even if it meant admitting that she and Stuart were lovers. When she was done, her mother let out a deep sigh.

"Oh, Dusty. To think that wretched Dr. Hughes almost ruined everything. What a malicious toad. He has no business calling himself an archaeologist." Her expression softened as she regarded her daughter. "I'm proud you stood up to him. You did the right thing."

Dusty's heart swelled with joy. Having her mother validate her actions made her even prouder of the choice she'd made.

"Thanks, Mom. It wasn't easy. Dad's the one who convinced me to go back to Troy and fight."

"I'm glad she did," Stuart said. "It took a lot of courage on her part."

Dusty's mother looked between the two of them. "This romance of yours. It's serious?"

"It is." Dusty gnawed on her lip as she waited for her mother's reaction.

Instead of casting a disapproving frown, her mother smiled. A true smile, not the tight-lipped one she displayed when she was feigning interest or appreciation. "I always knew you were right for each other. Didn't I tell you that in June? But no, you didn't listen. As if I couldn't see the writing on the wall. A mother always knows."

"You were right." If her mom wanted to gloat, she wouldn't get any argument from Dusty. "Now that you know what happened, can you please be extra nice to Mort?"

"Of course. Any friend of my daughter deserves the full VIP treatment."

"Thanks. I owe you one." As she said it, Dusty realized she owed her mom more than that. She needed to admit she'd finally taken control of her future. "There's something else I need to tell you. When I was on this dig, I made a decision." She tensed up, afraid to keep going, until Stuart came and stood behind her, placing his hand on her shoulder for support.

"What is it?" her mother asked.

*Be firm. You can do this.* "I'm withdrawing from grad school. I'm sorry to disappoint you, but academia's not the right path for me. I should have realized it a lot sooner, but I didn't want to let you down." She took a deep breath. "I want to pursue my art. I still plan on doing archaeological illustration, but I'm also looking into other options. I'm actually working on illustrations for a children's book series about time travel." She ducked her head. "Sorry."

"This isn't just another of your whims? You've informed your graduate adviser?"

"Yes. She was in Greece, doing research, but she got back to me this week. She said I could take care of the paperwork in September." Dusty laughed nervously. "To be honest, I think she was relieved to hear it."

Her mother gave a firm nod. "Good. I'm glad you came to a decision."

Dusty stared at her, afraid she'd misheard. "You're not angry? I thought you wanted me to get my doctorate."

"Honestly, Dusty, if you'd just *listen*. I wanted you to figure out a course for your life. I never said it had to be grad school. But I wanted you to stop running and decide on something. If it's art, then so be it."

An immense weight lifted off Dusty's shoulders. "Thanks."

"You're welcome. Since you've got a plan in place, I see no reason why you can't pursue it while staying at our condo in Boston. Or in London or Cairo. Or wherever you choose."

She gazed up at Stuart. "Right now, Boston's perfect."

"Good. Your father will be pleased to hear it." Her mother stood up. "When we have time, I'd like to hear more about this children's book series. Unfortunately, I have a busy schedule today. I'm meeting with a curator from the Archaeological Museum, then I'm off to visit a colleague at Istanbul University. But I have one last thing to say."

She nailed Stuart with a flinty glare. "You're like a son to me, but if you hurt my daughter, I will make certain you end up in a pit deep in the Sahara Desert. Do you understand?"

He flinched. "Understood. But I'd never hurt Dusty. I love her."

"I'm sure you do, but men make stupid mistakes. Don't be like that." She raked her gaze over the two of them. "Tomorrow night, I'm dining with a few prominent Egyptian archaeologists. Dusty,

I'd like you to be there, and Stuart, you could benefit from the networking."

Dusty was about to protest but thought better of it. "Sure. Just tell us when and where."

"I'll text you the details. Please dress decently. I don't want the two of you looking like you just rolled out of bed." With an arch of her brow, she added, "I'll let myself out."

Dusty said nothing until she heard the door close. Then she burst out laughing. Somehow, she'd found the courage to tell her mother that she was giving up grad school, pursuing art as a career, and sleeping with Stuart. And she'd escaped unscathed.

Stuart wiped his forehead. "Your mother is still as intimidating as ever. I can't believe she threatened to throw me in a pit."

"She'd never do it for real. Only if you break my heart."

He took her hand and pulled her up beside him. Placing a tender kiss on her forehead, he regarded her with affection. "I wouldn't. I love you, Dusty."

"I know. I love you, too."

Enfolded in his arms, she looked over at the Sea of Marmara, shimmering in the distance. The world was wide-open, just waiting for them. Next week, they'd be back in Boston. And in November, they'd get to go to Amsterdam. After that—who could say? Troy? Another adventure? Either way, they'd be writing the next chapter of their story together.

Stuart bent down and whispered in her ear. "Want to go back to bed?"

"Absolutely. But then we're buying a rug."

∽

Thank you for reading *Troy Story*.
If you enjoyed this book, please consider leaving a review.
Thanks! Your support is much appreciated!

Want a free novella from the Romancing the Ruins series? Sign up for my newsletter to receive a copy of *Lost & Found in Mexico*, a romance set in Las Vegas and the Yucatán Peninsula.

The Romancing the Ruins series will continue with Book 3, a rivals-to-lovers romance featuring TJ and Emilia set in Italy.

**Website and Newsletter Signup:**
www.carlalunabooks.com

# ACKNOWLEDGMENTS

This is the part of the book I always enjoy writing because it's like my own Academy Award acceptance speech, where I get to thank everyone who's helped me on my journey.

Thank you to:

My readers—for taking a chance on the Romancing the Ruins series. Leaving Blackwood Cellars behind to write books set in the archaeological world was a big leap, and I'm glad you've stuck with me. I wish I could give you all a delicious slice of baklava!

My wonderful team of professionals—Bailey McGinn, for her fabulous job with my cover; Serena Clarke at Free Bird Editing for her meticulous copy-edits; and Sandra Dee at One Love Editing for the final proofreading polish.

My beta-readers—for making this story *so* much better: Jennifer Rupp, Laura Luna, Gail Werner, Michelle McCraw, Liz Czukas, and Susan Keillor.

My writer friends—including my local writing group, the FITWIGS (Lolly, Jennifer, Lisa, Virginia, and Shlomo), my indie author squad (Michelle McCraw, Ofelia Martinez, Kristin Lee, Brandy Shaw, and Jazz Matthews), and my friends Amy Reichert and M.K. Wiseman for advice, support, and encouragement. I also have to include my midwestern retreat crew (Carrie Lofty, Natalie Caña, Brandy Shaw, Liz Lincoln, and Liz Czukas), who provided me with loads of brainstorming help and lots of laughs.

My critique partner—fellow romance writer Tricia Quinnies, who held me accountable until I'd finished this book, even when I got hopelessly stuck.

The Turkish contingent—the helpful staff at the Dersaadet

Hotel in Istanbul and the Hotel Des Etrangers in Çanakkale (the same hotel Heinrich Schliemann stayed at back in the 1870s!), as well as the local tour guides who showed me around Istanbul, Troy, and Cappadocia. And I can't forget Dr. George Bass, the former head of the Institute of Nautical Archaeology in Bodrum. If not for his invitation to spend five months there in 1993, studying the remains of a medieval shipwreck, I might not have fallen in love with Turkey.

My research sources—in studying the past excavations at Troy, I relied heavily on the work of Dr. Eric Cline, Professor of Classical and Ancient Near Eastern Studies at George Washington University (and my former TA on the Cyprus dig that inspired *Field Rules*). For questions regarding academia and academic protocol, I was aided by my good friend (and fellow archaeologist) Dr. Robert J. Beardsell. Any errors in this regard are 100% my fault.

My inspirations—the character of Dr. Louisa Danforth was inspired by two brilliant women I admire greatly: my former graduate school adviser, Irene Bierman, and my aunt, Sharon Dunlap Smith. The inspiration for Dulcinea "Dusty" Danforth came from my mom, the late Dulcie Luna. Like Dusty, she was a talented artist who didn't fit into the academic mold. Though she never got the chance to publish her children's book, she left behind some incredible artwork.

My family—my two (adult) children, Tasmine and James, who have grown up embracing the spirit of travel and adventure. Their support means more to me than I can say. Then there's my husband Mike, who has been by my side every step of the way. Not only has he talked me through some tricky plot points, but he also endured a road trip in which we spent the entire time listening to an audiobook about the history of Troy. Here's to many more adventures together!

# ABOUT THE AUTHOR

Carla Luna writes contemporary romance with a dollop of humor and a pinch of spice. A former archaeologist, she still dreams of traveling to far-off places and channels that wanderlust into the settings of her stories. When she's not writing, she works in a spice emporium where she gets paid to discuss food and share her favorite recipes. Her passions include Broadway musicals, baking, whimsical office supplies, and pop culture podcasts. Though she has roots in Los Angeles and Vancouver Island, she currently resides in Wisconsin with her family and her spoiled Siberian cat.

**For sneak peeks, giveaways, and book recommendations, sign up for Carla Luna's newsletter:**
www.carlalunabooks.com

# ALSO BY CARLA LUNA

## THE BLACKWOOD CELLARS SERIES

### Blue Hawaiian
Broke, single, and jobless, Jess Chavez feels like the family screwup when she flies to Maui to attend her perfect sister's destination wedding. But sparks fly when Jess reconnects with her roguish ex, Connor Blackwood. A secret fling offers the perfect escape from family drama, as long as Jess can keep from falling in love again.

### Red Velvet
When April Beckett's plus-one bails right before a big family wedding, her best friend, Brody Blackwood, offers to take his place. Now they have to convince everyone they're lovers—while sharing a cozy cottage in the Northwoods of Wisconsin. But what happens when the fake relationship starts to feel real?

### White Wedding
When Victoria Blackwood is tasked with planning her ex's Christmas wedding, she doesn't think her life could get any worse. Until she discovers the caterer, Rafael Sanchez, is the lover she ghosted five years ago after a steamy fling in Baja. To pull off the perfect wedding, they'll need to keep things professional. But it won't be easy, not when the fire between them burns hotter than Christmas in July.

# THE ROMANCING THE RUINS SERIES

## Field Rules

Digging up the past takes on a whole new meaning when graduate student Olivia Sanchez is forced to team up with her ex, Rick Langston, while working at an archaeological dig in Cyprus. Given that their last fling almost led to their academic ruin, they can't afford to repeat their past mistakes. But as they work together under the scorching Mediterranean sun, the heat between them proves impossible to ignore.

Made in the USA
Monee, IL
29 August 2023